# www.queenmotorhome.com

*A novel by*
**Patt Fero**

ISBN number: 1-4196-9677-7

This book is a work of fiction. Names, characters, places and incidents are the prodcuts of the author's imagination or are used fictitiously. Any resemblance to actual people, events or locations, either living or dead, is entirely coincidental and unintended.

Published by:

BookSurge Publishing
www.booksurge.com
1-866-308-6235
orders@booksurge.com

The Goldmind Company, Inc.
PO Box 25693

Greenville, SC 29616

# DEDICATION:

*To my Queen Mother, "Amazing Grace", the most beautiful woman I have ever known and who was real royalty. I aspire to be more like you and hope I have lots of your genes. I so wanted you to be able to read this book when published. Guess I'll have to over night a copy to Heaven. I love and miss you.*

*Amazing Grace - September 11, 1922-January 28, 2007*

# ACKNOWLEDGEMENTS:

As this is my first published novel, I suppose I get the right to ramble some. I sincerely hope that I haven't forgotten anyone. Firstly, to my wonderful husband, Jim, the love of my life, who helped me through my doubting moments and dark hours, and continued to encourage me to move forward. He has been my biggest cheerleader and always believed unconditionally in my future success as a writer.

To my longtime Queen friends of almost forty years, Queen Ingrid, Queen Chrissy and Queen Laurie. To all of my other wonderful Queen friends, Jan, Dot, Georgie, Peggy, Denise and Lynn who kept me inspired at all times.

To my brother John and his wife Robyn, and my sister Nancy, who encouraged me to keep going and not give up. To my daughter Stephanie, son Richard, and stepson Jonathan and his wife Betsy, who never once voiced concerns about my sanity in attempting this, although they probably secretly questioned it and whispered to each other behind my back about the same, they never gave a hint to me that they were thinking that I was completely crazy. To my stepfather, Charles, a writer himself, who always offered encouragement and inspiration.

To Mark, a salesman at a local RV sales lot, who allowed me to befriend him and spent time with me even though I was not a serious prospect for purchasing a RV. Mark educated me on the features and operations of RVs and motor homes.

To Sandy Richardson, my fabulous editor. We were introduced through a referral and never met in person until after our first edit run. Even so, we clicked like two Queen "southern soul" sisters with our first phone calls and emails. I told Sandy about two weeks into the project that I felt like she had crawled into my brain one night while I was asleep, and we woke up the next morning as one! I cannot offer enough praise and gratitude for her expert editing skills and of course, her never-ending patience and encouragement.

To David Wells, my illustrator, who identified with my characters and story plot from our first meeting and immediately had the ultimate vision.

To John Schulz, my brilliant website page designer. You are so creative and multi-talented.

To all of the beautiful people in my life that I know and to all of you I have yet to meet when I take to the road in my motor home and ride out into the sunset.

To all the Queens out there. Remember, you can be Queen for Life, not just for The Day!

And finally, it just goes to show…Believe it, See it, Act on it, Receive it… and Don't Give Up!

# www.queenmotorhome.com

Patt Fero

# Contents

# On the Road Again…

203

# S. O. S.…

215

# Heading Out…

231

# Crazy…

237

# The Rescuers…

249

# On the Edge…

263

# Rescue Rendezvous…

273

# The Homecoming…

287

*Nothing can prevent your picture from coming into concrete form except the same power which gave birth to it...yourself.*

Genevieve Behrend

Out of Here…

# Chapter 1

## You Can't Always Get What You Want

I didn't laugh so much anymore, and fifty-something felt way more like eighty-something than it should have. Ten-hour days for seven days a week, board meetings, crammed work schedules, and social obligations defined my life. My husband's business was in a lull. That big house we bought cost plenty, and driving a Mercedes wasn't cheap. Investments we'd made demanded more input than they gave out. The list went on and on. So what was I to do? A six-figure income and corporate benefits had become necessary evils. I was stuck.

At least, until the new CEO called me into his office.

"Charlotte, North Carolina, is growing every day, Leslie. And we're growing with it, so we're making some organizational changes. Most of your responsibilities will be shifted to others, which will eliminate your position here. But we're prepared to offer you a phase out program for three months. This way, you can help train the others with regards to your specific work areas. You've been a loyal and hardworking employee for many years, and we know you'll want to ensure that this transition goes smoothly." Mr. Yancey smiled in my direction, but his eyes slid to my left shoulder.

Why you short, fat, stupid, male chauvinist PIG, I thought. I should have seen this coming from the first time I met him. Since I had the most tenure, and because I'm female, he was threatened then and had remained that way.

"With all due respect, *MISTER* Yancey, this is totally not fair. I've given the best years of my life to this company; my work and my loyalty have been exceptional, and I deserve more consideration than this. I can't believe you're firing me!"

"Leslie, Leslie…we're not firing you, rather your position will be, as I said before…eliminated. There's a big difference."

His eyes did the slip n' slide again. I thought about my best friend Liz and how she mimicked him after their first meeting. She said he reminded her of her third husband. With that, I lost it.

"Big difference my ass! You really expect me to hang around and train my replacements? Think again, buddy-roo. I'm done here. I'm resigning immediately and you can take this job and your phase out offer and …and…" Somewhere in the back of my mind, my mother's voice reminded me to bite my tongue.

Mr. Yancey's right hand moved to his tie, dipped under his collar, and circled the front half of his neck. His mouth sagged to one side.

"Well, it's regrettable that you feel this way, Leslie. The company could really use your help in this restructuring."

"Forget it, Yancey. I'm out of here." I left his office, grabbed the few personal items from my desk, and headed for the main exit.

As I drove to my husband's office, the thought hit me, "Unstuck! Unplugged! Unburdened! Wow!" I barged in on Bob without even a hello to his secretary.

"Leslie! What is it? You look ….weird."

"Weird? No, I don't look weird, Bob. This is the look of a woman who is, who is……." I smiled. "Bob, I just got canned. Rather, Yancey offered me a transition of three months and severance, but I quit instead." My husband's green face seemed almost fluorescent as he sat slumped in his black leather chair, head in his hands. "Bob? Bob, are you okay? You look… sick."

"Leslie, I can't believe this. You quit your job?"

"No….yes,…well, was I supposed to hang around for three months, baby sit the new kids, teach them how to run the business that I worked so hard to help build, and let them put me out to pasture like some old…some old broken-back plow horse?" I plunked down into the chair opposite his desk.

"Ah, Les, I'm sorry, baby. I'm just surprised. It's all such a shock." Bob came around the desk to hug me and take my hand. "This is just so sudden. And well, you know how preoccupied I've been with my business not doing so great right now. This is just not the best time for this kind of news, baby. To be honest, we could really use that extra three months of your salary until things pick up here."

I looked up at my handsome husband. Any woman would be proud to call him hers. And I was...only..... He slumped against the desk, holding my hand.

I cleared my throat and began again. "I don't know why you're so surprised. I told you how things were at the office. We both suspected that something was up. Do you really think I should have stayed? Belittled myself? Accepted their crumbs. Let them USE me some more?"

"Ah, baby, come on, now. Maybe you should rethink this. I know you're unhappy there. I know you want something else, but honestly, we need the money. Call Yancey back. Tell him you've rethought the offer. That you'll stay for the transition."

My mother's voice bounced around inside my head again. Deep breath. Another.

Think before you speak, I reminded myself.

I pulled my hand away from Bob and stood up, brushing at the wrinkles in my skirt, buying time.

"Bob, how can I say this. Let's see...." I looked my husband in the eye and continued, "I'm sick and tired of having to be the one that STAYS in order to pay the bills. I've been doing that for years. I'm miserable. I need to leave that job with some smidgen of self-respect in tact, so don't give me that stuff about you need my check. You make me feel like that's all I am to you....a PAYROLL CHECK! I expected you, of all people to take my side.

"And as for finances, you've got investments and real estate you can cash in. Hell, I've got them, too. Take them. I don't care about them anymore. It seems the more we have, the less we have because for you, it's never enough. We're in a rut, Bob. Work, work, spend, spend, work some more. You even admitted you didn't like the people we're forced to socialize with these days. What's the point?

"You know I love you. I love you more than life, but I want more than mortgage payments, assets on paper, fancy cars. I want a LIFE. Sell your damn business if it's not going well. You said you hated it anyway. Let's get out of here. Neither of us are happy living this way. It's crazy." I sat again and broke down completely. Something I hate to do.

"Baby, baby…I hear you. I do understand. I hate all this rat race, too. But now's just not a good time to sell the company or any of the real estate. We'd lose money. We just need to regroup and figure this out. Look, you've got all the expertise and experience anyone could want. I'm sure you can find another job right away. Come on, now. You should just get focused on that."

Focused, I thought. If you only knew how focused I am right this minute. And if you call me "BABY" one more time, I'll bop you in the nose. I'm not a baby! I'm not a paycheck, and I'm not some old shoe to be thrown away, either. I looked up into my handsome husband's eyes.

"You're right. I should get focused. And I will…but it won't be on another job, Bob. You're not listening to me. I'm done with all this. I don't know what I'll do, or how, but I've got to change course here. I love you, but something has to give. I'm going nuts living like this."

Just like Yancey's, my husband's mouth slid to one side. A trail of open mouths seemed to follow me that day.

I took the back way home, driving through my old college campus, humming along with the Stone's "You Can't Always Get What You Want," soaking up the atmosphere of the place that always calmed me—the place that rang with memories of all the hopes and dreams of my younger years. Happy years. Years when my best friend Liz and I planned and dreamed of traveling the world, living lives totally different from the two that now seemed to hold us so fast, years when we still had hopes of getting all we wanted.

Memories raced through my mind, taking me back, back, deep into the summer of 1961, into my dad's Buick LeSabre station wagon. Cherry red with a white top. All six of us piled into it headed west: California or Bust!

I was fourteen, stuck then too, only it was in the rear seat facing backwards with one of my three siblings. Rita Hayworth and Rock Hudson paper dolls and Disneyland brochures surrounding us. A sleek Airstream motor home slid up behind us, then passed with a *WHOOSH!,* the silver sides sparkling in the desert sun, hubcaps spinning wildly. It glided like some great flying bird of freedom. I waved to the driver, and he waved back.

"Barbie," I said to my sister, " when I grow up, I'm going to see the world. I'm going to own one of those shiny, silver homes on wheels just like that one and go wherever the road takes me."

Barbie stuck her finger in her mouth and gagged at me. Bert and Sue giggled from the middle seat. And up front, Dad blurted out yet another verse of "Side by Side."

That motor home dream had followed me all the way back east that summer, right through high school, into and out of college, and through all these years of married life.

And I wasn't alone in my fantasy. I reached for my cell phone and dialed Liz, but got voice mail and had to leave a message.

"This is www.queenmotorhome.com calling. Cancel work tomorrow. I'll be at your house at 9:00. It's D-Day!"

For years, through marriages, divorces, children, careers, whatever, Liz and I had used this code phrase as a signal to each other that something had gone wrong, and we needed to talk. We fantasized often of chucking it all and hitting the road, but never did it. Jobs, children, husbands…always something or someone holding us back, keeping us stuck.   But not anymore. Why couldn't we have what we wanted?   Suddenly I knew exactly what  to do. Better still, I was certain I could convince Liz to join me. It was time to make our fantasy a reality.

# Chapter 2

## Didn't I Blow Your Mind

"Oh my, God!" Liz exclaimed as I made my way into her back door. She took one look at my get-up and howled with laughter, streaking her perfectly made-up face with mascara trails.

I rushed ahead of her into the kitchen.

"What in the world is going on with you? You look like some kind of left-over, Harley-riding, 60's hippie." She scanned me from the bandana tied around my forehead, to the huge black sunglasses on my face, down to my tee shirt, worn, faded jeans, and scruffy tennis shoes.

"We've gotta talk," I said, pushing her gently toward a chair. Liz sat with her mouth slightly askew, breathing in quick gasps, trying to stifle yet more giggling.

Not yet able to look her in the eye, I rested my head on the table and mumbled, "I did it."

"Did what? Leslie, what in the world has happened now?"

I raised my face slowly to my best friend, studying her. Could she handle what I was about to say, I wondered? Sure she can, I told myself. Liz laughed at everything. She had a great attitude about life, but she was extremely timid about most things... except when it came to marriage. She had married more men than most women our age have dated. Not that she was a slut, or anything—she was smart, beautiful, stylish, but plain lousy at choosing good men.

Yet another of her third husband's long losing streaks at the tracks catapulted Liz into near-murder mode. Number three was already well on his way out, but the bets he placed that day finished their marriage for good. Carl, her present and fourth husband, who won big on the same horses, happened upon the scene just in time to rescue Number Three from her tirade. With quintessential Southern chivalry, he suggested a few quiet moments apart and substituted her usual mild mint juleps with six Kentucky Bourbons. Afterwards, neither Liz nor Carl could recall who proposed to whom that very day. Liz married him as soon as her divorce was final, only to discover that betting on the horses had been his main occupation since his college football days. He suffered greatly from what she called "Post PRO-BALL Failure" syndrome, and ever since their marriage, she'd been cheerleading Carl along from one job to another. Now, he was "settled," teaching and coaching, and Liz seemed resigned that he was a lot like the other husbands she'd had. He was not the hero she had dreamed of, but rather, just another man, a weak and needy man. But to give her credit, she maintained a good attitude, even toward her ex's.

"Liz, I did it. I quit my job."

I took a deep breath and gave her yesterday's full story. Then I launched ahead. "So, after all of that, I just knew it was time to do what we've always talked about doing. I went scouting for our motor home. I dressed up just like this and went over to *Danny's RV World*. And that Danny person! You wouldn't believe! He had a wad of tobacco as big as an apple in one cheek, and he sort of rolled it along as he crossed the sales lot to meet me."

Frown lines formed around Liz's mouth.

"Don't worry;" I rushed on. "I made up a good story right on the spot. I told him that my sister and husband and I were thinking of surprising my Mom and Dad with a motor home, that Dad just retired, and we want them to travel while they are still able. Then I said how we knew absolutely nothing about RV's, and he asked me all these questions like what manufacturers, what sizes, features, and all the other options. It got so confusing.... So I told him I just wanted to look around by myself to get some ideas.

"Liz, you wouldn't believe how many styles there are. It's a whole different world with pop-ups and pop-outs, hitches, antennas...anything and everything we could possibly want.

"I realized right away we were going to need someone we could trust, so I blew off ol' Danny Boy, and did some research at home. I found several more dealers right here in town. And today, my friend, you and I are going to find our dream mobile."

"You really quit your job?"

I nodded. "Liz, I'm not going to stay mired down in this so-called "life" Bob and I have mistakenly created. I love him, but I want a LIFE. I want a REAL life. And apparently, what he wants from me is a monthly paycheck.

"I realized yesterday that losing my job was a sign….a sign that it's now or never. Bob won't change unless I force him to. And if he doesn't force, well, then, I guess…I guess I'll have to leave him."

"Whoa girl! Leaving is my forté. You can't leave Bob!"

"Liz, I can, and I will. This is our chance, and you're coming with me. It's what we've dreamed of for years. Remember, no guts, no glory!"

Liz shook her head from side to side. "But Carl and Bob will have pluperfect fits when we tell them all this. And what about our kids?"

"We won't let the men know about any of this until we're set to go. We'll find the RV, store it someplace, stock it, learn to drive it. We've talked about this for years. We've got the money. Liz, listen to me. We've worked so hard all these years. We can do this. All we need is a couple of weeks to get ready. When we're set to go, we'll leave Bob and Carl letters, and we'll write the kids, too. We'll say it's a wild, wonderful vacation, and then, if it turns out to be something more, well, we'll deal with that later."

I reached into my bag and pulled out a large manila folder filled with the on-line research I had done the night before, a yellow legal pad, and several colorful RV brochures I picked up from Danny's.

"See, I've thought of everything. We'll go through these brochures; I'll look the models up on line. We'll make a list of what we want, decide what we want to pay, and then we'll go shopping. I've mapped out several lots for us to tour—not Danny's, but there's *Paradise RV World*, *Rainbow RV*, *Sunset Park*, and one called *Sisters on Wheels*. We'll tell the same story I told at Danny's. . . Oh, and you'll have to sort of dress for the part, okay?"

Trance-like, she stared at me.

"We'll take care of insurance on site—most of these places sell their own insurance. I think I've thought of everything. I wasn't a corporate executive for nothing, huh?" I took a deep breath.

"Liz, it's time. It's OUR time."

I watched as her hands twisted in and out, one over the other. What she needs, I thought, is a dose of glamour. With her, anything sparkly works miracles. She was a real girly-girl, in that way. So, I reached into my purse and felt around. There it was; the tissue crinkled in my hands: my tiara. I unwrapped it and made a show of dusting off the stones with the hem of my tee shirt. Then I placed it very gently on my head and looked directly at Liz.

"Are you with me?"

# Chapter 3

## Drive It Home

Three lots, increasing disappointment, and five hours later, we pulled into the last motor home dealer on our list. Surrounding us were four wheelers, motorcycles, pop-up campers, mopeds, and several other varieties of recreational vehicles neither Liz nor I recognized. We gaped at the spectacle of choices.

"Hello, girls. Welcome to *Sisters on Wheels*." I nearly jumped out of my seatbelt, not having seen the woman walk up behind the car, but before I could respond, she leaned down and through the open window. Bright rouge circles highlighted a moon shaped face topped off with a lion's mane of gray hair.

"I'm, Della," she said, twisting her lips just so to spit without turning her head. Tobacco chewing must be the fad for motor home dealers, I thought. The stocky woman ran her hand across her black tee shirt sporting the company name. Her braless bosom distorted the letters so that they ran down her more than generous midriff like white goopy cake icing revealing only "sist son eel."

I glanced over at Liz. Her sucked-in cheeks and widened eyes told me laughter was dangerously close to escaping right in this woman's face. To avoid that embarrassing fiasco, I hit the release button on my seatbelt and climbed out of the car.

"Hi, Della. We, um....we're searching for an RV as a retirement surprise for our folks, and we're hoping you can help us."

"Sure, I can, honey. My sister Lerline and I have been in the business more than twenty years, and we know everything there is to know about RV's." Della paused, eyeing my costume, especially the bandana around my head. Then she shrugged slightly, as if brushing whatever doubts away, and said, "Follow me."

"Wait," I choked out, not wanting to waste any more time. "We sort of know what we want. We've narrowed the choices to something with a sofa and dinette that converts to sleeping space, a queen bed, firm mattress, and maybe one of those overhead cab bunk areas."

"And," Liz chimed in, pulling at the ribbons on her straw hat as she came around the rear of the car to join us, "we want a large viewing window by the dinette, real wood cabinets, and a microwave. We, I mean the folks, like all the creature comforts and nothing cheap, mind you."

Della grinned. "No problem, girls. I've got just the thing."

We followed her through a narrow passageway between two rows of humongous RVs and turned right. Della stopped abruptly, boots planted solidly in front of a vision from my childhood dreams. It was long, lean, and sparkled in the late afternoon sun. Liz and I took one look at the hood, then at each other, and nearly wet our pants laughing.

"Well now, I'm taking all that happiness as a good sign," said Della, eyeing us quizzically.

I reached across the hood and traced the two-inch letters with my fingers: Silver Queen Screamer. Perfect. A silver queen for two real-life queens.

"May we look inside, Della?" Liz asked.

"Sure, you can, honey. Right this way. Della unlocked the side door, flipped a lever and two gleaming metal steps eased up and out of the doorway. "Comes equipped with easy step access, so's your, um, "folks" don't have to strain getting in and out."

"Oh, that's great. Mom will love this." I smiled sweetly.

"Ohhhhhh!" Liz swept up the steps and into The Silver Queen. "Real cherry cabinets! And look at this luscious blue and green color scheme."

"Yep, this is a pretty one, alright. And it comes with its own GPS system."

Patt Fero

"What's a GPS system?" Liz and I asked at the same time.

"That, dearies, is a Global Positioning Satellite System. Kind of like a built-in navigator and compass system so you can find your way around if you get lost, gives you mileage from one point to another, and gives you your exact location in case you need to call someone for help.

"And," she continued. "The Screamer comes with a generator which is attached on the left outside there, in case you run into any power troubles. There's a DSL system for a computer if you want it, but you have to prepay for access. Everything else is standard. No extra cost."

Liz and I wandered through the motor home, touching, sitting, opening cabinets, and checking every inch. I watched her eyes light up at each new gadget she discovered, and I felt a lightness in my chest that hadn't been there in years. We're really going to do this, I thought.

"Why don't you girls take her for a spin. See how she handles?"

"Uh," I hesitated. I didn't want to admit I had never driven such a big vehicle, but one look at Liz's pale face and I knew I had to move.

"Sure, great idea." I jumped into the driver's seat. Della handed me the keys and pointed out the dashboard features, explained the gears, mirrors, brakes. I was certain she knew our secret, but she was kind enough not to voice it out loud.

"Have fun," she said and climbed out of the vehicle, closing the door firmly behind her.

"You can't drive this thing," Liz whispered frantically at me. Her hands went into their twisting, twining dance again.

"Relax. I drove an eight-gear truck once when I was moving. How hard can this be?" I didn't tell her that when I returned that truck, several gears were burned out.

I eased the gears into drive and took my foot off the brake, but then stopped suddenly.

"Wait!"

Liz, not yet in her seat belt, flew forward, but caught herself before crashing into the dash.

"What?" She gasped.

"First, buckle up. Now..." I reached into my purse and heard the familiar crinkle of tissue paper. "Get your tiara, out, Liz. This is our inaugural drive. The Queens are on their way!"

Liz giggled, and in seconds, tiaras in place, we were off.

The interstate seemed a bit much to take on for our first drive, so I stuck to the frontage road. The Silver Queen glided along, smooth as a ship on calm seas.

"Yeah, baby! I'm loving this Screamer! Feel the power! Feel the free-dom…..YESSSSS!" I shouted out the window at some grazing cows.

As we rode on, Liz began to relax. Soon she was snooping through the console compartments, her eyes widening with each new discovery of the little extras tucked here and there. "Drive It Home" blared from the Bose on the dash, as we cruised back to the Sisters' sales lot.

I slid the Queen back into her slot, and Della appeared again out of no-where.

"I think I'm in love. She's fabulous!" I said as Liz and I climbed out.

"Good! Let's make a deal," Della rubbed her hands together and turned to walk toward the sales office.

Liz looked at me, almost panicked. Decision time. And it was indeed a BIG decision.

"Uh, well, I actually think that Leslie and I need to discuss this before we say a definite yes." Liz backed slowly toward my car. She was going to bolt on me, I knew, so I took that as my cue.

"Sold!" I shouted.

Della and Liz both looked stunned.

"I mean, of course, we want to buy it…today….no time like now, right Liz? Now Della, I can tell you're trustworthy. Just give us the best price you can."

Della looked back at Liz, then at me, and without turning her head, twist-ed her lips just so and spit out another wad of tobacco. How did she do that, I wondered.

"You know, I've seen all sorts coming and going around here, but you two really beat it all. I don't know what's up with the costumes and tiaras, and it ain't none of my business 'long as it ain't illegal. So, I'll just go get the paper-work, and you can drive the Screamin' Queen home." With that, she shuffled off.

Liz all but flew at me. "What are you doing? You're just going to write a check today? We don't even know how to drive that thing! And where in the world are we going to hide it between now and when we leave." She stopped, gasping for breath.

"Liz, this is it. You know it, and I know it. We're buying that baby, and we're hitting the road. No more waiting. No more talking. It's a done deal. You'll thank me after it's all over." I turned and marched straight to Della's of-fice. Liz reluctantly followed.

Liz and I signed form after form. Della treated us right based on the price information we had researched. She even called in Lerline to write us an insurance policy for The Screamer. Lerline, dressed in mechanic's coveralls and a baseball cap, wiped her hands on a grease-stained rag and wrote up the policy in minutes.

"You sure you don't want to activate the satellite service?" She looked from Liz to me.

"No, our parents will NOT need computers," snapped Liz cutting her eyes at me.

Still partly in corporate mode, I almost panicked at the thought of not having my computer, but I had promised Liz there would be none. I shook my head. "Okay, ladies. That's it. Congrats and all."

"Your folks are gonna love it, I'm sure." Della winked at Lerline and tossed the keys to Liz who missed, and then stared at them like they were two boas doing the dirty in her lap.

"Della?" I asked as sweetly as I could. "We're going to need to store The Screamer for just a while before we, um, before we take it to the folks. Would you know of a place close by?"

"No problem, sugar. Lerline and I rent out spaces in the back all the time. You can pull right into one of those garages, close the door, lock her up, and come back whenever you want to get her."

I looked at Liz, but she stayed focused on her lap.

"Good. Sign us up." I dared not hesitate. Liz looked as if she might up and fly away on all of us.

"Oh, and one more thing," Della said. "You might want to outfit the RV with a CB radio. They're handy in a highway emergency. You can always get in touch with the truckers. They're real good about helping out."

"You're right. Definitely get us one of those, too."

"I'll put that in tomorrow, first thing," Lerline grinned. "What's the handle?"

"Handle? What's a handle?" Liz looked as if one more new thing was going to push her over the brink.

"Oh, you know," I said, nudging at her shoulder, praying we didn't sound as ignorant as we were. "It's like our CB name. A call signal. You say things like: this is The Silver Queen Screamer calling Hit-the-Road-Jack, 10/4, over and out." I glanced over at Della, proud I knew what a handle was.

Liz stared at me.

"So you want to go with "Silver Queen Screamer?""

"Yeah…that's it. The Silver Queen Screamer." I took the keys from Liz and tossed them to Lerline. You do what's necessary. We'll come by tomorrow afternoon and get her settled in the garage."

I shoved Liz toward the door, but as she walked to the car, I turned back to Lerline. "You know, why don't you just hook that satellite up while you're at it. I'll pay you for all of it tomorrow," I whispered out of Liz's earshot.

"Sure thing," she grinned. "The satellite service comes with a complimentary website for one year. The satellite people even give you a bumper sticker with your web address right on it, so's you want forget. You got a special name you want on it?"

After all the years of dreaming, it took me only a second to answer. "Oh yeah, I do. That would be: www.queenmotorhome.com."

"That's a good one. Goes right along with those crowns you two are wearing. Your parents wear 'em, too?" Lerline looked up at me from beneath hairy eyebrows.

I knew she was suspicious, but I just smiled back at her. "Oh, no. It's a private joke thing between Liz and me. Uh, Lerline? Let's keep this a little surprise between you and me, okay?"

"No problem," she said, shaking her head.

I hurried to the car where Liz, still looking pale, sat shaking her head from side to side. "What are we doing? What have you talked me into? We've just bought a HUGE motor home. We're going to leave our husbands and hit the road for God knows where with nothing but a CB radio between us and road stalkers! I can't believe…"

"It's okay, Liz. Don't fret. This is a good thing, you'll see."

"Sure," she said, and slumped down in her seat. At that moment, she looked like a lost child in Halloween drag…mascara smeared, tiara lopsided on her head. I reached over and straightened it for her. She looked up and slowly, slowly, smiled.

"You've lost your mind, and obviously, I've lost mine, too, because I'm following right behind you," she said, and we both laughed all the way home.

# Chapter 4

## See, See Rider

After some absolutely necessary fibbing to Bob and Carl, we returned to Della's lot late the next afternoon. The men thought we were at yoga class.

Throughout the afternoon, we scavenged discount and grocery stores stocking up on any and everything we thought we might need.

"I don't know how we're going to fit all this in The Screamer," Liz whined. "It's not that big, you know."

"Liz, Liz, Liz," I crooned. "Relax, we'll get it all in. There are tons of storage compartments. Not to worry."

We had dressed a little more normally since we didn't have to disguise ourselves from Della and Lerline. No way would they ever come in contact with the husbands, and if they thought us a little weird, they were just too damn nice to mention it out loud.

"She's ready to go," Lerline grinned when we pulled into the lot. "Let me show you about this CB." She climbed up the easy stairs leaving us to follow.

After demonstrating all the gadgets and gismos, Lerline motioned for us to follow her. We walked to the rear of The Screamer, and there on the rear bumper was the sticker with our web address: www.queenmotorhome.com. I was thrilled. Liz looked bewildered.

"Now Liz, don't get upset. It's not what you think. It's not a website. It's just a bumper sticker, kind of like 'California or Bust.' Lerline got it for us, and I wanted to surprise you. It's our identity!"

Liz raised one eyebrow at me, and said, "Well…it IS our special code, so whatever."

I guess she felt the same as I did: after all those years of using that code between us, now, we were really acting on it. We had a REAL moving, driving, on-the-road-motor-home fit for two queens: US!

While Lerline gave me a crash course in all of the mechanics of the motor home, Liz took charge of stocking the cabinets and shelves with all the things we bought.

Lerline covered The Screamer from back to front.

"This here, is what we call black water. You got to dump it a lot!"

"What's black water?"

"Toilet."

"Oh, I see." I vaguely remembered reading about that in my research and wasn't particularly looking forward to that exercise. Liz would faint dead away over it.

"And this is the gray water, which means water from your sink and showers."

Next came instruction on the electricity modes and how and when to use those, the water pump and water heater, heating system, propane tank, and finally the generator."

"Surely, our parents will stay only where there are plug-ins," I assured her.

"Uh huh, still….you're gonna need a generator."

Lerline didn't miss a button, switch, container, or hinge. I was overwhelmed with all the information she knew, and I guess I looked it because as she started to leave, she turned to me and said, "Don't worry. All this is in the owner's manual. You all will get the hang of it in no time." With that, she strode back to the office. I rushed in to locate the owner's manual and propped it on the console. It would be our Bible from now on.

The afternoon whizzed by. A slight rain fell, and the temperature dropped suddenly. It was early for this kind of weather.

As dusk fell, Liz turned to me. "Maybe we should postpone our driving practice. There's an early winter storm warning out, and the temperature's already dropping. I'm having serious doubts about being able to handle The Screamer as it is, much less on icy roads."

"Nonsense. We need to know how she handles in all types of weather. Just relax.

Put on your tiara and some tunes, and leave the driving to me." I grinned at my friend who sat with her feet in the seat and knees hunched up close to her face. She smirked back at me, but sat up and placed the rhinestone symbol of our new found lives on her head. I floored the accelerator. The Screamer squealed once, and we were off.

We drove to what used to be a Kmart not far from *Sisters on Wheels* and claimed the empty parking lot as our testing ground. I guided our Silver Queen right to the center, but when I went to brake, I missed and accelerated, instead. The Screamer squealed again and shot across the lot, hitting a frozen patch of rain and turning a perfect 360-degree donut.

"Wow! That was as good as any county fair ride, huh Liz?"

"Liz? Liz?" I poked her shoulder. She sat staring straight ahead, pasty white in the late sunlight. "I don't think I can do this, Leslie. I feel very….very…intimidated. Can't I just be the cook, navigator, and general slave? Do I have to drive?" She turned such big sad eyes on me, I almost agreed, but caught myself in time.

"Absolutely not! You do have to drive, and you can do this. Now get over here and buckle up." I scrambled around the console and unsnapped her seat belt, pulling her over to the wheel. After buckling my seat belt, I turned to Liz and said, "You're on the throne; so let's go."

Liz rolled her eyes at me, straightened her tiara, and reached for the steering wheel. She shifted the gear stick and eased her foot onto the accelerator. Slowly, The Screamer moved forward. "Okay, I'm doing it! I'm doing it!" she shouted.

All went well for the next twenty minutes or so. Liz cruised calmly around the lot. We sang while the wipers swished and swayed in time with the oldies playing on the Bose. The rain fell. The temperature outside dropped. The Screamer sped up. And sped up. And sped up some more. She began to rock and lean more heavily to the side with each circuit Liz made.

A little concerned, I turned to her. "Uh, Liz, I think you've definitely got the hang of it now, but, uh, don't you think we should slow down just a tad?"

"I'm in love," she answered and winked at me. The Screamer bounced suddenly and hit another patch of ice, sailing out of control toward the vacant Kmart store ahead.

Our "Whoa-ooooooooo's!" were accompanied suddenly by blaring sirens.

Liz hit the brakes. The Screamer jerked, slid, and reversed herself to face the swirling blue lights head-on in the darkening lot. We watched as the two officers crawled from their cars, hands on their pistols.

"Okay, Liz," I whispered. "Just let me do the talking."

She nodded.

One officer skirted the right front bumper, backed off a few steps, and stood directly across from my window. The other one walked to the driver's side.

"M'am, roll down the window, please."

Liz obeyed.

"Drivers license, registration, and insurance card, please."

"Officer," I said, "We just bought this motor home, so we don't have all that yet. But I do have the Bill of Sale and a paper stating we've bought the insurance."

"Hand it over, please."

"Officer, REALLY, we are so very sorry. We really didn't mean to do whatever it is we did…" Liz began, then dug in her purse to find her license.

I leaned across her. The officer to my right took a step forward and rested his hand on his gun. I looked back at him. He seemed nervous.

"You see officer, we just bought this motor home and wanted to practice driving it before we give it over to our parents, so we could teach them, and then, it started to rain and sleet, and well, things just got a little out of control."

"I see."

"We didn't realize the lot was so icy, and we would never, never intentionally squeal tires or cut doughnuts or…."

"And YOUR identification, m'am." He didn't smile.

I handed over my license and sat back. Now he'd know our names and addresses, and if this got back to Bob and Carl, Liz and I were doomed. I put my hand up to over my eyes. Liz slunk deeper into the throne. The officer walked back to his patrol car and got on the radio. His buddy stood stiffly by my window.

"You lied to the police! I can't believe you lied to the police!" Liz whispered.

I watched as the officer fiddled in his car, wondering what might show up on the police computer that would warn him to contact our husbands immediately. The thought of Carl and Bob finding out about our plans at this point spurred me to action.

"Officer! Stop! Wait!" I jumped from The Screamer and ran toward the patrol car. Immediately, the officer standing to my side stepped back, then reached for his gun, and started after me.

"Don't shoot her!" Liz cried behind me.

Shoot? Who? My mind flew from one thought to the other until I realized she meant me. Don't shoot ME!

I stopped, and immediately my legs slid sideways over the icy pavement. One went one way, the other went another. The patrolman chasing me couldn't stop in time. He skidded into me, and we both fell.

At that, the officer in the car jumped out and skated his way to us. Liz came from the other direction. The officer beneath me wrangled his way to his feet, and both officers stepped away from us. "What are you doing?" Liz whispered in my ear as she helped me stand.

Though I'm certain it was only seconds, it seemed that minutes passed before the officer spoke. "Are you alright, m'am?" He seemed unable to speak. He just stood there staring at us.

"Yes. Yes, sir. I'm fine. I just....I just..." Liz poked me in my back.

"Yes, m'am?"

"Uh, it's just that I wanted to tell you that um....well, you see, our husbands don't know about the motor home plan yet either. It's sort of a surprise for *everybody*, and I thought that maybe you might decide to call them and, and......that's why I was trying to stop you just now. I didn't mean to... to...."

"It's okay, m'am. I wasn't going to call your husbands." He looked over at the other officer and winked. "You girls aren't sneaking out of town, are you?" He smiled.

Liz jumped in before I could. "No sir. No sir. Like she said, it's a surprise for everybody—even us...we just up and bought this thing without any real planning at all."

"I see," he said as we all walked back toward the motor home He pointed to the hood. "Silver Queen Screamer, now that's an interesting name for a motor home, ladies. Is it something you chose?"

"Why, no sir, it's not. It came with the motor home. It is interesting, isn't it?" I smiled my widest, friendliest smile.

"Uh huh," he answered. "And those crowns on your head, I suppose they came with it, too?"

I reached up to straighten my tiara, having forgotten I even had it on.

Thankfully, he didn't wait for an answer. The officer handed our licenses and the paperwork back to both of us.

"Ladies, I've seen just about everything, but this is a first. I'm not going to charge you this time. It's right nice what you're doing for your folks, but for now, you two better head on home. It's a good idea, but tonight's weather doesn't bode well for practice driving. And another bit of advice: You might want to tell your husbands about all this. Maybe they can help you out with the driving lessons. This is on my beat, so if you come back to practice again, I'll keep an eye out for you. No problem. But for tonight, I suggest you head on home."

He tipped his hat and left us. His fellow officer pulled at the wet seat of his pants where they stuck to his backside and walked to his car.

"You lied! My God, you lied, again, to the police!" Liz mumbled as she climbed into the passenger seat while I claimed the throne this time.

"I didn't LIE exactly. Our husbands *don't* know about the motor home, and it *will* be a surprise to them, right?"

Liz shook her head, and then burst out laughing.

I drove slowly back to *Sisters on Wheels*.

We passed the RV where Della and Lerline lived. No lights shone from within.

"Looks like the old girls turned in early," I said as we glided silently toward the storage unit. "Now, I'm going to need your help backing this into the unit."

"No problemo!" Liz answered and jumped from The Screamer to open and lift the unit door. It squeaked loudly. She flipped on the overhead light, looked around, and then came back.

"You sure this thing's going to fit in there?" she asked.

"Della said it would. You get in the back and wave me in."

I maneuvered The Screamer into position and looked back at Liz.

"Ready?"

"Ready."

I eased my foot from the brake and gently pressed the accelerator. "Here she goes," I mumbled.

In the rearview mirror, I could see Liz frantically waving me on in. "Just a little more," she called to me.

Slowly, slowly The Screamer inched her way toward the far wall of the unit.

"Halt!" Liz yelled.

"Halt?" I asked, sticking my head out the window and looking back at her.

She grinned and shrugged. "I always did want to say that."

I shook my head, cut the ignition, and climbed down from the throne.

I had backed into the unit with plenty of room on either side, and I was about to brag a bit about this when I noticed that the front end stuck out beyond the door.

"Liz, I've gotta come back a few more inches. We can't close the door."

Back into the driver's seat I crawled, and back to the rear wall of the unit went Liz.

Inch by inch, The Screamer moved. I put the gear in park and revved the engine once more for luck. Then I heard a hacking cough from behind me.

Turning off the ignition, I called out, "Liz? Where are you? What's wrong?"

"Help!" She called and coughed again. I pushed the door open and scrambled to climb from the RV, but I stumbled, and this time, my knees, rather than my rear, took the brunt of the fall. The keys flew from my hand and up under the motor home.

"Help!" Liz called again. "I'm stuck. I can't get out, and those fumes just about gassed me!"

"Coming…" I stretched and turned and stretched the other way, but I couldn't reach those keys no matter how I positioned my body.

"Uh, Liz…."

"Hurry!"

At the rear of the motor home, Liz stood pinned between the bumper and the unit wall.

"Liz, don't panic. Now, listen, I'm sorry, but I've dropped the keys, and I can't reach them. We're going to have to figure something else out. Just stay calm. Are you hurt?" I added, realizing I hadn't asked before.

"No, I'm not hurt. I just can't get out either side." I watched as she pulled and twisted her body from side to side.

"Well, can you turn one leg and get it up on the bumper, and then lift the other?"

Liz struggled for some time, but finally managed to maneuver one foot so that it rested on top of the bumper.

"Okay, good. Now, lean over and grab that spare tire holder on the back and try to twist and pull your other leg up here."

Liz did as I asked, and soon she was crouched, hump-backed on the back of the motor home. Her arms wrapped around the spare tire, her legs bent at the knees, and her feet balanced shakily on the bumper.

"Okay. Now what?" She asked. Her face was smushed against the rear of the motor home so that her words came out garbled sounding like "Oh! Ow….at."

"Now, just up above you is the rear windshield wiper. Reach as high as you can and grab it. Then you can pull yourself up to stand on the spare and from there, climb on top of The Screamer and over the hood to the ground. Then we're good to go!" I smiled at my friend.

She struggled. And struggled. And struggled some more. I tried to push on her rear from one side, and finally, using the spare tire and the rear wiper to hoist her body, she was on top of the motor home.

"Great," I said.

"Yeah, great!" She answered me. "Now while I'm up here doing the snake, you go find the damn keys." Liz didn't sound happy.

I crawled up under The Screamer as far as I could, but still couldn't reach them. Then, I remembered my tiara. Of course, my beautiful, USEFUL tiara, I thought. I took it off my head and used it as a hook to snag the runaway keys. Then I slithered my way back out. I heard Liz making her way across the top. Not thinking too clearly and in a hurry to rescue Liz, I climbed in The Screamer to start the engine thinking I could move it backward just enough so she wouldn't have to squeeze herself between the door top and the motor home top. She might just get stuck again, I thought. The Queen roared to life, and I jerked the gear into reverse.

Immediately, Liz screamed. I slammed on the brake, and over the windshield, Liz slid. She landed with her face pressed against the windshield, arms splayed to either side. Her tiara hung from one ear. Hanging upside down, she snarled at me and then stuck out her tongue. I opened my mouth to say something to her, but before I could Liz somersaulted her whole body and landed on the hood like some splayed porno hood ornament.

I ran to her. "Are you okay?"

"I hope this night isn't an omen of what's to come on this crazy escapade," she said and began to giggle, and so did I. Laughing so hard, we didn't hear Della and Lerline come up.

"You two alright?" They yelled at the same time as they rushed to us. They stood barefooted, each wearing a man's plaid flannel robe. Hairnets studded with blue satin bows covered their pink plastic rollers.

Della and Lerline stared uncertainly at us. Liz and I looked at them, and then at each other. We knew there was no stopping what was about to happen. It started deep down in our bellies, gurgled upwards, and then exploded from our mouths—laughter. Bone shaking, rib-hurting guffawing. And then, well... we wet our pants.

# Chapter 5

## What's Love Got to Do With It?

I watched Bob sleep, thinking what a nice guy he actually is and how much I would miss him, BUT....and that "but" loomed large between us now. Bob was handsome, viral, and true. Just the kind of husband most women want. But I wanted one who could share this adventure of midlife and beyond with optimism and a sense of freedom. I didn't want to be tied down to things. I didn't want to have to think before I could have fun. I just wanted to live.

"I love you, honey," I whispered. "Please don't hate me when I leave."

"Huh? Huh? What's the matter?" Bob mumbled.

"Nothing. I love you. Go back to sleep."

The next morning, Bob left for work, and I went into action, piling luggage, bags, and boxes in the car trunk. The house was clean; the lights off. There was a casserole in the fridge for Bob to have later. A huge red heart magnet on the fridge held my letter to him. He couldn't miss it.

That letter turned out to be the hardest part of this whole scheme. I had struggled with what to write. In the end, I settled for what was my best attempt to explain and, hopefully, leave the door open.

*Dear Bob,*

*I love you very much. Please read this with an open heart.*

*Remember how the Queens always joked about running away and living together? Well, we're doing it. Liz and I are leaving today. We've bought a motor home and are riding off into the sunset, after all. The most important thing for you to remember is that I'm not leaving you. I'm leaving the "stuff." The stuff I tried to explain to you last week: the corporate crap, the routines, the games we have been forced to play. I'm in a real rut, and I need to get away.*

*Everyone always expected me to do the "right" and normal things. I was always the strong one, the practical one. But now...well, you're so wrapped up in your business. Rex has his own life at college. And for once in my life, I just want to do something for me. If I don't, I'll go crazy. And Bob, you know, this is actually cheaper than a shrink.*

*Please trust me. Try to be happy for me. Liz and I will be fine, so don't try to find us or send someone after us. I'm not certain just where we're headed, but we'll stay in touch. Please don't worry. Go to Sisters on Wheels RV Park just off I-85 and pick up my car. Inside, you'll find letters for Billy, Mom, and Rex. Everything's going to work out just fine, Bob. Love you.*

*Leslie*

*P.S. Last night was* **WONDERFUL!**

I locked the back door and drove over to Liz's house. We were on our way.

Or maybe not. Liz bounced down the stairs wearing what she called her "N Cognito" outfit: black stretch pants, long black pullover, and she finished the whole get-up with black flip-flops and designer sunglasses. She dragged several totes behind her.

"Liz, where are we going to put all of that stuff? You always bring too much!"

"Don't lecture me! As you pointed out yesterday, there's plenty of room in The Screamer. I *NEED* my stuff," she answered. Her stuff included not only clothes, but also an electric frying pan and enough hair products to open up a beauty supply store.

"Don't look at me like that," she whined. "It's hard to pack for the rest of your life, you know. And one of these totes has all our Queen stuff in it. I bet you didn't think about bringing that, huh?"

Actually, I hadn't. The Queen items included framed pictures and photo albums of our weekends away throughout the years we'd known each other. There were monogrammed wine glasses, our own special Queen tee shirts, teddy bears, feathered boas, toy microphones, the works. We had dreamed and pretended for years about the Queen motor home. And suddenly, it was a reality. We were hitting the road.

"Did you leave the letter for Carl?"

"Yep. Inside the refrigerator, taped to some pasta sauce for tonight."

I eased the car out of the driveway and headed for *Sisters On Wheels*. Liz looked back as we drove away. Tears puddled in her eyes.

"What's wrong with you? Don't tell me you're having second thoughts NOW!"

"No. I'm not." Liz sniffed and reached for a tissue in her purse. "It's just that this is so BIG for us. We've fantasized about this for so long, and I....I don't know. What if Bob and Carl don't understand? What if they don't forgive us? What if we forget something or there's a flat tire, or we meet up with thugs, or ....."

"Enough! We're not going to meet up with thugs. Anyway, if we did, we're covered. I brought my pistol!"

"Oh, well, THAT makes me feel safe!" Liz sniffed one more time and tossed her tissue into the litterbag hanging from the console.

"Seriously, Liz. Everything's going to be just fine. And as for Bob and Carl, they know we love them. They'll get over it." At least, I hope they will, I thought. But somewhere deep inside a little voice kept asking, "Then why didn't you tell them face to face?" I didn't want to explore the answer to that.

"We've planned. We've saved. We've covered every possible scenario. I'm a little nervous, too, but we made a pact years ago, and unless you telling me right now to scrap all this, we're leaving today. It's a dream come true for two really nice people who deserve it—US—you and me. And if the guys don't understand, well, then, we'll deal with all that later. Remember: no guts, no glory."

"Okay. But the thought of you with a gun really does scare me. So, let's don't talk about it." She settled back into the seat and took a deep breath. "I'm ready."

The *Sisters on Wheels* lot was empty, but that was fine with us. The fewer witnesses, the fewer lies we had to tell. When we raised the storage unit door, The Silver Queen Screamer gleamed in the morning sunlight. I unlocked the driver's door and swung it open. "Welcome home, Liz! Welcome to our future!" My heart was full.

We unloaded all the totes, boxes, and bags and packed everything away inside our new home. We had everything we needed. I even stashed away a case of vodka and some fresh oranges for little celebrations on the road.

"Okay, Liz, give me your other letter. I'll put it with mine inside the car and lock it up. The guys will find the ones at home and then these for the boys and Mom."

Liz's eyes welled up again.

"Now what?"

"It's just that I rewrote those letters a hundred times trying to find the best way to explain to Carl and Billy, and I'm still not sure they will understand. I don't want them to think I don't love them."

"I know. I know." I hugged my best friend. "I had a hard time explaining, too. Did you do what I told you to do last night?"

Liz blushed. "Uh huh."

"Well, then. See. We left our men with food, clean homes, and a great night of sex. What else could we do to make this easier for them? Besides, it's not like we're never going to see them again. Once we get organized and on the road, we can call or send email or..."

"Email? NO! You promised no computers and no email! You've spent your whole life married to a computer and a company that didn't appreciate you. You said we were leaving all that behind!" Liz looked dangerously close to losing it.

"Okay. Forget email for now. We'll send postcards. Postcards are nice. Everyone likes postcards, and we'll work out a contact plan after we get on the road. We'll figure it out." I patted Liz's shoulder. "Now, give me your letter."

I parked the Mercedes at the edge of the lot and carefully placed the letters on the front seat of the car where Bob couldn't miss them. I had a fleeting image of my mother reading hers. Now, that would be a Kodak moment for sure.

"You girls takin' off?" Della strode up behind me.

"Oh, yeah. We're, uh...our parents' anniversary is this weekend."

Liz steered The Screamer up beside me, horn blaring.

"Um, Della? My husband will most likely come tonight to pick up the car. Is it okay to leave it parked right here?"

"Sure thing. I'll keep an eye out for him. Oh, and here's a little something for your trip. It might come in handy." Della handed me a book entitled *A Dunce's Guide To RVs*. Safe journey to you and your folks," she said as she walked toward a customer just pulling into the lot.

"You drive first!" Liz called down, sliding sideways into the passenger seat. I climbed up on the throne, buckled up, and took a deep breath.

Liz tapped me on the shoulder. "You have the maps? I don't want to end up like those guys in *Deliverance*."

"Yes, Liz, I have the maps—right there in the console. Now, one last thing." I reached into my purse and pulled out my tiara. Liz grinned at me and did the same.

Crowns on our heads, we pulled away from *Sisters on Wheels*.

A thrill ran up my spine. Long ago, happy memories crowded out the last bit of nervousness. "Let's sing," I said to Liz, and burst out with a full chorus of "Side by Side." She belted out the words right along with me. As I turned onto the highway, I looked back once more. Della's image filled the rearview mirror. With one hand shielding her eyes from the morning light, she waved good-bye to us. Even from a distance, I could see the hairy eyeball look she gave me. Her suspicions were still there, all right. I waved back, and we were off!

# Chapter 6

## Running Scared

Miles down the freeway, I noticed Liz's smile fading.

"Okay, let's play the 'no more' game. I'll go first. Let's see…no more checkbooks to balance!"

Liz cocked her head to the side, and then smiled. "No more high school football games!"

"No more board meetings!"

"No more Prom Moms that need interior design!"

"No more…" Before I could get the words out, Liz beat me to them. "No more SNORING!" We both laughed.

I-40 took us over the Blue Ridge Mountains. Truck traffic was heavy, and several blew their horns at us as they dove down the steep declines. After the initial excitement of actually hitting the road, Liz and I both settled into a comfortable silence. But that got too close to being serious, so I suggested she turn on the CB radio.

"What channel are we supposed to use?" She asked.

"Channel 19 is for the truckers, and Channel 9 is for emergencies," I answered, proud that I could remember all that Lerline had told me.

Liz fiddled with the knobs, and the CB crackled to life. "Bingo Bud. Come in. This is Moose Man. I detect a bear in the air, so better slow down."

"Ten four, Moose Man, thanks for the warning."

"Bears?" Liz gasped, turning her head right and left, desperately seeking what Moose Man had described.

"Rendezvous, to Pie Face," said another voice. "We have half a dozen alligators up ahead."

"Ten four, man."

"Alligators?" Liz pulled her feet and legs up as if expecting one to crawl from beneath the seat.

"Relax," I said. "Alligators are tire treads lying on the road. And bear in the air is a radar check conducted by helicopter."

"Just how do you know all this, Miss Smarty?"

"The internet, my friend. I looked up a bunch of stuff online in preparation for our trip."

"You and that damned computer! I'm so glad we don't have one with us." I let it slide, and Liz settled back in her seat once more.

Trucks whined past us up the inclines and whizzed down the declines, blowing their horns sometimes three, four, or five times.

"Are they trying to tell us something?" asked Liz.

"I think they're just being friendly," I said and backed The Screamer down into second gear. Behind us, semis veered into the other lane.

The CB crackled to life again. "Hello, Silver Queen Screamer, come in."

"Oh no! Somebody's taken our name." Liz leaned forward to listen more closely.

"Silver Queen Screamer...come in please."

"Liz, that's us. Somebody's calling us! Pick up the handle and answer him."

"What? Who? It might be a. ...murderer! We can't just talk to strangers!"

"Answer him, Liz, or I will, and I'm not sure I can handle this motor home with just one hand on the wheel."

Liz picked up the receiver. "Uh, This is....this is Silver Queen Screamer."

"Say 'go-ahead.'"

"Uh, go ahead."

"Hey there, Screamer. This is Ponderosa Man. That's quite a handle you got there!" There was definite laughter that followed across the radio bans. "Where you girls headed?"

"What do I say to him, Leslie? Is he flirting with us? I haven't been flirted with in years!" Liz turned around thinking she might see him, but realized she couldn't see through the rear of the motor home.

"Give me that thing." I snatched the CB from her hand and sat up straighter.

"Hey there, Ponderosa Man. We're heading for the sunset. Any road construction up ahead?"

Liz rolled her eyes at me. I grinned.

"Watch for a detour about a mile ahead at Ed's Pit Stop. It's a great place for lunch."

Liz shook her head no, no, no. I smiled again, feeling devilish.

"That's a 10-4 Ponderosa Man. Thanks for the tip."

"What ARE you doing?" Liz's voice had gone several octaves higher than normal. "You're going to eat lunch with a truck driver at a place called Ed's Pit Stop? Have you lost your MIND?"

"Liz, settle down. It's a public place. Besides, I'm hungry and a truck driver can be a good friend in case we need help. You need to loosen up some, girlfriend."

She didn't answer me, but she did take out her compact and put on some lip gloss.

"Liz, this is a truck stop. Nobody gives a shit how we look. Let it go!"

We pulled into Ed's. The parking lot looked like a trucker convention. We walked into the smoky diner. I was dying for a cigarette, and enjoyed breathing in the second hand smoke. There were no empty tables, so I was about to tell Liz we'd just eat at the counter when a bear of a man stood up in the back corner booth and waved to us.

"Silver Queen Screamer?" He called out.

All eyes turned to stare at us. There were snickers and whispered comments as we walked to the rear of Ed's. I heard something about "you think those two really ARE screamers?"

The big man motioned for us to join him. I pushed Liz in the back to hurry her on.

"Hi, I'm Leslie and this is my best friend, Liz." The two of us squeezed into one side of the booth. "Thanks for the tip about the good grub here." I was feeling real hip using what I thought of as trucker lingo.

"Nice to meet y'all, ladies. And what we have here at Ed's isn't called grub, we call it food." His smile stretched from lobe to lobe. "So, where are you two headed?"

"No where in particular. We're just taking some time off from our usual lives and traveling a bit."

"Ran away from home, did ya?" Ponderosa Man leaned over the table toward us.

Liz fidgeted at my side.

"Well, I wouldn't say ran away, exactly…we just …um…." Liz turned to me, her eyebrows raised.

"Actually we're taking a vacation sort of from our usual selves," I told him.

He nodded. "I know about that, all right," he said. "By the way, my real name is Ray." We shook hands all around.

Liz reached for a menu. "Do they have anything low carb here, Ray?"

He laughed. "Did you hear that fellers? This little lady wants to know if Ed sells 'low carb!'" The whole diner burst into laughter.

Liz blushed and looked from Ponderosa Man to me. "Okay, then, well, …. if I'm letting go of the make up, then I'm squashing the freaking diet, too." How about something high carb?" She smiled her best smile at Ponderosa Man.

"Now that, Ed can get ya!" He answered and held up his hand to the waitress. "Margie, bring us all one of those western omelets with sausage and biscuits."

"Oh, and some extra butter," Liz added. She was going whole hog on this one.

We sat back to wait on the food. Ray eyed us both, and then twisted in his seat to lean forward on his elbows. He looked at us dead on.

"If you don't mind me asking, ladies, why are you two wearing those crowns?" We both giggled. "We're queens," I answered.

"Queens? You mean you two, uh…you two sleep together?"

Liz and I inhaled gulps of air. We hadn't thought of our title in that respect, but. I decided to have a bit of fun with old Ray before telling him the truth.

"Why, yes, Ray. We do…sleep together. We have ONE bedroom in The Screamer, and neither of us wants to sleep on the sofa bed."

He stared at me, and then let out a huge guffaw. "Ah you two. You had me going there. I see what you mean. So you're not like….like…lovers or anything?"

Liz and I looked at one another and smiled.

"No, we're not lovers. But we do love each other. We've been best friends forever, and we've always dreamed of taking off in a motor home for a grand adventure. The 'crowns' as you call them, represent something entirely different. I'm not sure you'd understand though. Anyway, we're not lovers."

"You're not in any kind of trouble, are you?"

"Well, we didn't kill anyone or rob any banks if that's what you mean." Liz was a little indignant.

"So, you just up and left? How 'bout jobs and families? Don't you have those?"

"We've been planning this for many years, Ray. It's a dream. Something we've always wanted. Our children are in college, and our husbands...well, now just seemed the right time to try it out, that's all. Honest."

He nodded. "Dreams I know about." Ray tugged at the bill of his cap and stared at his hands. His voice came out harsher and sounded more distant than it had before. "I wanted to chase a few myself, but when my ex died of cancer, that left just my daughter. She's partially handicapped, and I love her, but she doesn't have much to do with me. Must be nice to just quit the real world." He stared just above our tiaras.

Liz and I squirmed. Other than our husbands and sons, we hadn't been concerned with how others might react to our adventure. On the surface, it probably did seem a bit irresponsible. I wanted to explain, but the high carbs arrived, and all three of us dove into the meal. It was some minutes before the conversation picked back up.

"So where are you headed with this dream of yours? You have a plan?" Ray scrubbed at his mouth with a paper napkin, and then folded it neatly beside his plate.

"Not really. We've got maps and a campground guide book, and an open road before us!" I laughed. A certain light-heartedness began to settle deep within me, and I was enjoying it.

"Well, you girls best be careful out there. There're some bad people on the road these days. Best you keep to the main roads and campgrounds. And if you need me, just call out my handle. If I can't get to you, I'll find a buddy who can."

Before we could thank him, he stood up and pulled his cap farther down toward his eyes. Without looking at us or saying another word, Ray strode out of Ed's.

# Chapter 7

## Mixed up, Shook up Girl

"Drive!" Liz gasped as she climbed into The Screamer. She was red-faced and sweating.

"What's wrong? What happened?"

"Just drive—NOW!"

I put The Screamer on the road and asked again, "Liz, what's wrong?"

My best friend turned to me, her eyes wide, her breath still coming in tiny little sips. "I love truck stops." She sighed.

"What?"

"I love truck stops. More specifically, I love truck stop showers. Leslie, you'll never guess…you've never even dreamed….what I saw…."

"What Liz?"

" I decided to run to the ladies room after I paid our tab, but I took a wrong turn and ended up in the …"

"Men's room?" I was getting exasperated.

"Nooooooo! The truckers' SHOWER ROOM! And there was a man…a *big* man, a big *TRUCKER* man….Leslie, I swear, I've never in my life ……"

"WHAT?" I practically screamed. "Did he try to touch you?"

"If only…." Liz sighed, licked her lips and turned her wide eyes back on me. "You should have seen him, uh, *it*. It was HUGE! He was HUNG like a stallion! I'm gonna dream about him the rest of my life!"

I nearly wrecked The Screamer. I laughed; Liz laughed, and yes, again, we wet our pants.

I eased us off the interstate and pulled into a Wal Mart parking lot.

"I've got to change my clothes," I gasped, still fighting down the giggles.

"Me, too," said Liz, "but it was worth it. And Liz, he looked back…he looked back at *ME*! I guess fifty-five is not so over-the-hill after all, huh?"

We changed our clothes and finally hit the road again. This time, Liz drove.

"I'm still a little nervous about driving her," she said. "Those practice sessions we had helped, but these roads are bears! I hope I don't get carsick. Or get vertigo! Oh, I had forgotten that. Every time I ride in a car in the mountains I end up with vertigo! Leslie, you better drive."

"No! You've got to get used to this. Besides, I think the worst is over as far as the steepest grades. If you start feeling sick, I'll take over, but for now, The Screamer is all yours." I reclined my seat and closed my eyes, ready for an after lunch nap.

Fifteen minutes later a semi passed and laid on his horn. He lingered in the passing lane right beside us.

"Leslie! Wake up. Look over here. What does he want? Why is he riding right beside us?"

I straightened up in my seat and leaned across the console to get a look at our friendly trucker. He wore a leather jacket and a black Stetson. A cigarette dangled from between his teeth as he smiled and waved at us.

"Just keep going, Liz. Keep your eyes on the road. He's just messing with us. Don't panic. I can see other trucks coming up behind him, so he'll have to get out of their way."

The CB crackled. "Hey there, Silver Queen Screamer. This is Gigolo One. Where you two lovelies headed? I'm headed to the Corral West Bar over in Norris and I'd love the presence of your company tonight."

"Gigolo One! My God! What kind of name is that?" Liz turned to me. The Screamer swerved.

"Let me handle this, Liz. Hey there, Gigolo One. This is The Silver Queen Screamer, What's your specialty?"

"Leslie!" Liz swerved again. I put my free hand over hers on the steering wheel trying to steady the motor home.

"My specialty little ladies is the horizontal disco, and I love Screamers!" With that, the big rig nudged closer to The Screamer.

"Oh my God!" I realized too late that I had walked right into this and even held the door open for him. Liz turned toward me, her face pale.

"I'm sorry, Liz. I shouldn't have opened that can of worms. I was just being friendly. Oh, God…okay, okay. I'll just use my best boardroom voice and get rid of the creep. Don't worry."

Before I could conjure that particular ball-busting part of my repertoire, the CB crackled again.

"Gigolo One, this is Ponderosa Man. Advise that you move along. Out of sight, preferably. If not, *I'll* meet you at the Corral West Bar tonight and show you the Vertical Rambo tango. Get my drift?"

"Leslie, that's Ray. He's saved us!" I reached for the CB, but it crackled to life before I could call Ray.

"Silver Queen Screamer, this is Ponderosa Man. Is everything okay?"

"Oh, Ray! It's so good to hear your voice."

"Ponderosa Man, Screamer. I don't know any Ray."

"Oh, sorry, Rrr…I mean Ponderosa Man." I had forgotten that real names aren't used on CBs. "We're fine. That gigolo man has moved way ahead of us now, thanks to you. Where are you?"

"Just ahead. I heard the exchange. Keep it in the road, ladies. There's a lot you don't want to tangle with out here. Understand?"

"10/4. Ponderosa Man. Over and out!"

We drove on into the early dusk, both a little shaken from the encounter. We both realized that two women traveling alone had to develop some real road smarts, quick.

The Screamer's dashboard glowed softly in the gathering dark.

"There's our exit for the campground," I told Liz, pointing to the huge green sign on our right. "Just a quarter mile up and at the top of the ramp, take a left. It's just a few miles down that road."

"Thank God!" sighed Liz. "I'm about whipped."

"Me, too." I replied. I glanced at the clock on the dash: 6:45. Bob would be coming home about now. I closed my eyes and saw him: guiding his car carefully into the garage, unlocking the back door, slamming it. He'd toss his briefcase on the dryer and his overcoat on the kitchen chair. He'd call out his usual corny: "Honey, I'm home."

Then he'd trudge over to the computer desk and flip through the mail.

After a few minutes, he'd realize I hadn't answered. He'd wander through each room of the house, searching, calling, " Leslie-pooh, where are you?" When he realized I wasn't home, he'd make his way back to the refrigerator for a beer. He'd reach for the door and finally see the heart magnet holding my letter. He'd snatch it off the door, grab his beer, flop down in his easy chair in the den, and then, finally, open my letter.

# Meanwhile…

# Chapter 8

## Oh, Girl!

Bob read and reread the last few lines of Leslie's letter. *"Please don't worry. Go to* Sisters on Wheels *RV park just off I-85 and pick up my car. Inside, you'll find letters for Billy, Mom, and Rex. Everything's going to work out just fine, Bob. Love you. P.S. Last night was* **WONDERFUL!** *"*

Billy and Rex walked in just as he reached for the phone.

"Carl, what the hell are those two women up to now? I came home to a weird letter saying they were going on a trip, and I was to pick up the car and more letters at some RV park. Do you…."

Before he could finish, Carl interrupted. "Yeah, I got one, too. I don't know what's up. Is this one of their crazy jokes, or have they finally completely lost their minds?"

Bob motioned to the boys to come into the den. "Carl, the boys are here. I'll bring them along, and we'll pick you up in a few minutes."

On the way to *Sisters*, the younger men took turns guessing at why their mothers had taken off on their own.

"Dad, what's going on? Did you two have a fight? Did you hurt her? Are you getting a divorce? Why would mom just run away like this, and in a RV at that? She can't drive one of those." Rex poked his father's shoulder with each question he asked.

"Son, I'm as surprised as you are. And, NO, we didn't fight. I didn't hurt her. There's no divorce. It sounds like your mom just wants to drop out of society for a while, or some such foolery."

"Maybe they're getting Alzheimers," Billy added. "They're pretty old, you know."

"We, I mean they, are NOT old, Billy!" Bob all but shouted.

"Well, when do you suppose they might be coming back?" Carl whined. "Liz didn't say. Do they think we're just going to sit around here, all patient and ever-loving while they toodle across the country trying to find the meaning to the rest of their lives?" Carl was known for his impatience and frat-boy arrogance, and he treated most everyone just like he treated the kids he coached: Bust your butt; do it my way, or else.

"Maybe they need a shrink." Billy suggested.

"Yeah, can't you see 'em both sprawled out on couches, and some poor shrink sitting over in the corner drooling on himself cause he's so confused by them?" Rex nudged Billy in the side, and the two laughed out loud.

At *Sisters on Wheels*, Bob pulled up to Leslie's Mercedes. He unlocked it and retrieved the letters splayed across the front seat: one for each boy and one for Anne, Leslie's mother. He tucked that one in his jacket pocket and handed the other two to Billy and Rex.

While the boys read, Bob and Carl walked away to talk privately. "I should have seen this coming," Bob confessed. "You know, some jerk at her company was going to phase her job out, so she just up and quit. I tried to talk some common sense into her. But she wouldn't listen...oh no, she just went on and on about feeling like some kind of pay check to me, and hating the house, the mortgage, all our friends, everything. But I never suspected this! They won't stay away long."

"Who the hell knows with those two. You're not really okay with this. I don't see why we should give them any time at all. We should call the police, have them tracked down and make them come home. This is just another of their whims. They've always been trouble together, and this is just one more thing!" Carl paced in front of Bob.

"Hey man, wait. Maybe they'll call. I'm worried, but you know, they aren't dummies. I'm sure they think they can handle this...think being the operative word, here. We'll hear soon enough if they can't. Let's just give it a couple of days."

Later that night, after waiting hours for the call that didn't come, Bob held his own private pity party. He hadn't wanted the boys or Carl to know how shook up he was. He drank his scotch and listened to all of Leslie's favorite songs. He opened her closet and slid his hands down over her clothes. At the dresser, he picked absentmindedly through her jewelry.

When he finally turned in, he reached over to Leslie's side of the bed, pulling her pillow to him. It smelled just like her, and in the wee hours, he finally fell asleep to the sound of his own whispers: "Come back. Come back."

By morning, there was still no call or message from Leslie, so Bob tackled the job of phoning Anne.

"How about lunch today with your favorite son-in-law?"

"Why Bob! I'd love to. Kit's Kitchen at noon?"

Bob was already seated when Anne came in the restaurant. She carried a small brown bag, and Bob could only guess at its contents. He stood to seat her and kiss her on the cheek.

"Is that a surprise for me?"

"How'd you guess, darlin'? My latest batch of blackberry preserves." Anne replied. At 75, she looked more like 60. She could be the poster woman for the golden years: attractive, energetic, fashionable. But her young looks never got in the way of being the perfect grandmother or mother-in-law. Bob considered himself very lucky indeed and loved her like his own mother.

"Thanks, Anne. No one makes them like you do."

He helped her sit and returned to his own. "I've got some news, Anne, but I'm not quite sure how to tackle telling you. I guess the first thing to say is that Leslie's fine; we're not getting a divorce or anything, but well, she's …." He looked at his mother-in-law, listening so attentively, and he realized he couldn't explain it to her any better than he had been able to explain it to himself. Maybe a divorce was what Leslie really wanted after all, he thought.

"Hell," Bob hung his head as he reached into his jacket pocket. "She left you a letter. Maybe she explained it to you better than she did to me."

*Dear Mom,*

*Liz and I have finally done it! We've bought a motor home, and we plan to travel for a while. But by now, I am sure you've already heard that from Bob. I hope you'll forgive me for not telling you in person. Everything has happened so fast, but in a nutshell, my company was going to can me, so I quit. Those testosterone pricks finally got to me. I just couldn't stay another day. On top of everything else, I guess I just finally went over the cliff.*

*I love you, and I know that if anyone can understand, it will be you. I'm asking you to support me in what is probably perceived by everyone else as one of the craziest things I've ever done.*

*I just need to get off the fast lane train for a while. I promise you that we'll be careful, and I also promise that I'll contact you soon. Please stay in touch with Bob and Rex while I'm away. Help them understand. I'll tell you all about our adventure when we return.*

*Leslie*

"Let's have some lunch, Bob." A hint of a smile touched the corners of Anne's mouth as she refolded the letter and placed it in her purse.

"Lunch? Is that all you're going to say after learning that your daughter has gone off the deep end and run away with her crazy best friend in a motor home, for God's sake? Leslie told me she was in a rut. She said I made her feel like nothing but a paycheck. I thought we had a pretty darn good life going, and then she ups and does something like this."

"Relax, darlin'. I'm just gathering my thoughts."

The waitress interrupted to take their orders, and after what seemed to Bob an entirely long time, Anne finally began to talk to him again.

"Now, look. Leslie's a smart, savvy woman. She's capable, energetic, and creative when she has to be. Over the years, I wanted to do much the same thing that she's done. Just chuck it all, and take off! Just never had the opportunity, or the guts. I love to travel, but at my age now, it's very tiring. Leslie's at the age where she can and wants to travel. Tell me Bob, when was the last time you two traveled anywhere together?"

Bob shrugged his shoulders.

"My point, exactly. Now, here's the thing. You need to let go of this for a bit. I know you're concerned for her, but trust me, give her some space and a little time. Don't go traipsing after her at this point. She'll be in touch soon,

I'm certain. And I'm also certain that, in her own good time, she'll be back. Can you do that, Bob? Can you just let it go for a while?"

"I don't know, Anne. I really don't know. Besides, it's not just up to me. There's Carl to consider, too. He was ready to call the police last night. And what about the boys? Who's going to help them understand all of this?"

Anne reached across the table to pat Bob's hand. "Don't you worry about my grandson. He's more worldly than you think. I'll have a heart to heart with him and Billy. You just get that silly Carl under control. Everything's going to be just fine. You'll see."

Their orders arrived, and Anne made a show of unfolding her napkin and fixing it just so on her lap.

"Let's bless the food, now, Bob."

And they did, only Anne added a silent plea to the end: "Lord, let me be right about my wayward, impulsive daughter."

# Long Gone…

# Chapter 9

## Mama Said There'd Be Days Like This

"Here we are!  Our first camp night in The Screamer."  In spite of being weary, Liz's voice oozed with excitement.

A large woman in a Led Zepplin sweatshirt and baggy sweat pants stepped from the office trailer and met us at the gate.

"Hi, there.  I'm Leslie, and this is Liz."

She gave us the once over while she ran her hand through her silver and black hair—obviously a great color job—no one had natural silver highlights that perfect.  She would have been pretty except that her eyelids bagged and her facial skin sagged.

"I'm Beulah.  I run this place. What can I do for you?"

"We'd like to get a space for the night."

"That'll be twenty dollars," the woman answered.  She stepped back inside the tiny office and returned with a folded map and a couple of flyers.  "Here's a map.  I've marked your spot on it.  It's #33. Take a right here past the office and go down ten spaces. We have electric, water, and sewer hookups at each site. And there's a grill you can use, long as you clean it afterward. No loud noises. No parties." She looked us over once again, and then continued. "If you need anything, just knock on my door, but try not to come after 9:00 at night. Oh, one more thing: don't leave food around. We've had some bandit coyotes recently."

"Coyotes?" Liz's voice cracked on the word.

"Not to worry. They won't bother you if you don't bother them. But best not leave anything tempting lying around."

Liz nodded mutely. Her eyes huge in the glow from the dash.

The woman turned as if to leave, but then stopped. She looked directly at us.

"Ladies, I hate to be nosy, but what's up with the crowns? You two aren't 'weird' or anything, are you? I run a clean place around here, and I can't...."

"*Weird*? Us? Well, I guess the crowns might seem a little strange, but anyway, it's a long story, but I assure you we are not 'weird' in any kind of, you know, in any 'sexual' way." Liz used her fingers to make quote marks around the words weird and sexual.

"Uh, huh," Beulah answered, slowly. "Well, have a nice evening, then."

Liz put The Screamer into drive and pulled forward, but immediately stopped and backed up to Beulah again.

"You know, we'd just love to have you over for breakfast in the morning. That way, we can explain the crowns, and maybe you can give us some pointers on other camp grounds and points of interest in the area."

Beulah looked us over once again. Then as if something clicked into place, she shrugged. "Sure. I'll be there early if that works for you two."

"Great," said Liz, using her Miss Congeniality smile.

We made our way to the site. Liz backed in like a pro.

"I'll get the hookups. You mix us a drink," I said.

"Vodka with a twist of fresh orange coming up." she said.

"I'm ready, baby. Pour me a strong one."

The hookups and plugins went smoothly, so I took time for a cigarette. In no time, I stepped back inside The Screamer to wash up.

We took our drinks up to the cab.

"Liz, watch this," I said as I pushed the pop-out button. "I just love doing that. It's a lot more fun that hookups".

"Too cool!" Liz said, as we sat, feet propped up on the dash. We nibbled on pretzels and sipped our drinks. "The stars are so bright up in these mountains. I feel like they're closer than ever."

"Mmmmm," I replied. Too relaxed to enter into much more of a conversation.

"You must be more tired than I am," Liz said, laughingly. "We've had quite a day. Why don't I fix our supper, and we'll get showers and hit the sack."

"No, let me do supper," I said. "You get your shower."

"No argument, here," Liz answered making her way to the rear of The Screamer.

I rose to pull out the things I had packed away for tonight's meal. It would be our favorite: calamata spread, green olives on melba toast, fresh tomatoes on wheat bread, cream cheese, and salami, topped off with fresh cantaloupe.

Before I finished pulling everything together, Liz yelled. "What's with the shower?"

"What do you mean?" I hurried back to the rear.

"There's no water. I turned it on, but nothing's happening." She answered.

"I must have hooked up something wrong," I sighed. "I guess I need to read my dunce book that Della gave me. Let me go check it out."

"No, don't bother right now. Let's just eat," Liz said. We took our plates back up to the cab, so we could star gaze again.

In the quiet aftermath of the meal, a thought suddenly hit me.

"Liz, don't you think it's a bit odd that our cell phones haven't rung? I thought we would have been bombarded with calls from the guys by now."

"Oh, I'm sure we will be. They're probably hunched over some bar tonight, telling each other what crazy dingbats we are. I figure they'll stage a holdout for a few days. They most likely think this is just a whim, and we'll be home in a couple of days."

"Mmmmm," I answered. "But even mom hasn't called."

"Look, of all the people in the world, Anne will understand this perfectly. She's always been your biggest cheerleader, and she'll make it all okay with Bob and Rex. Anne's the least of our worries. It's Carl that's most likely to go off the deep end. Knowing him, he'll want to call out the Marines—or the police at the very least." She tugged her sweater closer around her shoulders.

"We did the right thing, didn't we?" I asked softly.

Liz turned toward me. Her tiara sparkled in the moonlight filtering through the windshield.

"The right thing? Ha! I'm the one who's supposed to have all the doubts, here." She poked me in the ribs. "Of course, we did the right thing. You and me, babe. We're the Queens. And we're hitting the road."

I smiled at my friend. "Right. We're hitting the road. It's just that it feels so different from our usual routine, you know. After all these years, I'm not the one behaving responsibly. Suddenly, I'm not the usual me. I'm different. I'm a…"

"You're a runaway girl, that's what you are!" Liz quipped. "And I'm right there with ya." Using her fake opera voice, she burst into the chorus of "Side by Side."

"Okay, okay." I couldn't help but laugh. "No more singing, P-L-E-A-S-E. Let's call it a day." We made our way back to the bed, each grabbing an extra blanket. I had forgotten how cold early fall in the mountains can be.

Sometime later, a noise outside The Screamer woke me.

"Liz, did you hear that?"

"What? What?"

"That noise," I whispered.

"Honey, if it's lighter than Carl's snoring, I don't hear a thing!" she mumbled.

A rap on the door jerked us both to sitting positions.

"Who can that be?" Liz whispered.

"I…I don't know. God, you don't think it's Bob and Carl. Or maybe they sent the police after all."

Liz scrambled to peek out the window.

"Get down. They'll see you. I'll get the gun; you get the Billy Club," I whispered back to her. The Billy Club was only a walking stick, but in these circumstances, any weapon might help us. Liz fumbled around in the closet. "Shhh…be quiet. Don't turn on the lights."

Finally, we crept toward the door. "Okay, on three, you open the door, and I'll point the gun." I positioned myself in the "shoot 'em up" posture I had seen on television so many times. Liz shook herself like some dog shedding water. She was pumped, I could tell.

"Ohhhhhhh," Liz quietly whined, but on three, she wrenched the door open.

"Don't move, or I'll shoot," I yelled.

"Yeah, and I'll knock your dicks in the dirt!" Liz raised the Billy Club high over her shoulder.

Three guys sporting sparkly get-ups with chains and high-heeled boots gaped at us. We screamed. Then they yelled.

"Oh, damn, hold on ladies. Don't shoot, please, don't shoot. I think we might have the wrong address," the middle one said.

"Talk," I said using my best wise guy imitation.

"We, uh, we saw the bumper sticker, and I guess we uh….well, we thought it was an invitation?" His explanation ended on an up note like a question.

"The bumper sticker? Invitation? What the hell are you talking about?" Neither Liz nor I had a clue.

"You know…the one on your rear bumper: www.queenmotorhome.com. And then there was, of course, the name on the RV: Silver Queen Screamer." The middle guy seemed to be the ringleader. The others didn't speak, just nodded their heads in quick agreement with their friends explanation. "We're sorry. We didn't mean any harm."

They turned to leave and bumped into Beulah and her 12-gauge shotgun.

"What's going on here?" she asked. At her side was the biggest dog I've ever seen, a beautiful Saint Bernard, who circled the boys, sniffing. They froze.

"It's okay, Beulah. It seems these young men got routed the wrong way. I don't believe they meant any harm. It just startled us. Sorry about the noise."

Beulah eyed them and us carefully. Then she grunted. "Okay, then. I'll be going. An old woman needs her sleep, so I don't expect to be woke up again tonight. Come on, Lulu."

She got three or four yards down the dirt road, and turned back toward us. "I wouldn't want to have send Lulu back either. Understand?"

All together, we said, "Yes, M'am!"

I looked at the three boys more closely now. They weren't much older than Rex and Billy.

"Well, since we're all wide awake, how about a cup of cocoa for everyone."

Liz stared at me, her mouth already forming a protest.

"Have a seat at the picnic table, guys, and we'll swap some stories. Hot cocoa coming up." I dragged Liz back inside with me.

"What are you doing? Do you want to get us raped and killed?" She all but jumped up and down.

"Relax, Liz," I whispered. " We're totally safe. Look at them. They're not much older than our boys, and they're GAY. We're in no danger of being raped. And murder is not what they came looking for."

She followed me out to the picnic table. The night was cooler than I thought, so I lit a fire in the grill. Liz brought out some extra blankets and passed them around.

"My name is Leslie, and this is my friend Liz. She's my best friend since way back. And believe me, you don't want to know exactly how long that is." The boys smiled and sipped their cocoa.

"I'm Winston," the middle one said. He had red spiked hair and sported a black glove on one hand. I was reminded of Michael J. "These are my friends, Ronnie and Kenny."

Ronnie's clothing was fairly normal, but he had no hair. He looked smoother on top than a boiled egg. Kenny, on the other hand, wore dreadlocks and some sort of genie pants.

Liz remained speechless.

"So…let's swap Queen stories." I looked from one to the other. They looked at each other, and then back at me. No one said anything.

"Okay, then. We'll go first." I gave them the long version of how Liz and I had always wanted to buy a motor home and take a trip together. Explore our world. Stretch our minds. The boys stared as if I was speaking a foreign language.

"We, uh, made up this secret code www.queenmotorhome.com to use whenever life got to be too much, and we needed a break. And well, it happened. Life got to be too much. So we bought The Screamer and headed west. She came with the name, and the bumper sticker represents our code. We've always considered ourselves, at least in our small part of the world, to be queens. You know, the regular kind."

"We even have tiaras," Liz blurted out. She rushed inside and grabbed them as if she had to show them to be believed.

The guys blinked. One by one they checked us out, head to toe. I could almost hear them thinking: "Geez, they're weirder than we are."

But they didn't say it out loud. In fact, Ronnie surprised us all when he said,

"That's pretty cool. I wish my mom had run away a long time ago. My life sure would've been different. Instead, she hung around and slept with half of Dallas. Instead of bedtime stories, I got to listen to her scream out 'Oh baby, oh baby, give it to Mama!'"

"I made up my mind way back then to run when I could, and I did."

Winston nodded his head as if in agreement. "Yeah, my story is 'bout the same. Except my dad was still around. He was useless. Drunk all the time. My mom got real depressed and was put in a home. Dad ran. So, I ran, too."

Liz reached over to pat his hand.

Kenny hid behind his cup. Winston spoke for him. "Kenny doesn't talk about his past. He's got this lisp, so he doesn't really like to talk much about anything."

I saw tears shining in Liz's eyes. My best friend was an absolute marshmallow.

"My God, how sad!" cried Liz. "How old are you boys?"

"Winston pointed first to himself, then to Kenny and Ronnie. "Twenty-one, Twenty-two, and twenty-one," he said. "We met at a gay disco one night and decided to hang together. We had visions of traveling being one big, fun adventure, but so far, it's nothing like that. We sleep in the car most nights trying to save money for food. We even stayed a couple of nights at a homeless camp. I guess in reality, we are homeless." Ronnie pulled his blanket closer around his shoulders.

"But you Queens sure have a nice gig here," he said, waving toward The Screamer. "That would make travel a big, fun adventure, for sure." The other boys nodded in agreement.

"One day maybe we'll have an RV, too. We've gotta land somewhere first and get some jobs to earn the money, though." Winston said. "We've talked about getting an Airstream."

"Oh, we looked at those, too," Liz piped up.

We sat for a while longer, each of us lost in our thoughts, staring up at an endless night sky. I didn't know about Liz, but I was feeling a little shame-faced and ungrateful. Here we were running away in style with our Screamer and the money to back us up. But those poor boys had the real reasons to run. Life wasn't fair. I don't know why I sometimes think I can make it that way.

"Tell you what guys. It's getting awfully late. How about bunking with us tonight? Then tomorrow, we'll have a big country breakfast before you take off."

The three of them looked ready to run.

"Oh, I'm sorry. I didn't mean it that way. I just meant, well, we've got a sofa bed and a dinette seat, and then there's the overhead bunk area. Plenty of room. You all look like you need a good night's sleep."

Liz's face was plum purple. I could already hear her arguments against this, but I was determined. It wasn't much, but giving those boys one decent night's sleep and a hearty breakfast would help sooth my guilty conscience.

Without a word, the boys rose and followed us in. We gave them extra sheets and pillows, and then turned out the lights. They whispered softly to each other as Liz and I made our way to the bedroom.

Before she could start her arguments, I held my hand up and explained my reasoning. She held her tongue, which was something new, but I did notice that she locked the bedroom door before climbing into bed.

"Good night, Liz. Sleep tight. It'll all be over in the morning." I smiled to myself.

Liz tossed and turned to face me. "Good night! And if you feel something long and hard in the bed tonight, don't get all excited. I'm sleeping with the Billy Club."

# Chapter 10

## I Betcha!

"Queeeeeeeensssss! Oh Queeeeeensssss! Wakey-wakey. Breakfast awaits."

"Leslie, wake up. They're calling us. Do you smell that breakfast?"

"Mmmmmm, do I. Eggs, bacon, and COFFEE! Come on!"

We scrambled out of bed and into our robes.

"Good morning, gentlemen," I greeted them. "Breakfast smells fantastic! But you didn't have to cook for us. How'd you make coffee without any water?"

"No biggy. We had some bottles in our backpacks, so we used those," Ronnie said. He was looking very smart to me this morning.

"Last night was the best sleep we've had in days. Besides, Ronnie's a great cook, and that's sort of his way of saying thanks," Winston explained.

A sharp knock sounded on the door. When Liz opened it, the mountain air drifted in, crisp and cold. Beulah and Lulu stood just beyond the easy steps.

"Good morning, Beulah. You're just in time for breakfast. The young men you met last night stayed over and this is their thanks for a warm spot to sleep in."

"Come ladies. Sit," Winston led us outside to the picnic table. I sat beside Kenny, who still hadn't uttered a word directly to anyone.

"Here we go," sang Ronnie. He placed the platters of food in the center of the table.

"My goodness," exclaimed Beulah. "This is a meal fit for Queens."

There was a second of silence, followed by a burst of loud, wild laughter. Beulah looked from one of us to the other.

"What?" she asked.

"Oh, it's just this whole queen thing is getting a lot of play lately," I replied, trying to pull myself together. "What with The Silver Queen Screamer on the front of the motor home, the queen motor home bumper sticker, our tiaras, and…." I hesitated.

Winston filled in the rest of the sentence, "And three real queens added to the bunch!" Laughter took over again. Even Lulu added to the ruckus with two staccato barks. It was some moments before things settled down.

Beulah slapped the table in an attempt to get our attention. "Okay, I get that you guys are 'queens,' but you ladies promised me an explanation, and I think now's a good time to hear it." She looked pointedly at Liz and me.

"Well, Beulah, in a nutshell, I guess you could say we are runaways." Beulah looked at us suspiciously.

"Oh, not from the law or anything. You see, well, we just needed to get away from our lives as we were living them."

"That's not so unusual," she replied. "But what about those tiaras you two wear? What's that all about?"

Liz and I looked at each other. Then we took turns telling our saga right up to last night's arrival at the Cozy Run Campground. Beulah listened quietly, with only the occasional grunt to a few of our comments.

Winston and Ronnie took over where we stopped, explaining their situations. Beulah shook her head in sympathy at the boys' stories, and then looked at Kenny.

"What about you? What's your story?" She asked.

Ronnie jumped in to explain about Kenny, and Beulah sat quietly studying him for a moment.

"A lisp ain't nothing to be ashamed of," she said. "You need to just spit it out, straight, and dare anybody to make fun of ya. That's what you're afraid of, isn't it—that people will make fun?"

Ronnie rose to pour more coffee for all of us. Kenny continued to stare at his lap, and just as I expected, Liz jumped right in to rescue him.

"Beulah, why don't you tell us your story? How long have you been in this business?"

"Well, mine started out similar to yours, ladies. Twenty years ago, my husband Joe and I finally had enough money to buy an RV and head out into the sunset. We'd planned for years. But just three days into our new life on the road, Joe dropped dead of a heart attack. I couldn't see myself heading on without him, so I figured the next best thing was to use his insurance money to open up this park. That way, I could enjoy other peoples' travel stories and still feel like Joe was right beside me hearing 'em too. It was sort of my way of fulfilling the dream without really traveling. I write all the stories down in a notebook and share them with Joe every night before I go to sleep."

Winston swiped at his eyes, and Liz reached for a tissue in her robe pocket.

The rest of us sat quietly, waiting.

"Now, if Joe was here, this is what he'd tell you ladies to think on what you left back home before you lose it. Doesn't sound so bad to me. Maybe you're just spoiled rotten and taking everything good in your lives for granted. Maybe the way to solve your life situation is to start out helping others less fortunate than you are. Get your minds on others instead of yourselves. That can fill up a whole bunch of empty spaces." She looked solemnly at both Liz and me.

"Now, I gotta go. Work waiting. You folks have a nice day, and thanks for the breakfast. It was real good."

"Oh, Beulah, wait! I wonder if you could take a look at the hookups over here. We don't seem to have any water." I led her over to the pole. She switched a couple of the plugins around.

"Try that," she called to Liz, who immediately ran inside to test the faucets.

"YES! We have water!" Liz called out.

"Thanks, Beulah. I guess I just got confused in the dark last night."

"No problem. See you later," she answered, and we all watched silently as Beulah and Lulu lumbered away. Between them, I could almost see the ghost of a man, his arm resting lightly across Beulah's shoulders.

"Well, I don't know when I've had such a great breakfast and such good company," Liz said trying to ease the strain of tension Beulah's talk left among us. I was already feeling guilty.

"Hey, you know what. She's a nice lady and her husband dying like that before they could live their dream was real sad. But I don't think you all are selfish. I don't know of anybody else who would have taken the three of us in like you did." Winston looked at his two friends.

"That's for real," said Ronnie. Even Kenny looked up and nodded once before ducking his head down again.

Liz supervised the boys as they cleared the table, while I sat watching the morning shadows chase the light across the campground sites. I knew she had taken Beulah's comments to heart, just as I had.

"Well, ladies, the dishes are done, the beds are made and it's time we headed out." Ronnie said. "We'll keep in touch using your web address back there on the bumper."

"Oh, that's just a bumper sticker. We don't have a real web site," Liz said primly.

"Why, not? You've got the satellite and all in there."

"No, Leslie promised me that, except for our cell phones, we'd leave the technology behind." She looked over her shoulder at me.

"I can understand chucking the corporate world stuff, but if you had an emergency, a website and email could come in real handy, you know. And you could email back home, uh, if you wanted to." Ronnie looked from Liz to me.

I could tell Liz was seriously considering this point. Of course, I wanted to jump at the chance to get the thing hooked up, but I knew it would be awhile before Liz came around on that one.

"Ready guys?" Ronnie called to his friends.

Winston and Kenny came from behind the motor home. Kenny held a handful of mountain holly toward Liz and me. The scarlet berries popped against the deep green of the leaves creating a bouquet as beautiful as any roses I ever saw.

"Tank you. I hope we tee you again tome day." He whispered shyly.

After a big group hug, the three boys lugged the backpacks across their narrow shoulders, smiled, and waved goodbye. So young, still, I thought as they made their way in their old, beat up Cadillac toward the highway. So young.

# Chapter 11

## What Kind of Fool

"I must be getting old," Liz complained after the boys left. "I'm pooped. What do you think about staying here another night?"

"I'm with you. It must be the excitement of the first day and all. Everything's catching up with us. Let's take the day and rest up. No one's called, so obviously we can relax about being hunted down right away. Maybe the guys are more understanding than we thought."

"Yeah, right," Liz answered. My friend never claimed to be above sarcasm.

Liz headed back to bed with a book while I went for a walk that turned into a run. Fall colors embraced me along the footpath, and the mountain air cleared away some of the cobwebs. I paced myself, slow and steady up the incline up and around to the top of the cliff. From there, I could see the curling roads and the rooftops of scattered homes that dotted the mountainside. A huge boulder provided a needed place to sit, and as my pulse slowed, I thought of Beulah and her impromptu lesson on thankfulness. She was right about a lot of things. We all had more than we could say grace over. But it was never enough. I knew this. Liz knew this. The thing was, we weren't sure our families understood this. What I wanted was exactly what Beulah had pointed out: a simple life lived with compassion for others and a full, thankful heart. But what I didn't want was what I had left behind: the rat race, the hurried, frenzied pace of life just to keep up appearances. So, it wasn't really a matter of not being grateful, I told myself. I knew I was lucky. Liz, too. We just didn't want all that to be thankful for.

A rustling in the woods behind me interrupted my thoughts. Whatever it was, it was big. A bear? A wolf? No, maybe a mountain lion. Did they have mountain lions in this part of the country? I didn't know. And truthfully, it didn't matter. Something big was heading straight toward me. I heard branches cracking, heavy panting. I eased down behind the boulder and armed myself with a ball-sized stone. Not much, but it was all that was available. I hadn't come prepared for a battle.

The crashing and panting grew louder. I crouched lower. The thing veered to my left. I followed the sounds. Bushes and brambles shook. I held my breath. My heart pounded. I stared so hard trying to see what was headed my way that my eyes watered. I lowered my head to wipe them, and at that moment something huge and hairy flung itself from the brush to my boulder and landed with its front paws on my shoulders. I screamed. Rolled to the side in a ball. A great tongue lapped at my face. Drool slid down my cheeks. I screamed again.

And then it barked.

I looked up to see Lulu straddling my prone body. She all but smiled at me.

"Oh, great! You made me wet my pants. Thanks a lot, Lulu."

She licked at my face again and I scrambled to my feet. There was no sign of Beulah anywhere, so I started back down the footpath.

"Ah, Lulu. Life can get so damn complicated." I patted her huge head and made my way back to The Screamer and Liz.

Liz sat at the picnic table sipping on a drink.

"I just talked with Beulah. We're set to stay another night. And you'll never guess what happened!" She called out as soon as she saw Lulu and me. "We got another CB call while you were gone. It came on all staticky, and then the big bass voice said, 'Come in Queen Screamer, this is Ponderosa Man!'"

"Hold on a minute. I've gotta make a change," I scooted past her into the motor home to change my clothes.

A few minutes later, she continued her story. "Ray says there's a big snow-storm heading this way around Turkey Day. He says we need to watch out for the weather and try not to be in the mountains when it hits. He wanted to make sure we knew about the emergency Channel 9. I told him we had all that stuff written down in our book, and we'd keep an ear out for the weather updates."

"Gosh, I hadn't even thought about Thanksgiving. It's just a few days away."

"Well, should we should move on or just stay put here for a while longer?" Liz asked. She scratched behind Lulu's ears. The big dog moaned with plea-sure, but left us as soon as Liz stopped her massage.

"Don't worry about it. It's not like the storm's going to hit tonight. You know what I'm dying for tonight?"

Liz smiled at me. "If it's sex, don't look at me!"

"Funny, funny. No, seriously. I'd love a big juicy cheeseburger and fries. Let's walk to that food place down the road that we passed by ."

"You mean 'The Joint'"? Liz asked.

"Huh?"

"The Joint. That's its name. I saw it when we came in yesterday."

"Okay, then. Let's go to The Joint and get us some more hi-carbs and fat for supper."

"You're on!"

We each stuffed a flashlight into our fanny packs, and I pulled my referee whistle cord over my neck. It dangled like some abstract jewel between my breasts. Maybe I'd start a new jewelry craze, I thought.

The Joint was filled with loud country music, smoke, the smell of grease, and several drinkers. We made our way to a booth in the corner of what looked like a dance floor. There were a few stares, and one low whistle. I winked at Liz. It had been a long time since either of us had heard one of those.

A waitress named Tilly meandered to our table through the crowd. She sported a red streak of hair down the center of her head and dangling three-inch earrings shaped like cowboy boots.

"What can I get you?" she asked.

"Two Michelob lights," I said.

"Honey, we don't have no fancy beer here. You can get Bud or Miller Lite."

"Oh, well then, I guess Miller Lite it is. And may we have a menu?"

"We ain't got none of those either. You can have a cheeseburger platter, a chili cheeseburger platter, a fried chicken platter, or a chili cheese dog platter," she recited.

Liz giggled. "Oooookedookey," I said trying not to laugh. "I'll have the chili cheeseburger platter," I said.

"Make that two," Liz added.

Tilly meandered away again into the haze of smoke. Liz leaned over to whisper across the booth.

"See that cowboy over there against the bar? The one that looks like Richard Gere, but with a Clint Eastwood smile? He's staring at us."

I turned slowly, so as not to seem to be looking specifically for him. He was staring all right. And he was a hunk. I pretended to look around the room again before I replied to Liz.

"Wow! Now that's a cowboy!"

We both giggled.

"Of course, you realize that the only reason he would likely be looking our way is that we most likely remind him of his mother." I said.

"Spoil-sport!" Liz sat back in her chair with a fake pout on her face.

Tilly came back with our food, and as we woofed down the meal, the music grew louder and the dance floor began to fill.

"I miss dancing," sighed Liz.

I drew deeply on my cigarette and blew smoke rings her way. She waved her hand in irritation and gave me a fake cough.

"Yeah, me, too," I said. "Why did we stop? The four of us used to go dancing all the time. It's been ages since we did anything like that."

I looked at Liz through the smoky haze. "I guess it just one more thing that dropped by the wayside while we were in the fast lane, huh?"

Liz wasn't listening. I turned to see what held her attention across the room, and there he was again—the hunk cowboy. And he was walking our way.

"I wonder what he wants," I asked.

"I hope it's me," she said dreamily. "Uh, just kidding, Leslie. No way is he coming over here, and he surely isn't going to want sex with me."

"Uh, huh," I said, as the cowboy stopped just in front of Liz.

"Hi, ladies," he drawled. "Nice to see some new faces in The Joint tonight.

My name's Warren, but most people call me Gig."

"Hi, Gig," I said, stifling a laugh at Liz who sat dumbstruck across the booth. "I'm Leslie, and this is my best friend Liz. We're traveling and just stopped in for a bite to eat. Seems like a pretty nice place, here."

"Yep, it is. Good food. Fine music. Would one of you ladies care to dance?"

"Oh, no, um, not me, but Liz here is a dancing queen. Give her a whirl."
I winked at Liz and waved to Tilly to bring another round of beer.

Liz didn't hesitate. She practically jumped from her chair and dragged Gig
out to the dance floor. For someone not so sure about taking this adventure,
she was certainly ready to go now. She was letting go and having fun. Meanwhile, I sat grilling myself on guilt. Had we done a purely foolish and selfish
thing?

Gig twirled Liz under his arm and drew her close for a slow dance. I watched
to make sure he didn't get too cozy, but Liz was smiling. She looked fine, but some
worry nudged at me. There was something familiar about the guy... "Gig?" It was
like a feather tickling at my memory, but too illusive to catch.

In the middle of my muddling, another man sidled up. He wasn't as pretty
as Gig, but he had great dimples. He introduced himself as Mac, Gig's friend,
and smiled so sweetly, when he asked for a dance, I couldn't turn him down.
Soon we swayed right next to Gig and Liz.

"Thanks for the dance, but I think I'll sit the fast one out," I said as the music changed. Mac bowed comically and followed me back to my table. I sipped
my beer and watched the crowd at the bar while he watched me. We tried for
casual conversation, but soon the clapping and hooting from the dance floor
behind us drowned out our voices as well as the music. I turned to see what was
up and nearly fell out of my seat. Liz lay on the dance floor with Gig straddling
her doing some very unsettling gyrations. I waved to catch her attention and
suddenly recognized the look on her face. In our college days, we used that
same look when we needed to be rescued from horrid blind dates.

I looked from Liz's face, to Gig's hips, and just as her expression registered
with me, so did Gig's name. Gig: short for? Oh my God! Short for Gigolo!
It had to be that CB Gigolo One. And what he was doing on the dance floor
most definitely looked like the horizontal disco to me.

But how did he end up here so near our campsite? Could he have followed
us? The thought unnerved me, but I didn't have time to dwell on it. I rushed
to Liz and grabbed her hand, pulling her to her feet. She stood there red-faced
and dazed. I swirled to face Gig. "Liz would NOT like to dance anymore."

"Oh, really?" Cowboy smirked. "How do you know what she wants
Ms.Queenie?" So, I thought, it is him.

I took a step closer. "Because we've been sleeping together for years, and I
KNOW her...get that? I KNOW her. Now back off, Gigolo One!"

The other dancers backed away, leaving us in the spotlight. Gig wedged
himself between Liz and me, using his hip to nudge me away. Liz stood limp
as he wrapped his arms around her again.

I took a step back and launched my body at his back. "Get off her, you pervert!"

There was a tussle. I reached for Liz, wrapping my arm around her waist. Mac entered the fray, tugging on my shirt, trying to hold me back. Gig snatched at Liz's arm from the other side. Liz stumbled forward, knocking him to the floor. She followed him. I followed her. My shirt ripped, and Mac stumbled to his rear end. We all hit the floor highlighted by the pulsing lights and whining guitars of the DJ's music.

After untangling myself and grabbing at my tattered shirt, I reached for Liz's hand. We scrambled away from the crowd, but Gig followed close behind us. He blocked the exit.

"Leaving so soon, ladies?" he smirked.

"Move it buster, or I'll…."

"You'll what? There ain't no Ponderosa Man to call now. You ladies are on your own and needing a lesson in being highway friendly, I think."

Liz blinked twice as if waking from a trance. She shook her head side to side, and held up her left hand pointing at Gig's face. "Back off, creep!"

Gig took a step toward her, and in one smooth move, Liz's right hand slipped to the Velcro fastener of her fanny pack, jerked it free, and slung the whole thing over her head like a great slingshot. It whirred over our heads. Gig backed away.

Liz inched closer and closer to him, forcing him away from the door. Finally, he threw up his hands in defeat. "Okay. Damn! I was just foolin' around."

Liz swirled the fanny pack one more time and brought it low and across his lower middle. We all heard the flashlight inside it strike home. Gig was stunned. His mouth opened, but no sound came out. Liz did a little celebration jump and grabbed my hand. We tore out the door and down the darkened road to the campsite. And for some time, we heard behind us, the distinct sound of laughter punctuated by Gig's curses.

# Chapter 12

## Rescue Me

Liz and I walked briskly for a short way down the road back to camp, but eventually we slowed to an easy stroll, enjoying the night. Mountain nights are beautiful. Cool, crisp. But it was dark. I was glad we had our flashlights—glad for more than one reason.

We walked in silence listening to the hoot of an owl, the cicadas, the occasional stir of tree limbs in the wind. Our tennis shoes made a plodding sound on the hard-packed dirt of the road. There was a distinct rhythm to our steps, and even our breathing soon blended as one. And then I heard it: a thud. I shook it off, and we continued down the road. But there it was again.

"Liz," I whispered, reaching to touch her arm. "Shhh! Don't be scared, but I think someone is following us."

"Ohhh!" Liz's voice sounded far too loud in the quiet night. I put my hand over her lips.

"Shhh! Listen."

We stood still. Liz's eyes over my hand were huge. We barely breathed. "There! There it is again." Liz's eyes widened, and I knew she had heard it, too.

I leaned closer to whisper to her. "Okay, we're about half-way back to camp. We're going to have to run, Liz. Can you do that?"

She nodded, and I realized my hand still covered her mouth. I dropped it.

Liz took a deep breath and whispered back to me, "You're the runner, but I'm a fast learner—especially when I'm being chased. On the count of three?"

We took off, our shoes slapping the packed dirt in steady beats. Behind us we heard another beat, between ours, out of place. Someone was definitely chasing us.

We saw no lights in the campground except for the few pole lights scattered down the entrance road. They gave us little comfort.

Liz fumbled the keys at the door, and I turned to look back.

"Oh my God! Hurry Liz! I see them. It's Gig and Mac. Hurry!"

We all but fell into The Screamer, but we were too late. The men caught up to us before we could slam the door. Gig jerked it from Liz's hand and yanked it wide open. We stood like deer caught in headlights.

"What are you doing here? What do you want?" I asked.

"Just one more dance, right Mac? That's all. You ladies left us high and dry back there. Besides, I think you owe me an apology for that swing you took with your bag there. In fact, I think you owe us a lot more than an apology." Gig's words slurred across his lips.

"Get out of here! Go away! I'm warning you…" Liz yelled.

Mac and Gig grinned at each other. Gig slammed the door against the side of the motor home and put his booted foot on the first step. I reached up to pull Liz away from the door, and my hand brushed against the whistle hanging from my neck. Perfect! I thought.

Before they realized what I was doing, I grabbed the whistle and blew. The shrill blasted through the night. I blew and blew and blew.

Gig and Mac covered their ears.

"What? Now you gonna call fouls on us, Queenies?" Gig swayed unsteadily and tried for the second step. Behind him, lights in the campers blinked on, doors creaked open, people peered from behind them.

Mac caught Gig before he toppled backwards, and then the two of them surged forward together. A blast rang out, and both men fell face first in the doorway. Lulu galloped up, growling and barking. Beulah stepped carefully up behind the men; her shotgun cocked and pointed right at them. Several other campers eased in closer, their own shotguns at the ready to back up Beulah.

"Okay, you two scalawags. Get up from there. These ladies asked you to leave, and you're gonna leave. I run a family place here, and you ain't welcome. So get goin', or I'll call some trucker buddies in to help move you out. You boys know Ponderosa Man, don't ya? If that don't work, well, there's always my shotgun here. I bet that'll help you along." Beulah fired once in the air.

Mac and Gig slid down the steps and backed away from Beulah and the dog. They inched their way backwards to the road, Lulu stalking them. Then they turned and ran. Lulu loped after them, half-heartedly barking and snipping.

Beulah turned to us. "I ain't had any trouble at all running this place til you two Queens showed up. It's been one thing after another. You two must be looking for trouble! Tilly called me from The Joint and filled me in on what happened up there. I suspected there'd be more trouble. That Gig is known for it around here."

With the commotion over, the other campers moved back inside their RVs leaving us to face Beulah alone. Lulu trotted back to Beulah's side.

"We're so sorry, Beulah. All we did was go for a meal, and they asked us to dance, and before we knew it, all hell broke lose. We didn't realize who Gig was at first. But we had already had a run-in with him on the CB. Ponderosa Man, the same one you know, came to our rescue then. Please don't be upset. We're really sorry. We'll be leaving tomorrow, and we promise, there'll be no more trouble."

Beulah shouldered her gun and looked up at us. "You girls, or Queens, or whatever you are, have no idea what you're doing out here on the road, do you? Last night was bad enough with those three homosexual kids, but tonight could have been real serious. You two better rethink this adventure of yours. I thought corporate types were supposed to be smart…guess you just don't have any street smarts, as they say.

"Did you two even notice all the campers ready to come help you out? They're good people. Hard working people. For the most part, they worked and saved for years to get their RVs. They live careful, so they can enjoy the time they have left. You two don't have a clue what it's all about.

"Look, it's not that I don't admire your courage. And I can understand you wanting to make a change, travel, get away from the rat race. But take my advice: go home. If you've gotta travel, take the husbands with you. You two are headed for some serious trouble."

Liz and I stared at the ground and shuffled our feet.

"Now, I'm going home and going to bed. I don't want to have to get up again, hear me? You go to bed, too. I'll leave Lulu with you as a lookout." She lumbered off into the dark.

Lulu led the way inside. Once there, we double-locked the doors. Lulu stared sleepily at us and let out a long whine. Liz went to the fridge to find a treat for her and came back with a slice of ham. She gave the ham to Lulu and walked back to the bedroom. When she returned, she pulled out a string of fake black pearls from her pocket.

"What's with the pearls?" I asked.

Liz bent over the dog and slipped the beads onto her neck.

"Every girl needs a little bling," she sighed. She looked up at me. "Do you feel we've been properly scolded? She made me feel like I was back in Junior High and had been caught toilet-papering a yard."

"Yeah, I know. Part of me wants to not like her, but the truth is, she's right about a lot of things. We are pretty naive when it comes to street smarts. We're too trusting that's for sure. My God, can you imagine what Bob and Carl would say about all this?"

"I don't even want to think about that," Liz replied. She yawned and Lulu followed. "But Leslie, do you think we'll be okay now. What's going to happen once we leave here and get on the road again. What if we run across Gig and Mac out there? Should we call Ponderosa Man and tell him what's happened?" She looked down at her feet. "Should we just go home?"

"No! We are NOT going home. Not yet. We haven't gotten off to a smooth start, but we're wiser now, and we'll be more on guard from now on. We'll let Ray know what's gone on when we hit the road tomorrow. I'll feel better if we find out he's somewhere nearby," I said.

"Tomorrow, I'll call Anne. Just to let her know we're okay. That way, she can get a message to the men."

"What about that snow storm?" Liz asked.

"Not to worry. We've got plenty of time to get out of these mountains before we have to worry about that. Now let's go to bed."

Evidently, Lulu knew the word "bed." She beat us to the back of the motor home and spread out flat on her belly in the middle of the bed. Liz and I stared.

"Well, I guess a dog as big as Lulu can sleep wherever she wants, huh?" Liz quipped.

"Fine by me," I laughed. We undressed and crawled into bed.

In the darkness, I felt the laughter before I actually heard it. The bed shook.

"Now what? What are you laughing about?" I sat up and looked toward Liz's side of the bed.

"Well, in just two days, we've taken up with three gays, been mauled on a dance floor, threatened with rape, lectured by an old woman with a shotgun, and slept with a 200 pound dog. I can't wait to see what tomorrow brings!"

# Chapter 13

## Hold Back the Night

"What?" Liz mumbled and turned her head toward the wall. Lulu lowered her big head towards the back of Liz's neck.

"AHHHH! She's drooling on me!" she cried.

"She wants you to let her out."

"Why can't you? You're closer to the door." Liz flounced over the side of the bed and stumbled toward the front of the motor home. Lulu lumbered behind her.

A few minutes later, Liz returned to shake my shoulder.

"Get up. Let's get going. You said you wanted to leave early."

I groaned, but made myself rise. After coffee and a light breakfast, I took care of the black and gray boxes, unplugged everything, and we were ready to hit the road. I drove up to Beulah's office and honked the horn. She stepped out, Lulu by her side.

"We just wanted to say goodbye, Beulah. And thanks again for all you did for us, especially leaving Lulu with us last night. We slept better just having her there."

"Thought you would," she replied. "She's a good watch dog, but it looks like she's turning into a queen just like you girls." Beulah leaned down to study the black pearls still around the dog's neck.

"Um, Beulah? We'd like to apologize again for all the trouble. Honestly, none of it was on purpose. And we've certainly learned some lessons. From the time this trip started, we just seemed to attract strange situations. I hope you aren't too upset with us."

"No harm done. But you two need to be more careful. I'm an old woman and don't get out much, but I hear all kinds of scary things are happening out there on the roads."

"Yeah, you're right," Liz said, looking down at Lulu. The great dog whined.

"Sounds like she wants to go along," said Beulah.

We laughed, but Beulah didn't. In fact, she all but scowled.

"I just had a thought," she said. "What if Lulu goes along with you for the rest of your trip. Living here with me isn't very exciting for her. She could use some good exercise, and she sure seems to like you two."

"Oh, I don't think...." Liz began, but I interrupted.

"You know, that might not be such a bad idea. I don't know exactly where we're headed, but we'll have to come back by here on the return trip, so we could drop her off, then. What do you think, Liz?"

"I don't know..." She rubbed the back of her neck, and I knew she was remembering this morning's drool.

"She's getting old, but she'd be good protection for you. In fact, it'd be a favor to me. Take her off my hands for a bit. I think she was some disappointed when we couldn't finish our own trip, and she's been stuck here in this camp ground ever since."

Liz raised one eyebrow at me as if questioning Beulah's sanity in regards to Lulu.

"I want her back, mind ya, but she'd probably like a little vacation." She rubbed her hand down the dog's back.

"I don't..." Liz began, but again, I interrupted. I punched her in the side. "Come on', Liz. Let's take her. It'll be fun."

Liz frowned at me, but I knew she wouldn't want to insult Beulah by refusing such a generous and kind offer. Besides, Beulah was right. We could use some extra protection.

"Oh, all right," Liz sighed. And as if she understood, Lulu backed away from the window and made her way to the door. Beulah rushed inside and came back a few minutes later with a huge plastic bag.

"Here's a few of her things: her flea meds, heart pills, treats, some dog food and dishes, a leash, and her favorite toy." She pulled a bedraggled Ken doll from the bag.

"She has a Barbie, too, but she prefers Ken," Beulah explained.

Trying not to laugh out loud, Liz and I climbed out of The Screamer and loaded up Lulu's things. While we exchanged phone numbers with Beulah, Lulu climbed into the motor home and immediately took her place behind the two front seats. She sat with both paws on the console and had a bird's eye view through the windshield.

With Lulu finally settled, Liz and I buckled up and reached for our tiaras on the dash. We turned to Beulah one more time.

"Bye! We'll see you before too long, and we'll take good care of Lulu." We waved and smiled as we pulled away. In the rear view mirror, Beulah stood shaking her head back and forth and waving us on our way.

A few hours down the road, I asked Liz to drive.

"I need to call Mom. There's a rest area just ahead, and Lulu probably needs to stretch her legs a bit."

We pulled off the interstate and glided into a parking space that was shaded by tall pines. After restroom breaks for each of us, Liz settled in the driver's seat, and Lulu pushed right past me to take over the passenger seat.

"Well! Lulu certainly has settled in, hasn't she? I guess I'll have to sit back here," I said making my way to the sofa to make my phone call.

Mom answered on the third ring.

"Mom, it's me, Leslie."

"As if I wouldn't know, even without caller ID. How are the two runaways? Where are you? What's going on?"

"We're fine, Mom. We're in the North Carolina mountains right now taking in the leaves and fresh air."

"Hummmphf. You take me for a complete fool, daughter? I know there's more going on than leaves and fresh air. But I'm glad you called. The husbands, by the way, are a bit frantic. Bob called last night. He met Carl, Rex, and Billy for a strategy meeting. Carl wants to call out the police force to find you. But they decided to give it a couple more days. I think they're expecting you two to turn tail and run home."

"I'm doing all I can to keep them at bay, but you do need to call them, Leslie. I know you girls well enough to know that you're being careful and that all of this has somewhat of a sound reason behind it, somewhere, but the guys, just don't get it.

"I envy you in a way. I always wanted to take off and travel, too. But I managed to talk myself out of it every time the idea struck. I guess I'll just have to live out that dream through you two. So, enjoy yourselves. I want all the details when you get home."

"Thanks, Mom. I knew you'd understand. And we will call Bob and Carl to let them know we're fine. But not just yet. We need a little more distance between us before we do. If we don't, they'll start a search for us and ruin everything. Please just tell them we're okay and not to worry. We're fine, and we even have a watch dog with us!"

"A what?"

"A watch dog. Her name's Lulu. She's a Saint Bernard. The lady who runs the RV Park we stayed at let us borrow her for the rest of the trip."

"Well, I never…." Mom was, for once, at a loss for words.

"Just tell the guys not to come after us, okay? We aren't ready to come home. Oh, and call the boys, too, will you?"

"I'll do the best I can, Leslie. And yes, I'll call the boys. But you two better be careful out there….dog or no dog. Have fun, but be careful. You're loved, you know?"

"Thanks, Mom. I love you, too. Talk with you soon. Bye."

"What did she say?" Liz called from the front.

"Everything's okay. She's going to handle the guys and talk to the boys. She says she understands but to be careful. Taking Lulu along wasn't a shock to her. She knows I'm crazy about animals."

Liz nodded. "I knew she'd be okay with everything. She's a good sport, and I'm so grateful that you shared her with me all these years. I miss my mom since she died, but Anne's been there for me time and again."

I grabbed our maps and brochures from the table and took two sofa pillows to sit on behind the console between Liz and Lulu.

"Our next stop will be near Nashville. There's a park called The Wanderer that's near Opryland. I always wanted to go there, but Bob didn't. So let's plan to visit that while we're in the area."

"Sure thing," smiled Liz.

Trucks and cars whizzed past us. Some waved, other's blared their horns.

"What's with all this attention we're getting?" Liz asked.

"Well, I'm sure we're not what they expect to see driving down the interstate. I mean, just look at us."

Liz glanced from me to Lulu and then broke into outright laughter. There was no denying we were a strange sight. Two middle-aged women wearing tiaras scrunched together near the driver's seat and a huge mammoth of a dog sporting black pearls sitting proudly on the passenger side.

"You know, Leslie," she said. "We've just got to get Lulu her own tiara." We giggled at the image, and Lulu barked happily in agreement.

Farther down the road, a call came in over the CB.

"Ponderosa Man to Queen Screamer. Can you read?"

"Ten-four, Ponderosa Man."

"What's the latest, ladies? My friend Tilly tells me there was some action at The Joint last night."

"Gosh," I said to Liz. "Our lives are an open book out on the road. Everybody must know everybody else."

"Yep, it was definitely an interesting night," Liz answered. "Your buddy Gigolo One showed up, and he's walking trouble for sure."

"Yeah, he's running out of welcome stations all around here. I'm glad you two were at Beulah's, though. Sorry you had to go through that. Most truckers are good neighbors. Gig's just carrying a lot of old baggage, I guess. He can be a real asshole at times. Say, don't forget about that weather alert. The storm's still brewing and it's a big one. Better stay tuned to the weather station."

"We will. Don't worry."

"Where are you headed now, ladies?"

I grabbed the CB from Liz. "Hey, Ponderosa Man. We're headed over to Nashville and maybe on to Memphis. We've added another traveling queen since we last talked with you. Her name's Lulu."

"Lulu? You mean Beulah's dog? Well, I be darned. I can't believe Beulah would give her away. She's a great dog."

"Oh, she didn't give her away. We're just taking her along for a vacation. Beulah thinks we need protection, and to tell the truth, after last night, I'm glad to have her with us. She's big enough to scare most anybody."

"Yep, she's big all right."

"Oh, and we're going to get her a tiara like ours, too."

Ray's laughter traveled over the radio waves. "I can see it now," he said. "The sight of the three of you will be causing wrecks all over the mountain. You two are too much. Call if you need help. I'm heading up to Virginia and Maryland, but I can still get to you or send help if you need it."

"Thanks. You be safe, too. Have a great Thanksgiving. Are you going to see your daughter?" As soon as the words were out of my mouth, I wished them back. I had forgotten what Ray said about his relationship with his daughter.

There was a heavy pause before he answered. "No, M'am. I'll have my turkey on the road with some trucker buddies, like always. You girls take care. Over and out."

"I wonder what the problem is between Ray and his daughter," I asked Liz.

"Who knows? Everybody has troubles, huh? It's a shame though, his being alone except for her and not being with her on holidays."

"Yeah, it is." We were both silent for a while taking in the last of the fall color throughout the mountains.

"Why don't we get off the interstate for awhile, I said to Liz. "We can check out some of those charming little towns tucked into the valleys."

"What towns?" asked Liz.

"You know. The ones they always show in the travel brochures. Look, there's an exit for Crossville right up here."

After lunch and a quick walk with Lulu around the town square, we headed back to I-40. Lulu decided to nap on the bed, so I sat up front again with Liz. Clouds rolled in from the west, and as we headed on toward Nashville, the rains came.

"How much farther to our exit?" Liz asked.

"About two hours. We take the Tobacco Run exit. Then it's about thirty minutes to the Wanderer RV Park." I punched in some tunes on the Bose and we reminisced about past escapades and how good life had been in our college days.

"But you know, this road adventure just may top 'em all, huh?" Liz and I giggled.

"Do you think we should call the guys? I'm sure Carl is chewing nails by now. I doubt Anne will be able to do much with him."

"Oh, never doubt my mother. She'll handle Carl and Bob. Let's just stick to the plan. With Mom handling that end today, I figure we've bought ourselves at least one more day before we have to take that plunge. You know, if we had a laptop, we could just email them. That way, we wouldn't have to listen to the yelling."

Liz looked sideways at me.

"Okay, well, just think about it. We can look up a Circuit City store and buy one. We'd have to have someone hook us up, but that shouldn't be too difficult."

Liz didn't answer. Our exit came up, and she wheeled us off the interstate and pulled into a convenience store. The guy behind the counter eyed us suspiciously as we wandered the aisles. We picked up a few staples and makings for tuna salad for supper. We chose some treats for Lulu as well. At the counter, the man outright stared.

"That be all, ladies?" He asked, his eyes fixed at a point just above our foreheads.

I noticed his cap right away. The words "I'm Bill" curled across the top of it. "Yes, Bill. That's all."

He rang up the purchases, bagged them, and then took our money. "Here's your change, M'am." Again, he couldn't seem to fix his eyes straight on at us.

"Thanks," I said. Liz and I turned to leave, but I looked back one more time. He was still staring just above our heads. I turned to stare directly at him.

"Excuse me, Bill. Is there something wrong here?"

"Uh, no M'am, it's just, um, well, Halloween is over, and I never saw people in these parts wearing crowns, that's all." His blush matched the red of his shirt.

"Oh, is that so. Well, for your edification BILL, we wear crowns all the time." I took offense at the Halloween comment. "It just so happens that we come from a long line of royalty, and it's our sworn duty to wear these when we go out in public. Sort of like wearing clean underwear in case you get in a wreck." I smirked.

Bill looked as if I'd slapped him, and Liz giggled behind me.

"And if you don't mind my asking, why are you wearing that silly ass cap that's says, "I'm Bill?"

Bill fidgeted with boxes of candy on the counter. His face reddened again. But this time, it was tinged with anger.

"I'm wearing this silly ass hat because my fat ass wife gave it to me for my birthday. If I don't wear it, she might sit on me and smother me to death. I apologize to you "High Asses" for asking you about the crowns. I was just curious, that's all."

I don't know what got into me and made me edge him on like I did. I embarrassed myself. He hadn't meant any harm, and truth told, I'm sure we did look silly with our tiaras. But it was our business, and we weren't hurting anybody. It seemed people just couldn't leave us alone.

"Well, I apologize, too, Bill. I guess we all have our burdens in life, huh." With that, Liz pulled me from the store. We raced across the parking lot in pouring rain. Lulu looked up from her nap as we piled inside, dripping water everywhere.

"What in the world got into you, Leslie? Why pick on that poor red neck? He didn't mean any harm. I felt kind of sorry for him. You and your sharp tongue and quick wit can come down pretty hard sometimes, you know. Besides, perhaps we should have chatted for a while. I'm sure he has a story, living way up here in the middle of nowhere. Wouldn't you have liked to hear his story?"

"I'm sorry. You're right. I don't know what got into me. I guess I just expect people to leave us alone. I'm tired of explaining. Why can't they just smile and go along with the joke instead of looking at us like we've escaped from the loony bin?"

Liz shrugged and began unpacking our groceries. "Hey, I just thought of something. How about the next time somebody comments on the tiaras, we just tell them straight out that we did, indeed, just get released from the asylum, and they made us all wear these silly crowns like prisoners have to wear those awful orange jumpsuits. That should give 'em a setback or too, and you won't have to lose your temper again." She grinned at me and we both had a big laugh. Lulu wandered up to the front of the cab, panting, as if she was laughing right along with us.

"I'll drive," I said and climbed onto the throne. Lulu took the passenger seat and Liz settled on the sofa with a magazine. The road ahead was slick with rain and here and there waters slid over the edges of the road like small waterfalls. I slowed The Screamer to almost a crawl.

Liz moved up behind the console to help me see. As we approached a small bridge, Liz grabbed my shoulder. "Look! Is that a person sitting out in all this rain?"

"I didn't see a thing, Liz. Why would someone be sitting out in this weather, for heaven's sake? You must be imagining things." I steered The Screamer across the bridge. Just on the other side was a sign: The Wanderer RV Park. There was no one to greet us, just a note sheathed in plastic and nailed to the open gate: "Open. Place your twenty dollars in the box and pick your spot."

"They sure must trust people around here. Leslie, do you think it's safe to stay without a manager or owner around?"

"Mmmm. I don't know. This is their off-season. Let's take a look around. If we don't like it, we'll leave." I steered The Screamer to the right. "Look, there are a couple of buses over there, and some motor homes to the left. See? I think we'll be fine, Liz."

"Okay," she murmured.

We chose a small pad tucked into a stand of pines just below two other RVs. The rain had all but stopped, but the trees provided a steady drip, drip from over head. It would be wonderful to fall asleep to that sound tonight. I got out to hook us up and plug us in while Liz fed Lulu and made our sandwiches.

"Man, I'm beat. Driving in that rain took everything I had." I stretched lazily across the sofa. Liz didn't answer. She stood staring out the door into the late afternoon.

"What's wrong?"

"Nothing. I just keep wondering if that really was a person on that bridge."

"Oh, no, you don't, Liz. We are not going out there to look for some homeless person. Are you crazy? Besides, it probably wasn't anybody anyway. Even it there had been someone there, surely the rain drove him or her to find shelter."

Liz turned and gave me that sad hound-dog look of hers.

"All right. Let's go. Lulu needs a walk anyway. And I need to drop off our twenty dollars in the box. But we're going straight there and coming right back. It'll be dark soon."

Liz took a minute to wrap up a sandwich and some chips. Then she poured the last of our coffee into a plastic cup.

"What are you doing, Liz?"

"That poor soul might be hungry. I just thought I'd take this along in case."

"Beulah's lecture got to you, didn't it? I've been thinking about it all day, too."

I reached over to hug my kind-hearted friend.

"Okay. Let's go. But I'm taking the gun and the whistle, just in case."

# Chapter 14

## Try a Little Tenderness

The dark closed in around us before we reached the bridge, and a chill breeze blew down from the mountaintops. A light mist fell, and a heavy fog swarmed at our feet. Liz and I walked side by side, but Lulu galloped ahead of us, ventured into the trees at the side of the road, and then circled around behind us.

"You know, this reminds me of some of those Nancy Drew mysteries I read as a child," I said to Liz. "And in the movies, it's always just as darkness falls that the wind picks up and with it comes trouble."

"Stop. You're making me jittery. Maybe this wasn't such a good idea after all." Liz pulled her jacket collar up around her neck. "It's really getting cold."

"Well, we've come this far. We might as well cure your curiosity and follow through. Then we can go back to The Screamer and watch *The Shining*."

"Great. Just what I need to see on a night like this." Liz swished her flashlight back and forth across the road in front of us, then to the side and up into the trees. The bridge was just up ahead, but the fog blocked any real vision as to what might be up ahead. Lulu trotted ahead and disappeared.

"This fog's getting really bad. I can't even see Lulu anymore. Let's turn back." Liz stopped at the edge of the bridge. "Lulu! Lulu! Come on girl!"

There was an answering whimper from somewhere below us.

"Come on, Liz. She's down there." I pointed my flashlight to the heavy brush below the bridge.

"I don't think we should go down there, Leslie. Lulu! Lulu!"

I made my way gingerly to the edge of the road and started a slow and careful trek down the embankment. Lulu's whines grew louder. "Come on Liz. I think she's found something."

Just as Liz joined me, a fog-muffled scream rose up from the blackness beneath the bridge. Lulu barked.

"Get off! Get off! What the hell are you doing you big oaf?"

In our rush to save the dog, we slipped and promptly slid down the wet, grassy slope. We landed with loud grunts at the edge of the branch. Lulu raced towards us to lick and paw at each of us. Then she whined and turned back under the bridge. We followed carefully.

There was silence in that blackness, and our flashlights barely penetrated it and the fog. But high up on the embankment just under the bridge header was a huge cardboard box. Out of one side stuck muddy tennis shoes. Lulu's rump stuck out of the box. Her tail wagged.

"That looks like legs and tennis shoes to me, Leslie."

We carefully made our way up to the box.

"Oh my! They *are* legs and tennis shoes. It's a person. A real person!"

"Hold it right there!" The voice was gruff and hoarse. I slipped my hand into my pocket and felt the gun, but feeling the cold metal jolted another thought: I hadn't loaded it before we left The Screamer.

"Get away from me! Leave me alone. And take this big slobber dog with you."

"Oh, please. We don't mean any harm. Don't hurt us, please!"

"Hurt you! I'm the one being mauled by this dog. It's about to lick me to death."

Something in the voice rang clear and true. This was no madman or thief. Nor was it a murderer or anyone who intended harm. This was a woman. I stepped forward and leaned over to look into the box.

She sat huddled in wet clothes. Her hair was matted beneath a thin scarf. A backpack lay at her side.

"Hi," I said weakly, and then cleared my throat. Speak loud and strong, I told myself. "Um, we are so sorry to disturb you. Lulu means no harm. In fact, she seems to rather like you. She doesn't lick people she doesn't like."

"Humpf!" was the only reply.

"We passed this way earlier and thought we saw someone on the side of the road. The weather turned so bad, and well, we just couldn't imagine what anyone would be doing out in this rain, and we thought we'd see if you needed, um…if you needed some help or something to eat?" I rambled on, fumbling the words, and Liz was no help at all. She stood speechless and peeked from behind me. Someone had to take control here. This woman might die of pneumonia if left outside.

The woman peered up at me and let out a gruff laugh. "Well, ain't that nice, missy. And just who are you? Some do-gooder? A detective? No, wait, I know. You two are royalty—have to be. I see those crowns." She laughed coarsely again and slapped her leg.

Embarrassed, I realized that once again we had forgotten the tiaras on our heads. How silly we must look to this stranger. I struggled to find an opening to a conversation with her. But Liz found her voice just in time. "Oh, these," she said, fingering her tiara. "No, you see…well…honestly, it's just all so silly and doesn't matter at all. What's important is that we found you and that you're not hurt or anything…are you?"

"Why, ain't that nice of you two strangers to care. No, I ain't hurt. I'm just waiting out the rain. You see, I'm what you call a Road Queen, and I'm gonna pull my crown out of that back pack there and slip on my gown for the Royal Road Queen Prom tonight. Why else would I be sittin' under a bridge in a rain storm?" She cackled and shook her head.

I swerved my flashlight and found her eyes. She was beautiful. Her skin, her teeth. Except for the wet hair and mud, she could have passed for some African Queen. I knew instinctively that we didn't need to be afraid. This was a woman in need of help.

"Please M'am. Is there anything we can help you with? You shouldn't be out here in this weather. You'll get deathly ill!"

"Been sick before. It don't matter," she said. "You can get used to lots of things given time. I don't need no help. Just take that slobbery dog and go. Leave me be!"

Liz gave me her "very concerned eyebrow arch" look. I knew before she said a word that we wouldn't be leaving without this woman.

"Please, don't misunderstand," Liz began. "We mean no harm. We truly just wanted to offer help if you needed it. Look! I brought a sandwich and some hot coffee just in case you...or whoever we found out here was hungry." She pulled the food and thermos from her coat pocket and held it out toward the woman.

She sniffed loudly and then looked us both up and down. With a grunt, she shifted her weight and reached for the coffee. Liz placed the sandwich just inside the box next to her.

I eased myself down to the ground and pulled Liz with me. The rain had stopped, but the world was dark and damp. A fecund smell rose from the dirt where we sat. Lulu backed out of the box and settled next to me. All three of us stared as the woman gulped down the coffee and gobbled the sandwich. When she finished, she folded the plastic baggie and slid it into her pocket. Then she leaned back against the far side of the box and stared at us.

"Thanks. Wasn't bad," she said.

"Oh, no thanks necessary. You are so very welcome. I wish we had brought more." I nudged Liz.

"So, how long have you been a Road Queen?"

"Long enough to know it's been too long," the woman sighed.

"By the way, I'm Leslie, and this is my friend Liz. Oh, and this is Lulu." I patted the great dog's head. "She's the one that found you. We're staying at the campground just a short distance on the other side of the bridge. We're, um...we're traveling a bit. You know, seeing a bit of the country." I felt embarrassed at the frivolity of our lives compared to what this woman had obviously experienced.

"Ain't that nice. Leslie and Liz, huh? My name's Darlene. Had me a dog once. But it died. Got hit on the highway one night outside Nashville. Had me a stray cat one time, too. But it left me."

Liz and I both sighed. "That's so sad," Liz said. "I bet you get lonely without your pets."

"Lonely? Hell, you don't know lonely, woman. The kind of lonely I got, ain't no mere animal gonna fix."

Liz and I looked at each other and we knew without saying it out loud, what we had to do.

"Darlene? I know you don't know us or anything, but well, we'd really like to help. Would you like to come back to the our camper with us and stay the night. We could give you a good meal, and you could shower and get into some dry clothes. We'd be really happy for you to do that...come back with us that is." Liz's eyes sparkled with what would soon be tears if we didn't convince this woman to come home with us.

Darlene stared straight ahead. "I ain't got no money. I ain't got nothing but what you see right here and in this pack. But I ain't into charity, neither.

I can take care of myself. Besides, I like to come and go when I please. Don't want to be be beholden to nobody." She shifted so that she sat nearer the open end of the box now.

"It wouldn't be charity, Darlene. We just want to make sure you get out of this weather tonight. More rain's on the way." I reached out to touch her arm. "Look, we're just two silly old Prom Queens trying to help out a Road Queen on her way to....where are you going, Darlene? We'll bring you back here in the morning."

She stared hard at us for what seemed like minutes. Lulu leaned forward and licked her hand. "Well, now, where I been and where I'm going is a story. A long one. One best told a bit at the time, I reckon. But never you two mind cause it ain't none of your business.

"But the truth is, I *could* use a shower. Ain't had a good meal in a while, either."

She stopped to scrutinize us again. "You two ain't funny or anything, or you?"

Liz looked at me, and I looked at her. There was nothing to do but be honest.

"Well, Darlene, it's like this. We're queens, but we're not those kind of queens. Don't worry. You're safe with us. And we'd love to hear your story."

We helped her out of the box and started up the embankment. Our flash-lights cast a faint path ahead of us. When we turned into the campsite entrance, Darlene stopped dead in her tracks and turned to look up at me.

"Hope nobody steals my box while I'm gone."

# Chapter 15

## You Beat Me to the Punch

Liz took Darlene inside while I checked the hookups and plug ins one more time. Lulu guarded the door, so I sat beside her and lit a cigarette.

"Okay, big slobber dog, now what do we do with her?"

She licked the side of my face. "Gee, thanks. You think love cures everything?"

I ruffled her fur. "You know, old girl, you may be right. Love just might be the answer for Darlene." For Liz and me, too, I thought. We had wanted a change, adventure, less in our lives. Poor Darlene certainly had less, but her life wasn't better. What real difference could Liz and I make in her life? A night or maybe two of warmth and food, but was there anything else out there for her? For any of us?

Liz opened the door.

"I found some clean clothes and socks for Darlene, but I don't know what to do about shoes," she said. "Maybe I should just take these," she leaned to pick up the mud-caked shoes Darlene had left by the door, "and scrub 'em and then dry them over night. I suppose that's the best we can do, huh?"

I nodded.

Darlene stepped from the shower wrapped in my housecoat. She patted at her hair with a towel. When she looked up at us, Liz and I both gasped. She was truly beautiful. There were lines and wrinkles that hinted at hardship, yes, but there was a glow about her—a glow that seemed to come from inside of her.

"Don't be thinking I'm beholding to you for a lifetime for it, but that shower felt damn good."

"Here, Darlene," said Liz. "I found some dry things for you. I'll work on your shoes after we eat." Darlene took the clothes and went into the bedroom to change.

Liz had made more tuna sandwiches. Those along with hot tomato soup, chips, pickles and potato salad sat waiting on the table. When Darlene stepped back into the dinette area, she took the end seat. Lulu stationed herself at her feet.

"Would you like a beer, Darlene? Or I can give you tea or water."

"No M'am, Liz, isn't it? I don't touch no alcohol. I had a bout with that, which is a long story, and I ain't never going near it again."

Liz and I looked at each other quizzically and then began passing the platters and bowls to Darlene. She heaped three sandwiches and mounds of salad and chips onto her plate. I refilled her soup bowl twice. When she at last wiped her mouth and tucked her napkin under her plate, the platters and bowls were empty, and I made a mental note to pick up more soup and tuna at the store.

"Mmmm," Darlene sighed. "That was fine, mighty fine. I do like good food."

"Well, it's certainly not anything fancy. Leslie and I are into cooking light. We stop and eat at diners and places for heavier meals."

Darlene's lips curved upward in a kind of smirk. I felt for Liz. She realized how she sounded to Darlene at the same time I did, and we were both embarrassed by our complacency. Darlene most likely thought this was a heavy meal.

"Darlene, we've only been on the road for a few days now, but we've met some wonderful folks. They all seem to have a story, and I'm certain you do as well. How about tell us about yourself."

"Ain't much to tell."

"Oh, but I'm sure there is. How did you come to be living under that bridge out there? Where are you headed? What are your plans?"

"Plans? Ha! Don't you know God and fate laugh at our plans. I ain't made no plans. Learned not to. 'Sides, like I said, it ain't none of your business."

I felt the blush creep up my face. I hadn't meant to sound nosy.

"Is that what all this kindness is about? You charging me that for the shower and meal? You two do this all the time, I bet: bring in people, feed 'em and them get em to tell their stories so you can go and laugh at 'em later?"

"No, Darlene. That's not it at all. I didn't mean to sound nosy. I'm sorry if I did. Liz and I are just interested. We're learning a lot about people and life on this adventure of ours. And we aren't laughing at anybody. Quite the opposite. You don't have to tell us a thing. Honest. Let's have some coffee and we'll get you back to the bridge in the morning."

"Sounds good to me. I'll just be right out front." Darlene got up and walked to the door. Lulu followed.

"Where are you going?"

"I'm sleeping outside here. I don't want to be owing nothing to nobody."

I was astonished, but decided not to push the issue. I grabbed a blanket and handed it to her. "You'll need this tonight. Would you like a pillow?"

Darlene laughed. "No, missy. I ain't had a pillow since I can remember. You can keep your goose feather pillows inside."

"Okay. Come Lulu. Time for bed."

Lulu didn't budge. In fact, she watched as Darlene settled herself on the concrete slab outside the door. I rolled out the aluminum awning to cover the area, but that wouldn't keep out the damp and cold. I didn't know what to do. I watched as Lulu settled herself up against Darlene like she belonged right there.

"Okay. Sleep tight." I shook my head and went back inside.

"Leslie, this isn't going to work. She can't stay out there on a slab of concrete with a dog. Why is she doing this?"

"Better yet, why are we doing this?" I asked her.

"I can't sleep in here knowing she's out in the cold and damp."

"But what else can we do, Liz? She doesn't want to owe us anything, she says. You know, I thought being this close to Nashville, we'd actually have a chance to experience something fun. Instead, here we are with a cantankerous, homeless woman who will eat our food and wear our clothes, but doesn't like us, and a slobber dog, who has decided she likes her better than she likes us. How do these things happen to us?"

I was ranting, and I knew it, but it felt good to just unload. Three days on the road, and we had met with more than a normal share of trouble. But before I could say more, the cell phone rang.

"Hi, Mom. Is anything wrong?"

"Everything's peachy, honey."

That phrase was a signal. When Mom uses it, it means just the opposite. I tilted the phone so Liz could listen, too.

"Mom......what is it? What's going on?

"Well, I met the guys at Scally's tonight. They were not pleased that you two had called me and not them. They were even more NOT pleased that I still didn't know where you are. Carl went on and on about calling his buddy at the precinct. He says he's gonna get in his Mustang and go out searching. Bob and the boys did try to calm him down, but Bob was close to giving in to the idea. They're worried…no, mostly, I guess, they're confused, and maybe a little bit angry—that's Carl and Bob, not Billy and Rex.

"Unfortunately, I am now the official referee between the two camps now. I'm not sure how long I can hold them back. You need to call them. And soon, or they'll hit the road and come for you. If you don't want to call them, send an email, at least."

"We don't have email, Mom. Liz didn't want me to bring the computer. I needed to get away from all that. However, we are set up for it, so I'll talk to her and we'll see what we can do. Are Billy and Rex okay?"

"Your sons are handling this better than the big guys, which doesn't surprise me. Those husbands of yours are both big babies. You've spoiled them. And really, girls, you know, they do love you very much. Just stay in touch with me and I'll try to stem the tide, so to speak. But you do need to think about the email if nothing else. They need to know what's going on, and they need to hear it from you."

"Oh, well, I don't think we'll be telling them all that."

"What do you mean, Leslie? I don't like the sound of your voice. Is everything all right? What are you two girls up to?"

"Oh Mom, it's just, well, this has not been exactly the journey we envisioned so far. First we met up with the gays, then there was the trucker incident…"

"What gays and what trucker incident?" Mom's voice was on the rise. Not a good sign.

"Oh, it was just silly, that's all. Don't worry. It's just that now we've inherited a dog and tonight we found a homeless woman under the bridge."

"Under the bridge? Leslie, what are saying? Are you out of your mind? Taking in homeless people? Dogs? Homosexual boys? My God. No wonder Bob and Carl worry so much? I thought you had better sense than this?"

"Mom, it's Okay. Really. We're fine. We're just …."

"Leslie, I've had too many margaritas tonight. I can't deal with all these details right now. Tell you what. I'll trust you to write this all down for me. It'll make fantastic reading when you come home. Right now, I'm going to bed. Call your husbands. Night."

I was about to launch into a discussion on buying a computer with Liz when she rushed to the door.

"It's pouring rain again. Darlene and Lulu cannot stay outside in this weather!"

We opened the door. In the dim light from the RV, we could see the two of them lying side by side. Darlene appeared to be asleep. I made my way over to them and touched her shoulder.

"Darlene, you've got to come inside. It's storming again. We've got a sofa bed, or you can sleep on the floor, whatever you want. But you can't stay out here in this. And neither can Lulu."

Darlene popped up to a sitting position. "You two are real control freaks, ain't ya? Well, if coming inside means that you'll leave me be and let me sleep, I'll do it. I wouldn't want Slobber dog catching cold because of me."

I helped her to her feet. The wind blew the rain sideways, so we hurried up the steps. Darlene and Lulu made it in just fine, but I slipped on the bottom step and sat right down in a puddle of water. By the time I got myself up and inside, Liz was plumping pillows for Darlene on the sofa, and Lulu was stretched out at her feet.

"You're dripping!" Liz said to me.

"No shit! I'm soooooo sorry," I snapped. I was tired, wet, and cold. I wanted to go to bed. And I did not like being called a control freak.

Later, Liz came back to the bedroom, and I told her that it pissed me off what Darlene had said.

"Well, she IS right. We ARE control freaks. And we ARE nosy. I guess we deserved to be put in our place, huh? Come on. It's just one night. We can do this this. She's probably had a really hard life and that's why she's so cantankerous. Tomorrow we'll try to get her to talk again. I have a feeling there's quite a story there."

I looked at my friend. She had tried so hard to make everything right for Darlene. And even now after being snubbed and called names, she was still searching for the positive in it. "I love you, Liz. And you're right. Darlene surely has quite a story."

# Chapter 16

## Have You Seen Her?

"Leslie, get up! Please get up! They're gone!"

I sat up out of a dead sleep. "Huh? Who? What?"

"Darlene's gone, and Lulu's gone with her. I can't find them anywhere."

"She took our dog? Why that ungrateful bitch!" I hit the floor, fuming all the way to the front of The Screamer. "After all we did for her! She just took off without a word! You better check around. No telling what she stole. I'll go outside and call for Lulu." I stuffed my feet into tennis shoes and grabbed a coat to cover my pajamas.

Outside, an older couple ate their breakfast at a picnic table. I walked over.

"Hi, I'm Leslie. My friend and I are staying right over there." I pointed to The Screamer.

"How do? Ethel and I wondered who'd be living in a camper called The Screamer. Real interesting name," said the old man. His smile seemed a bit sly, and she blushed.

"Our dog seems to have wandered away. She's a Saint Bernard, very large? Have you by chance seen her this morning?"

"No M'am. We just came outside a few minutes ago. It's real quiet here. You're the first sign of life we seen."

"Well, thanks," I said and made my way on around the campgrounds calling and searching, but there was no sign of Lulu or Darlene.

"Anything missing?" I asked Liz as I stepped inside The Screamer.

"Doesn't seem so. I checked all our cash stashes. The money's still right where we hid it," said Liz.

"I think we better go down to the bridge. That's most likely where Darlene headed. Lulu's probably there with her. I'll take care of the outside stuff. You get us ready to go in here."

A half hour later, I pulled The Screamer onto the wide shoulder of the road just over the bridge. The morning was still foggy and very damp. We climbed out and stood peering down into the fog that hid the underside of the bridge.

"I don't know about you, but I plan on giving Darlene a big piece of my mind." I pulled the collar of my coat snugly around my neck.

"Now Leslie, let's try to be diplomatic. Who knows, maybe she has a good reason for leaving like that and taking our dog." Liz looked worried.

"So you tell me how I should be diplomatic with a homeless thief. She may have had a reason for leaving, but she had NO right to take Lulu! We're responsible for that dog, and besides, I've gotten very attached to her." I cupped my hand around my mouth and called, "Lulu! Come on, girl."

Lulu bounded up the embankment and barked happily making circles around both Liz and me. We followed her back down the slope and under the bridge. Darlene sat in her box, munching saltine crackers.

"Before you get upset with me, I want to say I did not kidnap Lulu. She followed me. I told her to go back, but she wouldn't. Besides, I knew you'd come looking for her here, so I decided to just stay put. I'm right glad you're here. She's going to lick me to death if you don't take her away."

"Darlene, why did you leave in the middle of the night like some kind of thief? We did our best to make you welcome and comfortable. We were worried when we found you gone." I sat on the wet ground beside her, and Liz sat next to Lulu.

"I figured you two were gonna put me through the third degree about my situation, and I just didn't want to answer your questions. You two are nothing like me. We have nothing in common, so why should I tell you anything. You wouldn't understand. I didn't mean for Lulu to follow me."

Hearing her name, Lulu nudged Darlene's arm and then munched happily on the saltine handed to her. "She likes saltines a lot," Darlene commented.

I looked around at the underside of the bridge. I couldn't imagine living like that. I felt very sorry for Darlene, and I did wonder about what secrets lay behind those beautiful eyes of hers. She looked so sad and lonely.

"It's okay, Darlene. You don't owe us an apology. But you are wrong about one thing. We do have a couple of things in common We're all runaways. We might be running from different things, but still, that's a common thread. The other thing is that we're all queens. You're a Road Queen, and we're Motor Home Queens. So I think we could be friends just based on that. And you should have a tiara, too."

Darlene almost smiled at that. "All right. We'll make a truce. Now, you two need to get moving on with your adventures. You don't need me weighing you down and holding you up. Maybe our paths will cross again someday."

I looked over at Liz. She was pretty near a crying jag, but I knew that it was probably best that we leave Darlene. I stood up and brushed the back of my pajamas off.

"Okay, Darlene. If that's what you want. Come on Liz, Lulu." We started back up to The Screamer, but Liz stopped suddenly. "I don't feel right about this. Isn't there something we can do? What if we invite her to ride with us for a few days? What could it hurt?" Liz was the ultimate caretaker, from her sick relatives to stray kittens; you could count on her to take someone or something in. I often called her the Great Mother of All.

"Are you crazy? She doesn't want to be around us. She thinks we have nothing in common. Besides, she's not willing to tell us anything about herself. Maybe there's a good reason she doesn't want us to know about her. For all we know, she could be wanted by the law! Let's just get going," I said.

We looked around for Lulu, but she had disappeared again. I shook my head and sighed as we made our way back under the bridge. Lulu sat by Darlene's side eating another saltine.

"Lulu! Come!"

She whimpered and lowered her head, but didn't budge.

"I think this big slobber dog has a thing for me," Darlene said.

Liz gave me her look that said, ASK.

"I think you're right, Darlene. She really likes you. Did you put a curse on her or something? Maybe it's just the saltines, huh?" I smiled down at Darlene. "At any rate, we can't get going without her, so it looks like you'll just have to go with us."

"Humpf!" Darlene turned her head away from us. "I don't need no trip with the likes of you two. Just take your dog and go."

"Darlene, believe me, we'd love to leave, but we can't go without Lulu. We're taking care of her for a friend. What about this: Why don't you come along with us for a few days. You can see the country with us, have an adventure. You might decide we aren't so bad after all." I smiled down at her.

"You two offering pity or something? I don't need no pity. I'm fine just where I am." Darlene crossed her arms over her chest as if to block us out.

"Come on, Darlene. Go with us. We'll take it a day at a time. You can leave anytime you want. All you have to do is say so. Please...." Liz went down on one knee and gave Darlene her biggest smile.

"God! You two are something else. I'm thinking you're the ones needs some pity and care taking." She pulled at her sweatshirt. "I guess I could try it for a day or so. But I ain't making no promises, you hear? And if I say, 'stop', you gonna stop and let me off with no more long speeches of yours. I don't want to owe nobody nothing!"

"Great!" Liz stood up and reached to help Darlene. Lulu circled us yipping happily. The dog clearly understood what was going on. We started up the hill.

"Come on Lulu," I called, but she didn't budge. Instead, she sidled up to Darlene.

Darlene bent to pick up her backpack. "Come on slobber dog," she muttered, and Lulu followed happily behind her.

"What a morning!" I whispered to Liz. "I'm worn out already. And look at us! We're not even dressed."

"Oh, who cares? We'll change when we stop later on. Let's get going!" Liz seemed completely blissful at the prospect of having Darlene to mother. Lulu made her way up to the upper bunk, a tricky climb for such a big dog, but she had mastered the task. Darlene made her way to the sofa. Liz poured coffee for us and I took the driver's seat. When she slid into the passenger seat beside me, she smiled.

"Just look at her! All comfy, cozy already!" She said.

I turned to see Darlene had stretched out, feet propped up. Her eyes were closed and a smile lingered around her lips after each sip of coffee.

"Where are we going?" Darlene called to me.

"The Insane Asylum, I think," I whispered to Liz.

But to Darlene, I called out, "How about Opryland? Do you like country music, Darlene?"

# Chapter 17

## Kidnapper

We weren't on the road long before snores came from Lulu and Darlene.

"Liz, we need to talk." I looked briefly at my friend. Her "oh-no-what-now-look" settled on her face.

"We have to make some decisions about communications. I know you were against having a computer, but we've got to contact the guys soon. They won't hold out much longer, and then we'll be running AWAY from them. So, I say, we get a computer, have it hooked up, and we can email the guys. That way, we don't have to CALL and listen to their ranting and raving. We can buy some time by emailing."

Liz stared out the window for a moment and then turned to me. " I'm still not liking the idea. A computer in The Screamer will be a big temptation for you, but we'll agree to use it for communication and that's ALL! Deal?"

I smiled. "Deal! I've been thinking about how to get it hooked up, so when we get to Nashville, I'll take care of it."

The CB interrupted our conversation.

"Silver Queen Screamer, come in."

It was Ray. I smiled and Liz looked sideways at me. "If I didn't know better, I'd think you two have something going on like CB sex," she said.

I winked at her and reached for the CB, but she beat me to it.

"Go ahead, Ponderosa Man. What's up?"

"Nothing much. Where are you two queens headed?"

"Nashville."

"Better watch the weather. That storm's headed that way."

"Ten-four on that. We hope to take in Opryland while we're there. Oh, and we have some new company with us."

"Have you two picked up another dog?"

"No, a person, actually." Liz looked back at Darlene who was still sleeping. She lowered her voice when she clicked on the CB again. "She's homeless. We found her under a bridge. Her name is Darlene. Lulu took a real liking to her. So now The Screamer's carrying two motor home queens, a road queen and a giant dog!"

"Sounds pretty special to me," Ray answered. "Speaking of special. Turkey Day is just a few days away. Keep me posted on where you'll be. You stay safe. Over and out."

I happened to glance back at Darlene again, and she was sitting up staring at Liz. I didn't know how much she had heard, but it was clear that something was on her mind.

"So you two flirting with truckers, now?" She quipped.

Darlene and I were developing a relationship that definitely hinged on her pushing all my buttons. I decided to let her comment slide.

Farther on down the interstate, I noticed she had found a book to read. Lulu slept above her, on guard as usual.

"Well, she seems to have made herself at home, hasn't she?" Liz asked. "I'll go make some sandwiches for lunch. Maybe when we get to Nashville, we can actually do some exploring and get out of this motor home for a while."

"What's wrong? You sound frustrated."

"I guess it's just that, like you, I had envisioned lots of sightseeing on this trip, but so far, we haven't. It's a lot different than what I thought it would be."

"I know, but I thought that's the kind of trip you and I both wanted. You know: no day planners or schedules. Just going with the flow. I didn't have any expectations except escaping that prison of a life we had built back home. What's the matter? You want to go back home to Carl? Is that exciting enough for you? I'm sorry, Liz. I didn't mean to say that."

I noticed our exit coming up. "We'll be exiting pretty soon. I'll stop, so we can get some more supplies and let Lulu out."

Liz stayed very quiet. I worried that she was actually thinking of going home, and if so, well, so be it. But I didn't think she really wanted to do that. Maybe it's just the early travel blues, I thought.

According to the campground brochure, the RV Park was just three miles from the interstate. I was hoping to find an electronics store close by so we could get that laptop. Maybe Liz would feel better after we sent messages home.

I pulled up to the gas pumps at the first convenience store we came to.

"Liz, why don't you and Darlene go inside for supplies while I fill up The Screamer and walk Lulu out back? Oh, and don't forget a box of saltines. That should keep them both happy."

Darlene grumbled a bit about having to leave the book she was reading, but Liz convinced her she needed to move around a bit. Traveling, even in a motor home, can crimp up a body.

Up the road, I saw signs of a shopping strip mall. Maybe there'd be an electronics store there, I thought. We'd check in at the RV park and have supper. Then we could come back to town. Not having a regular car was getting a bit challenging. We had to hook up and unhook every time we wanted to go somewhere. The thought occurred to me that perhaps we needed to purchase a small used car and pull it behind us, but that could be another pain in the ass.

Liz and Darlene came back with two small bags.

"What is that weird smell?" I asked.

"Pickings at a convenience store are slim," Liz said. "I got hot dogs for tonight. Darlene wanted the fried oysters they cook up in there, so that's what you smell. I told her I'd never eat that awful smelling stuff. No telling how long it's been sitting out.

We need to go to a store soon. I'm craving fresh veggies, fruits, and specialty cheeses."

We loaded everybody back on board and headed straight to the Northfork RV Park. A sign out front read: "Closed for the Season."

"Oh, no," I said. "It's closed. That can't be. Surely there's someone around."

"Looks like someone lives back behind that office over there," Liz pointed out.

"Okay, I'll go knock on the door. Maybe they'll take pity on us and rent us a space for the night."

A young girl, who looked to be about twelve years old, answered my knock. She wore blue jeans and a sweatshirt, both of which hung on her skinny frame. But she had beautiful blue eyes. I couldn't help but stare at them, and the longer I looked, the more startled she appeared.

"Hi, my name is Leslie. The sign out front says the park is closed, but we are desperate for a place to park tonight. Are your parents here?"

"No, they're at the race park. They won't be home until later tonight."

Great, I thought. But I wasn't ready to give up.

"What's your name?"

"Rachel."

"Well, Rachel, do you think we could just park at one of the pads for about an hour while we have some dinner. We need to go back to the shopping mall in town, so we could come back later and ask your mom and dad about staying the night. Do you think that would be all right?"

Rachel studied me carefully. "I guess so." She said quietly. Then she seemed to remember something. "I'll have to charge you twenty dollars whether you stay an hour or all night, though. That's the policy. Oh, and the outdoor showers and toilets aren't working either. We closed up November the first, and they haven't been cleaned or anything."

Shrewd little cookie, I thought. She's been taught well, and I didn't question her. "Sounds like a good policy to me," I said and pulled out a twenty-dollar bill.

"Where should we park?"

"Take a left just past the house, and you'll see pads that will fit your RV. I don't believe Dad has shut off the water and electricity to those up near the house."

"Thanks, Rachel."

We found a spot about a half block down the first road and backed in. "Okay, let's turn the radio on and eat. I'll go check for power and water and get us hooked up. Hand me a cold beer, please Liz." Liz tossed me one from the refrigerator.

"Come on Lulu. You and I will take a short walk, too."

Outside, I hooked us up and checked back with Liz to make sure everything was working. Happily, we had power and water. Then Lulu and I walked to the end of the road and back in the late afternoon dusk. When we returned to the RV, Liz had the hot dogs ready, and Darlene sat at the table gobbling down her fried oysters. Lulu perched at her feet hoping for a taste.

"Darlene, whatever you do, do not give Lulu any of that greasy food. A large dog with diarrhea would not be a good thing."

We ate in silence as we listened to the radio. A weather message mentioned the possible storm but was unclear as to how fast it would develop and which specific direction it would take.

"Sounds like that storm system is pretty unorganized, and I'm not worried, so I think we should finish up our supper and head back into town. I want to find a computer store and get that laptop before you change your mind," I said to Liz. "While I do that, you can take Darlene to Walmart and buy her a decent jacket. That lightweight thing she's wearing isn't enough for the cold weather coming."

I went out to pull the plugs again, a chore that was beginning to wear thin. We found the strip mall I had seen earlier and luckily, there was a Walmart at one end. I pulled up to it to let Liz and Darlene out, but Darlene hesitated.

"I ain't taking no charity," she grumbled.

"Darlene, get out. It's not charity. It's a gift."

Grudgingly she stepped out. Lulu tried to follow, but Liz caught her collar and led her back inside the motor home. "See you in about thirty minutes," I said.

I headed down to Circuit City at the other end. Once inside, I studied the rows of laptops available. I knew what I wanted…just something simple, no bells or whistles.

A young man in his early twenties approached me. "Welcome to Circuit City," he said. "Can I help you?"

His nametag read "Reggie." That fit his skinny build and curly brown hair, but his Christmas tie and two earrings didn't.

"Yes, Reggie. I think I've found just what I was looking for." I pointed to the laptop. Reggie nodded.

"Good choice," he said as he walked to the register. "It's on sale, and we've got one left. Must be your lucky day! Do you need any accessories for this?"

"No," I said, handing over the cash I had dug out of a pair of boots where Liz and I stashed some of our cash. Liz and I had decided not to use the credit cards because if the guys checked, they'd know where to start. So, credit cards were out except in a dire emergency.

"Here you are," Reggie said handing me the shopping bag. "Anything else I can do for you?"

"Actually, there is. I'm traveling and our motor home is wired for a computer and connected to a satellite, but I'm not quite sure how to connect the dots. Is there anyone here that might help me? I'll be happy to pay for the service."

"I've got a break coming up," he said. "I could give it a try."

"Great!" Reggie grabbed a tool kit from under the counter and signed out for his break and followed me to the parking lot.

"Uh, just so you don't get frightened, you should know we have a BIG dog in here," I said as I unlocked the door. "Lulu's quite big, but she's harmless."

Inside, Lulu made me out a liar as she yawned down at us from the bunk.

"Wow! This is really nice. I've always dreamed of owning an RV one day. I'd like to go out west and see the country."

"Oh, I know all about those kinds of dreams," I told him and led him to the flip down desk by the sofa.

Reggie set to work right away, and I glanced at the clock on the dash.

"Oh, my God. I've got to pick up my friends down at Wal Mart. Can you work while I drive?"

"Sure. No problem," Reggie answered. "I have fifteen minutes before I have to be back on the floor."

Back at Wal Mart, Liz and Darlene climbed on board with several bags.

"We've got company," I said to them. "Reggie is hooking up the computer for us." Reggie smiled up at Liz from his position on the floor.

Darlene pulled her new jacket out of the bag and held it up for me to see.

"Oh, that's great! Model it for me."

Darlene grimaced at me. "It fits. I'm not putting it on right now, though. You can see it later." She shoved the jacket back into the bag and sat down at the table.

Reggie popped his head up and looked at me. "I'm not so sure they have this thing wired the right way. I can't seem to get it to work. Might be some crossed wires or something. I can probably fix it, but it's gonna take longer that my break time. What time is it?"

"Six-thirty," answered Liz.

"Oh man! I've gotta go. I'm sorry."

I was thinking fast. My withdrawals from email and technology was setting in big time now that I was so close to having it back. No way was I going to let Reggie leave and not have that computer working. Before I answered, I reached discreetly toward the door and turned the lock. Then I jumped into the driver's seat and revved The Screamer's motor. The tires squealed as we spun out of the lot and onto the road back to camp. Liz fell to the floor on top of Reggie. Lulu tumbled from the bunk, and Darlene slid right off the dinette bench.

"Leslie! What are you doing? Have you lost your mind?"

"Not yet, but I probably will if I don't get that computer hooked up. I'm having serious withdrawals, Liz, and I'm taking Reggie back to the park with us so he can fix it."

"But I have to get back to work," Reggie said. He stood up brushing off his pants. One large curl fell across his left eye. He looked pale.

"I know. And I'll get you back. I'll even lie to the manager and say I was sick and you took me to the hospital or something. But I need you to fix that computer."

"For God's sake, Leslie. This is like…kidnapping! You can't do this."

I ignored Liz's pleading and raced ahead down the road. We took the turn off on two wheels, raced past the office and back to our pad.

"Come on Reggie. Think of this as double overtime, and I'm paying cash. Here!" I took a wad of money from my pocket and thrust it toward him.

Reggie's eyes bulged at the sight of all that money. "Well, I guess for double time, I can try." He crawled back under the flip top desk.

"Now, I'm going to leave the three of you here for a few minutes. Liz, why don't you fix us a snack? I'll take Lulu and walk back to the office. Maybe Rachel's parents are home now."

There were no pole lights on to light the way, but with my flashlight, Lulu and I finally made it to the office. I knocked lightly at the door. Rachel's face peered through a small crack.

"Hi, Rachel. I'm back. Are your parents home yet?"

"No, they aren't. It'll be really late. They're at the races, and tonight they'll be real late. It's the Turkey Day Race in celebration of Thanksgiving."

"Oh, I see. Well, we're desperate for a place to hook up for the night. Please, can you just say 'yes.'? We'll leave early tomorrow morning."

"Well," she hesitated. "You give me another twenty dollars, and then you can stay."

I reached into my pocket to get the money.

Rachel's eyes followed every move.

"The folks probably won't notice you anyway. They're usually drunk. Just don't make a lot of noise."

"Deal!" I said and handed her a twenty. Lulu and I made our way back into the dark, but I could feel Rachel's eyes following us until we rounded the curve in the road.

# Chapter 18

## Hello Stranger

When I told Darlene and Liz about Rachel's demand for twenty more dollars, Darlene snorted out loud. "The world's full of cons and criminals. We should be right at home here."

I looked over at Liz. My patience was wearing thin.

"Be cool," Liz mouthed at me.

Poor Liz. She's right back in her mothering role. Darlene's just another child to her. And stupid me, I go right along with Liz on whatever tugs at her heart strings. Then the thought occurred to me that perhaps she came along on this trip just to mother me.

"Reggie, you probably missed dinner. Would you like a hot dog?" Liz asked.

He looked up at Liz, unsure whether or not to trust the offer. After all, we had all but kidnapped him. "Sure. I can always eat."

In microwave speed, Mama Liz set a platter of hotdogs and chips on the table. Reggie dove in. I sat across the table from him, watching and thinking of my own son. Rex was on his own now, although it had taken some tough love to get him there. I still subsidized his income some and paid the tuition, but basically he worked and supported himself. I wondered about Reggie. Was he in college? Was the job at Circuit City a part time gig, or had my kidnapping scheme cost him his livelihood? I felt a moment's guilt, but shook it off.

Darlene and Liz were engrossed in a Lifetime movie, so I took the opportunity to nose around a bit in Reggie's life.

"Would you like a beer, Reggie?"

"I would, but I better wait until I finish up with all your wiring. By the way, I noticed a web address on the bumper. Do you ladies have a website?"

I hesitated. Liz and Darlene were still zoned out on some movie. I leaned closer to Reggie and whispered, "No, but I sure would like one. Can you do that? Can you set up websites?"

"Sure no problem. It's easy. Just give me the name and the site address from the bumper. I can do that in no time."

I reached for Reggie's hand and squeezed it. "It's www.queenmotorhome.com," I whispered as if the very name were magic.

"I'm sorry if I frightened you by speeding you away from your job and all. I'm just a little desperate, but I promise, I'll take you back and I'll talk to your boss. I won't let you lose your job because of me."

Reggie's mouth bulged with hotdog, so he didn't answer out loud. He just bobbed his head up and down. I went to talk with the girls while he scooted back under the desk in a web of wire.

"Are you still not going to talk to me?"

Darlene stared past me, looking for Reggie. "You done done it now, Queenies. Why'd you kidnap that poor boy? You could of just asked him to come along later tonight. But no, you just rushed in and grabbed what you wanted. Just like this motor home of yours. Liz told me all about your little plan to run away. Sounds to me like the both of you are some kind of ungrateful for what you got in life. You don't have no idea what it's really like out here on the road. I think the both of you need some lessons in gratitude. You just spoiled rotten, that's all."

"Oh, here we go with that sharp tongue of yours, Darlene. What gives you the right to judge us and our reasoning anyway, especially since you are a guest here?"

"Humpf," was her only answer. Liz shook her head at me as if to warn me away from the subject. I sensed another lecture coming.

"Liz, Reggie has the computer just about up and running. I need to check in with Mom to see if anything is new before we contact the guys."

"Yeah, and when you do, ask 'em if they want you back? Bet they don't. Bet they're glad to be rid of two selfish queens," Darlene muttered under her breath.

"Darlene, I wasn't talking to you. Liz, what do you think?"

Liz didn't answer right away. She looked sympathetically toward Darlene and then back at me.

"Why don't we just have a nice, quiet evening here? After all the turmoil of the day, I'm just not ready to deal with anything else. Besides, I think you need to settle down a bit before we make contact with the guys."

"Whose side are you on anyway? Is Darlene making you feel guilty about coming on this trip? Do you want to just call it quits and go home? If that's it, you better tell me right now." I could feel my blood pressure rising.

Before Liz could answer, there was a loud thump on the windshield. Lulu barked and took a nosedive from her bunk. She scrabbled up into the drivers seat and proceeded to whine and bark. Darlene jumped up and ran to see what was going on.

"It's a cat. It looks like my stray Rosie cat!" For the first time since meeting her, Darlene smiled. She tap-tapped her fingers along the glass calling, "Kitty-kitty."

The cat followed Darlene's fingers, and Lulu bounced from seat to seat trying to get at her. The Screamer began to rock side to side. Finally I grabbed Lulu's collar and pulled her back to the bedroom. Meanwhile, Darlene opened the door and the cat leapt inside. Lulu smelled her and dragged me back to the living area.

The cat led the chase with Darlene, Lulu, and me right behind. A loud yowling started up followed by incessant barking. Darlene added her "kitty-kitty" calls to the fray and I threw in a few choice expletives.

"What's going on?" Reggie crawled from beneath the desk just in time for the cat to pounce on his head. Lulu rammed into his back and sent him head first toward the floor again.

"Do something, Liz," I cried, but she was doubled over in laughter.

The cat leapt upward onto Lulu's bunk bed. Below, Lulu howled like a banshee.

"Hush up, Lulu," Darlene said. "That's my Rosie cat." Miraculously, Lulu stopped her barking immediately. She gave one more whine and then sat silently staring up at the large calico.

It was a pretty cat, I had to admit. But we didn't need a cat. One pet was enough in a motor home. Darlene climbed up the ladder and retrieved the cat. Lulu watched intently. I expected another outburst at any minute, but Darlene returned to the sofa and put the cat in her lap. Lulu followed, positioning herself against Darlene's knees.

I was touched by the tender way Darlene stroked the cat. She even hummed a bit of a song that I couldn't quite catch. Surely, this couldn't be Darlene's cat. It was just a coincidence that it looked the same.

"I knew that mangy two timing stray would come back. She couldn't make it without old Darlene." Darlene muttered to herself and continued to pet the cat. Lulu stretched her neck over Darlene's lap and sniffed loudly at the cat. Then she gave her a big lick.

Oh, great. Now Lulu's gone soft in the head. Darlene really thinks it's the same animal, I thought. Now we have a stray cat to contend with. I felt the walls closing in.

"You're up and running!" shouted Reggie. He crawled from beneath the desk and fiddled with the laptop. Here you go."

"You are a genius. How can I ever thank you?" I hugged him hard.

"You did mention double pay," Reggie answered with a straight face.

"That I did," I smiled and went to get more money.

"How about that beer now?" asked Liz.

"Sure thing," he replied.

While Reggie played on-line a bit, I snuck away to call Anne.

"Hi Mom."

"Hi darling! What's going on?"

"Well, it's a long story, but we now have a computer on board. I was going to send the guys an email. Is there anything new we should know about?"

"Not really. And as I said before, you need to communicate with them some kind of way. It'll make my job a whole lot easier. Bob calls almost every hour asking if I've heard from you.

"By the way, the weather channel has been broadcasting watches for a big winter storm. Are you keeping track of the weather wherever you are?"

"We're right outside of Nashville and heading toward Memphis tomorrow morning. Don't worry about us and the weather. A trucker friend's looking out for us."

"What do you mean a trucker friend?"

"He's just someone we talk to on the CB. He's one of the good guys."

"Uh,huh. Well, you do realize that Thanksgiving is only two days away, don't you? And holidays make this kind of separation more difficult for everyone involved."

"Mom, what is this? A guilt trip? I thought you supported us in this. As a matter of fact, I do know Thanksgiving is looming, and guess what? It's the first year in MANY years that I don't have to worry about turkey and dressing and all the trimmings. For once in my life, I'm not even THINKING about getting the family together. Besides, Bob and Rex can eat with you. They like your turkey better than mine anyway."

"I don't know about all this, Leslie. You need to go ahead and send that email."

"I will. I promise. For now, I've got my hands full. And Liz and I will have a very nice Thanksgiving after all without all the fuss. We've got the homeless woman, a very large dog, and now a stray cat, and a young computer guru here. I'm sure we can rustle up enough food to give thanks over."

"Well, Leslie, what can I say? I do understand the need to get away from the routine for a while. And don't worry. I'll take care of Bob and Rex. I'll even invite Carl and Billy over to eat. So, you girls just take care. Clear your heads. Enjoy. Just be careful. I worry about you."

We said our goodbyes, and I wandered back to the kitchenette. Darlene, Liz, and Reggie were playing cards.

"I just talked with Mom. She's going to take care of Thanksgiving for us. She'll be inviting Carl and Billy over, so you don't have to worry. This is one holiday family gathering we can forget about. I guess being on the road makes it easy to overlook those kinds of things."

"No, it don't either," Darlene grumbled. "Being out here alone makes it easier to remember. You feel lonelier. In fact, that was one reason I was feeling a little down back under that bridge. My old home church is pretty near here. I've been wanting to visit again. Seems like I'm just supposed to. I don't know why. Say, you know, they always hold a big dinner the night before Thanksgiving at the church. And another thing, my old homeless camp where I hunkered down for a spell is right near there. Maybe we could go by there, too. I'd like to look up some of my old acquaintances if they're still around. Wonder if they fared better'n me. Never dreamed I'd be one of 'em." Darlene rubbed Rosie's fur with a gnarled, weathered hand.

"The church people would welcome us with open arms, and they'd feed us good too," she muttered.

"We don't need them to feed us, Darlene. We've got plenty."

"That so? Got plenty of food and stuff and money, I see. But you lacking a whole lot else." She actually sniffed at me and turned her face away.

"Having a meal at your church is one thing, Darlene, IF it's not out of our travel plans, but I have no interest in sightseeing at a homeless camp."

Liz's face tightened like it always did just before the tears fell. This was great, I thought. Darlene's now making plans for our holiday, and Liz is going to go right along with her. I don't get this. How did things get so out of control around here?

"It could be a nice change of pace for us, Leslie," Liz ventured.

"Oh, I give up!" I stormed over to the computer desk and summoned Reggie to the laptop. "Reggie, you say we're up and running?"

"Yes, M'am. Your email account is The Silver Queen Screamer. I hope that's okay. I took it right from the motor home."

"I don't think that will work. The guys could trace our whereabouts with that. Let's try something else. Any ideas?" I turned to Liz.

"Well, how about "getting away from it all"? Or "two Queens and a slobber dog?" Liz giggled. I rolled my eyes.

"I know. Let's keep it simple. Let's go with Leslie and Liz something or other. How's that?"

"Fine with me," Liz said.

"Reggie, can you find us one of those complimentary email service providers?"

"No problem." It was only a few minutes before he gave us the go ahead. "You're all set. You are now LeslieandLiz@stardust.com."

"Okay, so what do we say?" Liz, Reggie, Darlene, Rosie, and Lulu all gathered around me. "A little air would be nice, folks?" I grumbled. They stepped back but soon were peering over my shoulder again.

I thought for a minute and then began typing.

*Hello, darlings,*

*We are fine and want you to know that. We miss you and love you very much. Please don't come looking for us. We're traveling every day, and will try to email every day.*

*Love, Leslie and Liz*

"How's that, Liz?" I looked over my shoulder at her.

She read carefully, opened her mouth as if to add something, but then stopped herself. "Fine. Just send it."

I hit send. For better or worse, the deed was done.

"Well, Reggie. I guess we should get you back to Circuit City. Will your boss still be around? I'll go in and explain, or rather, we'll make up something that doesn't get me arrested for kidnapping and you fired for abandoning the post."

Reggie looked at his watch. It was past ten o'clock. "The store's closed now. It'll be tomorrow before I can reach the boss. He's gonna be really pissed." For the first time since stealing him away, I felt guilty about the jeopardy I had put Reggie in.

"Oh, Reggie, I'm so sorry," I said.

"I've got an idea," Liz said. "Why don't we just keep Reggie here with us tonight, and we can take him back first thing in the morning? You can talk with his boss then. I'm sure we can make this all come out okay."

I looked at Reggie. "Well, what do you think? Can you stand us for the night?"

"You bet! I was just thinking how cool it would be to sleep in a motor home." He grinned.

"Okay, let's figure out sleeping arrangements. Any ideas, Liz?"

She turned to look around as if she had lost something. Through the doorway we saw Darlene spread out on our bed with Rosie curled at her side.

"I guess, we'll let Darlene and Rosie have the bed," she said. Her mouth twitched holding back a smile. "You and I can do the sofa bed, and Reggie..." Lulu barked at us from the bunk. We all looked up. She seemed to grin down at Reggie, drool sliding down over the edge of the bunk.

"Cool, I can sleep up there with Lulu," Reggie said.

"You want to sleep with a slobber dog?" I asked.

"I don't mind," he answered. With that, we got settled in and turned out the lights. Only the dim glow of the stove light lit the motor home. Night sounds began to seep into the silence. Reggie and Lulu began a snoring contest. And from the bedroom, we heard the occasional grunt from Darlene and a purr from Rosie.

I turned to look at Liz. "Liz? I was just thinking....you remember the time we kidnapped Ron and Larry from that bar and turned the night into a scavenger hunt?"

Liz moaned beside me.

"Oh, and how about the Las Vegas trip and the island cruises?

"Leslie, what is the matter with you? It's late. Go to sleep!"

"Well, I was just going to say that of all the things we've done in the past, I think this motor home adventure will top it all. And I'm thinking we ought to just take Darlene up on the suggestion to go to her church for that pre-Thanksgiving feed."

Liz rolled over to stare at me in the dark. Finally, she spoke, "Why not? Now can we just go to sleep?"

"What's happening to us, Liz? Is it a good thing?"

Liz yawned and reached for my hand. "Oh, we're not so bad. Just think of this way: we're helping out strays. We're sharing our blessings." She poked me in the side and smiled. "Come on Leslie. Give it a rest."

I smiled back at her. "I guess you're right. Tomorrow we'll figure out where we go from here. I wonder what the guys will think of the email?"

"I don't know, and right now, I don't really care. We'll worry about them tomorrow. Good night." She flounced over and covered her head with the pillow. Soon, the night sounds lulled me to sleep, as well.

Back at home…

# Chapter 19

## You Send Me

The phone rang before Bob could dry off after his shower.

"Bob, this is Carl. It seems we have an email from the runaways. At least I think it's from them since the address is <u>Leslie&Liz@stardust.com</u>."

"What does it say?" Bob dropped his towel and walked to the computer.

"Not much. But then, what did we expect? The only solid thing I got out of it was that they are still alive. Nothing about where they are, who they're with, or what they're up to."

Bob pulled up his email on the computer and read the brief message. "Not exactly a warm, fuzzy love letter is it? Not knowing where they are could be a problem. There's a huge snowstorm moving into the southeast. I just hope the girls have enough sense to keep tabs on the weather. I can't imagine them driving a motor home in good weather, much less in a blizzard."

"So, what do we do? Email 'em back and tell 'em off or call the police?"

"Just hold on Carl. Let's think this through a bit more. I'm real anxious to talk to Leslie, and I do miss her, but maybe we shouldn't be in a hurry to respond since they took their sweet time in contacting us? Maybe a bit of their own medicine will do them good."

"Maybe you're right. Let them wonder about us for a while. Let 'em freeze their butts off in a snowstorm. That'll teach 'em to run away in a motor home."

"Carl, I didn't mean we need to get into a punishing mode over this. Let's just think about the situation for today. We can meet the boys tonight at Scally's and talk it over with them. Meanwhile, I'll call Anne and tell her that we've heard from them finally. How about meeting at seven tonight?"

"Great," agreed Carl. Bob hung up the phone and dressed for work. Before leaving the house, he dialed Anne's number.

"Anne, Carl and I got an email from the girls this morning. They didn't tell us much, nothing about their whereabouts, but at least we know they're still alive."

"Well, I'm glad they contacted you. I told them to get in touch one way or another. They must have bought that computer Leslie mentioned the other day when I talked with her. Oh, by the way, she did tell me that they are definitely not going to be home for Thanksgiving—kind of a rebellion against tradition is what I got out of it. I told them I'd cook for you, Carl, and the boys, so pass the invitation along."

"Thanks, Anne. We'll be there. I'll bring your favorite wine. I just don't know what to say about this runaway stuff. You sound like you've accepted it, though."

"Accepted it? I don't know, Bob. A part of me kept thinking they'd return by the Thanksgiving, but that obviously isn't in their plans. At any rate, I can feed you and keep you company. I think we should just let things be as they are for a while."

"I agree. Thanks, Anne. Talk to you soon."

Bob waited at Scally's for the others to arrive. Carl arrived and strode to the bar.

"I've been thinking all day and part of me says to just forget the girls and let 'em sit and wonder who's keeping us warm at night. I gotta tell you, Bob, I'm about done with all this. The neighbors are even talking. That story about Liz going to see an eccentric sick aunt isn't playing very well."

"I talked to Anne this morning. She talked to Leslie yesterday and she said the girls have no intention of coming home for Thanksgiving. Anne invited us all to her house for dinner. I told her we'd be there."

Before Carl could respond, Billy and Rex walked in.

"Hey guys. We got an email from your mothers."

"No kidding? What did they have to say?" asked Rex.

"Here. Read it for yourself." Bob handed the email print out to his son.

"Sounds like one of Mom's corporate emails, short and to the point, right Dad? Didn't really tell us much, but at least we know they're safe."

"For all we know, that could just be a guilt email after talking with Anne. After all, she told them to contact us. It's not like there's anything personal there. Just an obligation, I think. I gotta tell you, I think they owe us more than a couple of sentences that sound like something from Dear Abby regarding the correct response for running away from your husband.

"And, they probably don't have a clue that the snowstorm is headed their way. Maybe when we respond, we should give them a marriage warning instead of a weather warning, huh?" asked Carl.

"Look. We're all confused about this whole thing, and it's only natural to feel some frustration and anger. But, basically, they asked us not to respond or react, so I think that's exactly what we should do. Give 'em what they want. We can email them about the storm, but just leave the rest alone. I've got my laptop right here. What do you say?" Bob placed his laptop on the bar and turned it on.

"You better be the one to write the email," Carl said. "I'm liable to give 'em both a piece of my mind. What did we do to deserve this? Is this some sort of warped punishment for us?"

"We're all confused, Carl, but anger isn't going to help us here. I think the girls will come around eventually. Think of this way: if we had the opportunity to leave for a little adventure, would we have the guts to do it? At least they did."

"Sorry, but I'm not feeling like passing out medals to them, Bob. They're acting like spoiled rotten brats. And I'm also wondering if they're a bit deranged and in need of help. But I'll go along with you. Just send something short and to the point."

"Okay, any suggestions?"

After a few minutes of absolute quiet among them, Bob said, "How about this:

*Dear Leslie and Liz,*

*Thanks for writing. We've been worried about you. Hope you are well. We'll miss you at Thanksgiving. Big storm moving into Southeast. Don't know if that will affect you, but you might want to check it out on the weather channel. Please stay safe. We love and miss you.*

*Bob, Carl, Rex, and Billy.*

"Sounds way too soft if you ask me," said Carl.

"Come on, Carl. Put it aside, man. Let's just get this done. I'm mainly worried about their safety at this juncture. Besides, the truth is that we do love them and miss them."

"I think it's fine, Dad," said Rex.

"Me, too," chimed in Billy.

"Should we send it then?"

"No, wait a minute. I'll go along with the message, but I still think we should wait until tomorrow to answer. It won't hurt to have them wonder about us for one night, will it?" Carl asked.

"Boys?" asked Bob. Everyone nodded in agreement.

# What Does it Take?...

# Chapter 20

## Ain't No Big Thing

The smells of breakfast woke me and Liz the next morning. Reggie greeted us with a smile and cups of hot coffee.

"Reggie, this is so thoughtful of you. How marvelous to wake up and have breakfast waiting! What are we having?"

"I couldn't find bacon, so I opened up a can of corned beef hash, poached some eggs and made some toast. I hope that's okay with you. By the way, I checked your email account to make sure it was still working this morning. It looks fine, but you didn't have any mail."

"Oh, well, maybe the guys haven't received our email to them yet. But Bob usually responds immediately to his emails."

"Surprise, surprise! Guess those men got you to wondering now, huh?" Darlene made her way to the table and plopped herself on the sofa next to me. I didn't like the smirk she had on her face.

"Darlene, why do you have to keep picking on me and Liz? We've been nothing but kind to you, but you're always making snarky comments. I know you don't think we've handled the situation at home very well, but the thing is, we know what we're doing and you don't." At least, I hoped we knew what we were doing, I thought.

"Yes, M'am, I'm sure you do," Darlene sniped back at me.

Liz joined us at the table. "How wonderful, Reggie! Thank you so much for this fabulous breakfast. Now, if you only did hair and massage, you'd be a real keeper." Liz smiled teasingly at him.

"Actually, I used to do both. I'm also a pretty good chef, as you can see, and I clean, walk pets, and bartend, as well. We'd make a good traveling team." Reggie looked from Liz to me.

Oh, no, I thought. Here it comes. And sure enough before I could step in to stave off the invitation, Liz jumped right on it.

"Then you've just got to stay and travel with us. Life on the road can get hard, and we could use a man around, I think, don't you Leslie?" She looked over at me and raised her eyebrows as if daring me to disagree.

"Well, I'm not so sure you'd really want to spend the next few months on the road with a couple of Royal Runaways. And what about your job at Circuit City? You wouldn't want to give that up, I'm sure." I kicked Liz under the table.

Reggie spoke softly when he answered. "Well, I have a little life story myself, but that will keep for another time. I always dreamed about owning a motor home, but I'm not fooling myself. I'll probably never be able to afford one. So going along with you all would be sort of like living my dream for a while. I'll do anything you need me to do, and I won't complain one bit." He gave Darlene a quick sideways glance.

Liz's eyes welled up again, and I knew I had lost the battle. Besides that, I was curious about his life. There was yet another story to hear on this adventure. And who knew, maybe if Reggie opened up, Darlene might do the same. "Well, I guess we could try it for a few days. But let's just agree that none of us is under any obligation to stay together if it doesn't work out. Just like Darlene, here. Just say the word and you're free to leave, and vice versa for Liz and me." I looked directly at Darlene with this last part, but she seemed focused on putting jelly on her third piece of toast. But that didn't stop her from offering her opinion. "I think it would be great to have you along…help me to straighten out these two diz brains. You might bring some balance to the situation, I 'spect. Besides, you and me have something in common, I think. We should compare notes on the hell we've been through." She stuffed her mouth with toast.

"Wow! Great! Fantastic!" Reggie all but bounced around the motor home. "I've never been anywhere before! I'll even give you your money back for the computer hook up."

"No need to go that far, boy," muttered Darlene. "Here, take this slobber dog out for a walk, for me."

Liz and I got up to clear the dishes.

"Did you hear that?" I whispered angrily. "Darlene acts like she has the right to make decisions as to who comes along with us and who doesn't. And she talks like Lulu is HER dog and as if our money is HER money. Listen to her, ordering Reggie around already. How do we get into these messes?"

"Shhh! She'll hear you," Liz replied. "I guess we're just two bleeding hearts. But he is a nice young man, and he can probably help out a lot. And if we have to, we can always put them both out at the next town."

"Yeah, like we would!" I scoffed. "But seriously, Liz, we've got to agree on something here. The Screamer won't hold but so many bodies. We can't be the rolling lost and found for the state."

"Okay. But this is an adventure, right? And I think I'm loving it."

When we finished in the kitchen, Reggie came back inside. He hugged first Liz and then me. "Thanks. I promise I won't be a bit of trouble. I might even be able to help out with Darlene."

"What? What's that you saying, boy? I ain't needing no kind of help from anybody and specially not some wet-behind-the-ears-computer-nerd!"

"Sorry, Darlene. I didn't mean any offense. But after all, this isn't your motor home, and if you don't like the arrangements, then you can just…" Reggie looked over at Liz and me and winked, "…well, you can just kiss my grits!"

There was a second or two of stunned silence, and then Darlene let out the loudest guffaw I have ever heard, and that was all it took to get us laughing. When we finally caught our breath, we took turns showering and dressing, and with everyone helping out, we got unhooked and unplugged in no time. Reggie offered to drive the first leg, but I wanted to maneuver The Screamer out of the park. He was going to need some practice time before I turned him completely loose with her.

Just as I cranked up, Ponderosa Man called on the CB.

"Go ahead, Ponderosa Man. The Queens are here!" I answered.

"What have you been up to the last two days? I was getting worried when I couldn't get a rise on the radio."

"We're fine. We've just been holed up outside of Nashville taking care of some computer needs and picking up another friend."

"Another friend?"

"It's a long story, Ponderosa Man! But don't worry. Everything is cool. We're heading out in just a few minutes. We're planning on doing a little visiting somewhere between here and Memphis. A church and a homeless camp."

"Come back?" Ray sounded completely puzzled.

"Another long story. Anyway, we'll be heading west."

"Keep watch on that snow storm. Best to find somewhere to park and stay for a few days. It's headed right at you. I'll be on the road Thanksgiving Day, so if you run into trouble, just call."

"Ten, four. Over and out."

Liz came up front to see what Ray had said. "He's really a nice man. We're lucky to have met him," she said after I filled her in on his concerns about us and the storm. "What about the storm, anyway?"

Darlene piped up from the back. "When my toes wiggle on their own, it means a storm is coming on. The church is not far from here, so why don't we drive there this afternoon, stay on for turkey, and see what's up with the weather, then."

"Can you believe her?" I whispered to Liz. She just smiled and with that, we pulled onto the dirt road to leave the park.

# Chapter 21

## On My Own

At the park gate, I motioned for Reggie to take the wheel. Lulu lumbered up front with him. "What about your car, Reggie?" I asked. "Are you just going to leave it in the mall parking lot?"

Reggie looked down and then looked back at me. "I lied, Ms. Leslie. I don't have a car. I take the bus to work."

"Oh, Reggie. You didn't have to lie. But I understand. I remember when my Rex couldn't drive, and he wanted to impress a certain girl, he told this outlandish story about his jaguar being in the shop. I guess we all fall victim to the occasional story." I made my way back to the dinette where Liz and Darlene had pulled out a deck of cards.

Reggie smiled and eased into the turn, but then he hit the brakes hard.

"Ms. Leslie, I think you better come take a look at this."

I made my way back up front. Rachel stood by the gate, her blonde hair limp in the damp air. She carried a faded red backpack strapped across her back. I rolled the window out.

"Are you expecting another twenty from us, Rachel?"

"No M'am. I was just wondering if…if…." she hesitated and for a moment I saw tears in her eyes.

"What is it Rachel? What's wrong?"

She swallowed and took a deep breath. She glanced shyly at Reggie and then looked back at me. "I was just wondering if you have any room left in that RV?"

"What?"

"I need to go with you, Ms.Leslie. I have to get away from my parents. They didn't come home again last night. They do this all the time—get drunk and leave me here to run things for days. I don't want to do this anymore, Ms. Leslie. I'm scared out here by myself."

"Rachel, honey, we can't just take you away. That would be kidnapping."

Reggie poked me in the side. "That was different, Reggie," I whispered.

"Please, Ms. Leslie. Please don't leave me here. I wrote them a note. I told them I was leaving and not to come looking for me. You wouldn't be the blame for that."

I watched her shuffle from one foot to another. Her clothes hung loosely around her thin body. Her eyes seemed dull and listless, afraid, too. I couldn't stand to see a child afraid.

"Just a minute, Rachel." I made my way to the dinette and motioned Reggie to come with me. He switched off the ignition and followed. Outside, a cold, light rain had begun to fall.

"We need a conference," I said to Liz. "Did you hear what Rachel just said?"

Liz nodded her head.

"What's to conference about?" Darlene chimed in. "That poor girl is miserable and scared. She needs help. We should take her with us."

Again, Darlene assumed an ownership that wasn't hers, but this time, I couldn't fault her reasoning.

Before I could comment, she went on, "She reminds me of my granddaughter. She used to write to me, but then I got all these troubles, and well, I miss her. I'll take on the girl. You don't have to worry with her."

I was astounded at Darlene's generosity.

For once, Liz looked hesitant. "I don't know about this," she said. "It's fine for Darlene to say she'll take care of Rachel, but well, how? I mean, you can't really take care of yourself right now."

Darlene bowed up at that. "Who says I can't, Missy? I was doing just fine before you two Queenies came along. Just because I ain't living like you think I should, don't mean I ain't taking care of myself."

"I didn't mean that to hurt your feelings, Darlene," Liz said. "I just mean, taking on a minor without parental permission, that could be lots of trouble, and I don't mean just day to day. Even with her leaving a note, well, the law might see things differently."

"What if Rachel signs a note that says she ran away on her own will. We came along and gave her a ride, meaning she was hitchhiking, right? I wonder how old she is anyway?"

"Looks about thirteen to me," Reggie said.

"Yeah, and sounds like she's got a good reason to run away. Just like me. Not like you two." Darlene sulked.

"Okay, everybody. Let's think this through. I feel so sorry for her, and I don't think it's safe to leave her out here alone like this, so let's get an agreement written up. Reggie, get some paper. I'll write up something for her to sign."

I opened the door and motioned for Rachel to come in.

"Rachel, what are your plans after you leave here and then leave us later on? And how old are you anyway?"

"I'm eighteen, Ms. Leslie. And I don't have any plans. I just know I have to leave. I can get a job somewhere along the way, I'm sure. I won't be with you forever, and anytime you say leave, I will. I'll sign anything you need me to sign."

I looked back at Liz. She nodded. "Okay, if you're eighteen, then that takes care of the legal stuff, I guess. But I still think we need to have her sign that statement. Just in case." She came over to Rachel and hugged her. "Welcome aboard, Rachel."

Darlene smiled and waved for Rachel to join her at the table. "You hungry, honey?" she asked. "You, Ms Lizzie, get this child something to eat."

Liz smiled at me and opened the refrigerator to do as Darlene had told her. I was amazed at the control Darlene had over all of us already. How did that happen, I wondered. Oh well, for better or worse, our bleeding hearts had taken on another soul for this journey. We'd just make the best of it.

Reggie brought over the agreement for Rachel to sign. She wrote carefully. Liz and Reggie witnessed it.

"What exactly did you say in the note you left your parents, Rachel?" I asked.

"I just told them I was leaving home. It was time to be on my own. And I said not to come looking for me. I'd get in touch when and if I wanted to." She picked at her fingernail and then looked back up at me. "They won't care, Ms. Leslie. They probably won't even know I'm gone until they need something done. That's about the only time they have any use for me."

I took the paper from her and placed it in the desk drawer. When I turned around, Rachel held out her hand.

"Here's your money back, Ms. Leslie."

Darlene pursed her lips like she was about to jump in the conversation again, but before she did, I shook my head at Rachel. "No honey, you keep it. You may need it down the road."

She tucked the money into her jean pocket.

"Okay, Reggie, time to hit the road. Take a left out here and hit I-40. Then, put the pedal to the metal. Since we missed Opryland, let's try for the music district in Memphis."

"Here you go, sweetie," Liz said, placing a plate of food in front of Rachel. The girl's eyes widened and without a word, she dove into the food. Darlene poured her another glass of milk. "Drink up, sweetie. There's plenty more where this came from."

Liz and I made our way to the bedroom.

"I don't know what we're going to do with all these sad stories," I said. "We must be crazy taking on all these people and their problems."

"I know, but well, let's just think of it as our good deed for the year. Maybe Darlene will take Rosie and take up with someone at her old church or get off the homeless camp and Rachel might just go along with her. Reggie will probably choose a city somewhere. Then it'll be just the two of us again...except for Lulu."

I shook my head. We certainly had a full house now. Liz and I made our way back to the front of The Screamer. Lulu sat in the passenger seat beside Reggie like some giant interstate lookout. Rosie slept curled up in Darlene's lap, and Rachel nodded sleepily next to her.

"Let's check our email," I said to Liz.

"Nothing," she said. I guess we shouldn't be surprised. This is just like Carl to want to punish us."

"Ms. Leslie?" Reggie called.

Before I could answer, Darlene yelled back at him. "Get off at this next exit. We're going to my church for tonight's Thanksgiving service."

"Darlene," I interrupted. "Why do you call it your church? When was the last time you attended there? And let's get this straight right now..." I was loosing patience with her bossiness. "If the church is on our way, fine, we'll stop. If not, we're going to keep right on trucking down this interstate. There's a storm brewing, and I want us parked and safe out of its way."

Darlene snapped back at me. "Do you have any religion in you, woman? Do you remember that tomorrow is Thanksgiving? My church is not out of the way. It should be very close to this exit. And I think you and Liz could use a little church in your lives." She crossed her arms over her chest and pouted.

"Okay, Darlene. You're right. We should stop for Thanksgiving. Reggie, follow Darlene's directions. We're going to church."

Darlene heaved herself up from the dinette and plodded up to the passenger seat. "Get down, you ol' slobber dog, you." She tugged at Lulu's collar. When Lulu lumbered to the back of the motor home, Darlene settled herself in the seat and set to "getting her bearings" as she put it. I turned to switch off the computer, and when I looked again, Liz's tiara sparkled from the top of Darlene's head.

"Would you look at that, Liz?" I shook my head. "I've never in my life seen..."

"Oh, let it go," Liz said. "She's fine. Besides, you and I need to think groceries. We've got to make a stop soon or we'll be down to popcorn and canned soup."

"Reggie," I called, "Look out for a grocery store. We need to make a stop."

The two of us settled on the sofa. The motion of the motor home and the hum of the engine had me drowsy. Rachel snoozed beside Rosie. Lulu's head hung over the edge of the bunk. Up front, Reggie's head bobbed to the beat of music only he could hear. Darlene sat straight and proud, giving directions like the queen she thought she was.

I smiled. As frustrating as all this could get, it was interesting. Who would have thought our mad adventure and dash for freedom would have landed us in the middle of this hodgepodge of souls? I yawned, and my last conscious thought was that we should write a book.

# Home Base…

# Chapter 22

## When It Ain't Right With My Baby

"Have you contacted the girls?" Anne's voice sounded breathless over the phone.

"Actually, no. We thought we'd make them wait a bit since it took them a while to contact us." Bob answered.

"Well, what a macho kind of thing to do, Bob! Does this mean you're not in love with my daughter anymore? You and Carl need to get your heads together and start making some sense out of this mess. Don't you know the storm of the century is about to hit us? How can you two be so wrapped up in your silly pride instead of the safety of the girls?" Anne was obviously upset.

"Anne, just calm down, please. We don't know for sure where the storm is going to hit. I've been tracking it for the last few days on the weather channel. But we don't know where the girls are either. How can we decide what to do when we don't have any solid information? If you have any ideas, let me hear them. And in answer to your question, I still love your daughter very much."

"If that's true, then give up this macho stand-off, and go get her. I'm worried!"

"Anne, she doesn't want me to come get her. She wants to be left alone. She said so. Remember? Besides, I don't have a clue where to start looking for her. And if I do find her, then what? What if she doesn't want to come home?"

"I can't answer that Bob. All I know is you need to find her. You two have to figure out what your relationship is and where it's going. But you need to find her in order to do that. Leslie hasn't called me again, and I'm worried to death those girls are going to get into trouble with this storm. They don't know how to survive a blizzard."

"They seem to have figured out a lot of things I never expected them to know about, Anne. I think they'll be fine."

"You THINK they'll be fine? That doesn't sound good enough for me, Bob. I'll see you at 2:00 tomorrow for dinner. By then, I want to know what your plans are!"

Bob repeated Anne's concerns when he met Carl at Scally's that evening. Billy and Rex were home for the holidays, so they joined them at the bar.

"The wives aren't home yet, I see," chuckled the bartender. "Maybe they decided to ditch the sick aunt and head for the hills, huh?"

"Very funny," Carl replied, agitated. "Let's get a booth."

The four of them sipped at their drinks. Finally, Bob broke the silence. "Okay, it's time to make some decisions. Anne's worried about the storm. She wants us to go find the girls before they get caught in it."

"About time somebody starting making some sense around here," grumbled Carl. "I've been saying that since day one."

"If you're going after them, I'm going with you," Rex announced.

"Count me in," agreed Billy.

"Wait a minute," said Bob holding up his hands. "We need to think this through. How about if we send an email tonight, give it a couple of days. I think being away from home and family on Thanksgiving might just be the thing to make the girls come back on their own. What do you say?"

"Yeah, we don't want to look too eager." Carl tugged at the collar of his unironed shirt. "Maybe they'll get stuck in that storm and then really be sorry they left." The others frowned at him. "Not that I'm wishing 'em bad luck or anything," he explained.

"Okay, Rex, get us another round of drinks while I boot up this computer. Let's take a look at what we wrote last night and see if we're all still good with it."

Bob pulled up the draft and read it out loud.

*Dear Leslie, Liz, and Moms,*

*Thanks for writing. We've been worried about you. Hope you are well. We'll miss you at Thanksgiving. Big storm moving into Southeast. Don't know if that will affect you, but you might want to check it out on the weather channel. Please stay safe. We love and miss you.*

*Bob, Carl, Rex, and Billy.*

"It works for me—short and to the point," Bob said. "Leaves no doubt that we're together on this. We even reassured them that we love them. Ready to send?"

Everyone nodded yes. Bob hit the send button, and all four men slumped back against the booth seat as if relieved.

"Whoa! Wait a minute," Bob exclaimed. "The weather page just came up showing the live Doppler shot of the Southeast. The storm's been upgraded from this morning. It may reach blizzard strength before it's done. Looks like the hardest hit area will between the Arkansas border and western Tennessee."

The men looked at each other. Something like a premonition crawled up their backs, but they shook it off with talk of tomorrow's feast at Anne's. Meanwhile, the Doppler screen blinked green and red in the darkness of the bar.

# So, I was saying…

# Chapter 23

## Any Day Now

"We're almost there!" Darlene called from the front of the Screamer. It was 4:00, and she was in rare form.

"The supper usually starts around 6:00. You all got to get dressed. Pick something fancy. And find something for me, too. Do you have any hats? Hats is always good at church events. Rachel, do you have anything you might wear to church?"

"Not really. I never had any church clothes," Rachel replied, already showing a hesitancy about going to the supper. Liz pulled her to the bedroom. "Don't worry, we'll find something," she said.

"Darlene, we didn't bring any dress hats, but of course, you can always wear Liz's tiara," I sniped at Darlene. Her answer was to sniff in my direction.

Darlene guided Reggie right to the Praise the Lord Congregational Church, even though she claimed it had been years since she was there. Reggie eased The Screamer into the back parking lot. As we turned into the drive, a sign showed us Darlene was right about time for both the service and meal. But the sign also said to bring a dish.

"We don't have a dish to take to the supper, and there's nothing much in the cupboard. We can't go without taking something."

No one offered a solution. "Okay, then. Well, Darlene will just have to go alone, and the rest of us will go into town and get gas and supplies."

"Oh no, you don't. You just trying to dump a po' old homeless woman. That plan ain't flying. We all go. These church people don't care if you bring anything at all. They'll be just as happy with a donation in the offering plate. And you can sho' manage that, can't you, Queenies?"

"Honestly Darlene, I wasn't trying to dump you. Just go back there with Liz and find something to wear. Reggie, you're out of luck. We don't have anything in your size. We do need to get you some more clothes somewhere along the way."

Reggie nodded. Outside, the skies were graying and filling with clouds.

"How about turn on the radio, so we can check out the weather." I took the passenger seat Darlene had vacated.

In the back, Darlene opened the bedroom door to find Liz doing a complete makeover on Rachel. She wore a beautiful cashmere sweater on loan from Liz. Make up littered the dresser top. Her hair was coiled on top of her head, making her look more like the eighteen she was rather than the thirteen she appeared to be on first meeting.

"Lord, you look pretty. Spittin' image of my granddaughter." Darlene swiped at her eyes. Rachel smiled up at her.

"You can be next, Darlene," said Rachel. Darlene looked to Liz for confirmation. Liz nodded.

"Really? Well, let me go get a quick shower, then. I'll be back in a jiffy." Darlene hustled off to the small shower.

"You do look very pretty," Liz said to Rachel.

"Thanks. My mom never took any interest in me this way. I've been pretty much on my own since I was twelve, and I've been dreaming of leaving home for years, but I just didn't see any way to do it, until you all showed up at the park. I sure am grateful for the ride and the help."

Liz hugged the young girl and then applied her own makeup.

Up front, the automated voice came over the radio. " …a winter storm warning has been issued for parts of Tennessee. High winds and near blizzard conditions are expected for at least a forty-eight hour time period. Snow accumulation is expected to be between 10 and 12 inches. A travel warning is in effect."

"Sounds serious, Ms. Leslie," Reggie said. "Are we any where near it?"

"See if you can find a local station. Maybe we can get more specifics."

Reggie fiddled with the dials until he found a Nashville broadcast. We listened to a commercial and then heard the weather alert signal. My heart sunk to my stomach as we listened. "We are expecting the storm to last over the next couple of days. The Memphis area may be on the fringes but the exact path has not been determined. You are advised to stay tuned for updates, especially if you have travel plans."

"Well, maybe we'll be lucky and the edge won't be so bad," Reggie looked at me for validation. I nodded a vague 'yes' and turned up the radio volume.

"There are still two missing people from the outlying Nashville area. Reggie Thompson is a white male in his early twenties, with dark hair, and is approximately 5'8". Thompson was last seen as he left for a work break at the Circuit City store on Highway 36. After two days of no word from him, the store manager reported him missing, and police searched his apartment. There were no signs of forced entry or robbery.

The other is eighteen-year-old Rachel Wilson reported missing by her parents from Northfork RV Park. She's a white female, has light hair, and stands about 5'2" at 100 pounds.

Because the two are from the same general area, police are considering that there may be a connection. If you have any information on these two people, contact your local police department."

"Oh, God!" I said. "They're talking about you and Rachel. We'll be arrested for kidnapping after all. I hope no one at the church has heard this. Since we don't have clothes for you anyway, it's probably best that you stay in here tonight with Lulu and Rosie. We'll go to church with Darlene. That way if people have heard the broadcast, they won't notice just a young girl with us. We'll bring you some supper."

Reggie nodded hesitantly. "I can do that. I'd just as soon stay here anyway."

"We better plan to leave early in the morning, too. Let me check the book and see where the next RV Park is located. Oh, and Reggie, don't say anything about this to the others. They'll just worry. I don't need anyone freaking out right now."

Reggie left to give Lulu a quick walk and to let Rosie snoop around outside for a while. I pulled out the maps and brochures. The Crossroads RV Park was located very close to the interstate near a town called Millington, just outside of Memphis. It was open year-round and appeared to be the last park in the state of Tennessee. A ball of fear built up in my stomach: a storm coming, police alerts on Rachel and Reggie, and no word at all from the men. Things were piling up.

I switched to the CB. "Hey Ponderosa Man, are you there? This is The Queen Screamer, please come in."

While I waited for a response, Reggie returned. "Lulu must sense something. They say dogs can smell a storm. She was real antsy out there, sniffing around like crazy."

I didn't have time to worry about Lulu's supposed ESP. "Reggie, help me figure out this GPS system while I'm waiting for Ponderosa Man to respond." We bent over the instruction manual while Lulu yipped shortly at Rosie.

"Hey, stop that!" Darlene yelled as she came from the rear. Liz and Rachel followed her. "Wow, you all look terrific!" I said. Liz wore her black Chico's outfit with boots and scarf to match. Rachel glowed in the red cashmere sweater, and Darlene wore my brand new teal blue sweater and stretchy black pants. On her feet were my Ralph boots. A Hermes scarf circled her neck and low and behold, Liz's tiara sat high on her braided hair.

"I guess I should go change into something else," I said. "Reggie, keep working with that GPS."

I leaned down to whisper, "Don't say a word about the news or the weather."

He nodded, and whispered back, "I don't think it's working right, Ms. Leslie. But I'll keep trying."

I rushed to the back to freshen up. There wasn't much time to fuss over what to wear, so I threw on a pink sweater and black pants. Since my boots were busy, I had to settle for black tennis shoes.

"Got your money?" quipped Darlene as I brushed past her. I decided not to answer her. That ball of fear in my stomach was growing and my nerves were frayed. Better to let things be for now. We said our goodbyes to Reggie and left for church.

For the first time since meeting her, we saw Darlene walk straight and proud. Her face glowed with the make up Liz had applied, and she wore my clothes like they were made for her. Striding importantly, she led us across the parking lot and up toward the front door. She sniffed the air and commented, "You girls better pray hard tonight because I do smell a storm and my big toe is wiggling. Get ready to smile, now. Be nice. Mind your manners."

I smiled to myself. "Lead the way, Darlene. We're right behind you."

# Chapter 24

## I've Been Wrong Too Long

People stood in line out front to get in the door. I had never seen such a collection of hats, scarves, dangling beads, high-heeled shoes, boas, and big shiny earrings. The men wore suits that ranged from plaid to purple, from formal tuxedoes to leisure suits. Everywhere, there were black cowboy boots. A definite gaiety permeated the air.

"Welcome to the Lord's House!"

"So glad you could join us."

There were rounds of introductions, but I didn't hope to remember all the names. As for us, we were just Liz and Leslie. I whispered to Rachel to use the name Carol. She looked puzzled, so I said, "Trust me. I'll tell you later."

"Lord! If ain't Sister Louise. It's been so long. Good to see you. How are you doing?" Darlene wrapped her arms around a huge woman dressed in rose and pearls.

"Darlene! Darlene is that you? Lands sakes alive! What brings you here?"

We waited tensely on Darlene's explanation.

"I was just passing through. We're on a little vacation, seeing the world, you know. And when I realized we were so close by, I told the ladies we just had to drop into my old church. Come meet my traveling companions."

"Whoa! This story is bound to be good," I whispered to Liz.

After we were introduced to Louise, Darlene went on to explain our presence at the church.

"Leslie and Liz are my special travel companions and assistants. We're traveling by private bus. And this young lady here is ..."

Before Darlene could finish, Rachel jumped right in to say. "Carol....I'm Carol."

Liz looked astounded, but before she could comment, Darlene obviously picked up on something, and covered for Rachel. "That's right, this is CAROL," stressed Darlene. "She's Leslie's niece—on break from college and tagging along with us old folks for a few days." We shook hands and smiled all around.

"Well, come on in. The service is 'bout to start," said Louise.

"Assistants?" I whispered to Liz. "Can you believe the story she made up? Makes you wonder what her real story is for sure." Liz nodded.

We took our seats three rows from the back. "This will make it easy for you to leave if you start misbehaving," said Darlene.

"Why would I misbehave? I know how to act in church, Darlene."

"Humpf," was her answer.

A large choir in crimson robes paraded in as the last of the congregation squeezed into available seats. The wooden pews were overflowing, and the late afternoon sun streamed through beautiful stained glass windows, melting colors across the plain pine floor. The congregation hummed along with the choir.

Suddenly, a trumpet blared from the rear of the church. There was a drumbeat and the double doors flew open. The minister busted through, striding back and forth down the aisle, shouting, "Welcome! Welcome All!" A small band followed and the entire congregation stood and began to clap. Bodies swayed in rhythm to the beat. The mood was contagious. Darlene's face lit up. I said a silent prayer in thanks for this opportunity to share in worship and asked the Lord to watch over us all.

The sermon put most of us to shame for not being grateful enough for our many blessings. Darlene poked my side with her elbow every time the preacher said the word grateful. The room filled with hearty responses of "Amen" and "Yes, brother." The fear in my stomach gradually gave way to a deep and real joy.

The choir continued to entertain us while we waited for the supper to begin. It wasn't long before the minister invited us all to stand and say Grace.

"I hope there's a lot of food," I whispered to Liz. "I've worked up an appetite."

"Me, too," she answered. Rachel nodded as well. The poor thing needed to put some meat on her bones, and I had a feeling tonight's supper would help that along.

We filed out to the back wing of the church where long tables sported paper tablecloths depicting turkeys and cornucopias in traditional fall colors. We stood to the rear not wanting to be the first in line. Some of the men went out back to the parking lot to smoke. I noticed that several of them pointed to The Screamer. I worried that they might go over and investigate, so I took the opportunity to join them in a smoke.

"Excuse me, but may I have a light?" I asked an older gentleman who obliged immediately.

"Thanks," I said. "I'm Leslie. My friends and I are visiting tonight and we certainly enjoyed the service. It was lovely."

"Glad to have you, M'am. I'm Ben, Senior Deacon." The other men eyed me curiously.

"Say, is that fancy bus yours?" Ben pointed to The Screamer.

"Yes Sir, it is. We're traveling with one of your former church members, Ms. Darlene. She wanted to come tonight since we were so close by. We'll be on our way tonight to another RV park, unless it gets too late. In that case, do you think it would be okay for us to stay in the parking lot?"

"Why sure. No problem. I guess you heard about the big storm that's brewing. It's likely going to affect your traveling plans."

"Yes, sir. I know. We've been listening to the weather broadcasts. That's why we thought we'd go on to the RV Park as soon as possible. You know, hunker down there until the storm moves out."

One of the women peeked outside the church door to call us in. "Time to eat, fellas!"

Ben tipped his hat at me, and I went back inside to find Liz and Rachel.

Darlene had finagled them to the front of the line with her, so I joined them there. Darlene chatted away with several people standing beside her. Her face continued to glow with a happiness that made her absolutely beautiful.

"Where have you been?" asked Liz.

"I went to smoke a cigarette. I saw some men eyeballing The Screamer, and I was afraid they might go over to check her out. Thank God, Reggie had the sense to turn all the lights off."

"Why are we being so careful? And why is Rachel now Carol?" asked Liz.

"Oh, we'll talk later. Let's eat. I'm so hungry." I pushed her on up to the stack of paper plates, and we proceeded down the line filling our plates with all kinds of wonderful foods. There was fried chicken, ham, turkey, pot roast, peas, corn, potatoes, biscuits, rice, gravy and more desserts than I could count. Reggie was going to faint with joy when we brought this back to him.

Liz, Rachel, and I followed Darlene to one of the tables. For the moment, we were the only ones at that table.

"Well, Ms. Leslie, you are a first at this church, for sure." Darlene said.

"What are you talking about?" I asked.

"Going out there in the parking lot to smoke with the men. Our women don't do that kind of thing."

My face burned. "Darlene, I am so sorry. I didn't mean to embarrass you in front of your friends. But the men didn't say anything. In fact, they were very polite. The Senior Deacon even gave me a light."

"Course they were polite. Did they ask you any questions?"

"We had a brief conversation about the possibility of our staying in the parking lot here tonight. They said it would be fine, but we'll see after we finish supper."

Sister Louise joined us at that point. She brought a string of relatives with her and everyone made room at the table. Louise glanced at our plates.

"I guess I don't have to worry about you getting enough to eat tonight, Leslie," she smiled.

I had to think fast to come up with an explanation of why I had two plates of food in front of me. "No M'am! I just had to try a little of everything. And anything left over will go to Darlene's pets. They're traveling with us, and I'm in charge of taking care of them for her." Darlene rolled her eyes at me.

"So, are you still in Nashville working at that recording studio, Darlene? I heard you took some time off from recording, but that you stayed on in the business office."

Darlene coughed, and then wiped her mouth with a napkin. "Uh, actually I did stay for awhile, but then I decided I needed a vacation. So here we are." She smiled at Louise and kicked my shin under the table.

I had stuffed myself until I was nearly miserable.

"I guess I had better go feed the animals before they start creating a fuss."

"I'll go with you, Ms. Leslie." Rachel rose and picked up her plate.

"We'll be back for coffee and dessert," I said as we walked away.

Reggie opened the door at our quiet knock. He carried a small flashlight. Lulu and Rosie lay curled on the sofa in the darkened motor home.

"Gosh, I'm starved!" He said. "I could smell that food all the way over here. And the music was great! Sounded like you were having a great time."

Rachel went over to pet Rosie and Lulu and fed them bites of leftovers. I sat at the table beside Reggie while he ate, my back to Rachel so she couldn't easily overhear our conversation.

"Any luck with the GPS, yet, and have you heard the latest weather report?" I whispered.

"I think the GPS is a goner," Reggie said quietly between bites. "I tried everything I knew to try. But I did get the Memphis station again, and the storm is coming this way for sure. I checked the map, so I think I know where to head for the RV Park you mentioned. Looks like we should plan to stay there for a couple of days. 'Course, if we go to that homeless camp like Darlene wants to, it could put us way off track. I just don't think we ought to chance it."

"What about Ponderosa Man? Did he ever answer our call?"

"Nope, not a word from him, whoever he is." Reggie sat back from his plate and rubbed his stomach. He glanced toward Rachel and raised his voice enough for her to hear him. "That was terrific!" he said.

"Glad you liked it. Well, I better get back to the church." I stood to leave, and then bent over to whisper in his ear, "We'll try the GPS again when I get back."

I turned to Rachel then and asked, "Are you ready to go back?"

"I'd really like to stay here with Lulu and Rosie," Rachel said. "Can you just tell them I was tired and wanted to go to bed?"

"Sure, honey. Don't worry about it. You've had a big day after all. I'm sure Reggie will enjoy your company, too." I suspected that there was more to Rachel's wanting to stay than just the animals, but I didn't say so. As I left The Screamer, I noticed that Reggie's face was unusually rosy.

Back at the church, Liz and Darlene were both well into their fourth desserts. I grabbed a cup of coffee and a piece of cake and joined them. Darlene was holding court with former friends. I leaned to whisper to Liz, "We need to talk tonight."

"What now? What's going on?" She asked.

"Nothing really…we just need to talk."

# Chapter 25

## It's All Right

Reggie took his paper plate to the trash compactor and refilled his glass. "That was some great food. Ms. Leslie sure loaded my plate up."

"Actually, I helped. She didn't know what you liked to eat, so I suggested we bring you a little of everything. I wish you could have gone with us. You should have seen all the food! So, what's the news on the storm?"

Reggie hesitated a moment before answering. He wasn't sure what to tell her since Leslie hadn't wanted to tell the others they had heard on the radio.

"Tell you what… why don't we take Lulu and Rosie outside. It's dark now, so the church folks can't see us."

"Great. Let me get these nice clothes off. I'll be right out."

Reggie watched her as she walked back to the bedroom. She looked different from the girl they picked up at the RV Park. She really was very pretty, he thought.

"Okay, Reggie, I'm ready. Let's go." Rachel slung a jacket over her shoulders and led the way outside. They veered to the backside of The Screamer toward the woods and away from the church.

Rosie went her own way, but Lulu stayed fairly close by. She sniffed and rooted at the leaves and pine straw that covered the ground.

"Reggie, you didn't answer my question about the storm? That makes me even more nervous, like you and Ms. Leslie want to hide something from the rest of us."

Reggie stopped. "It looks like we're going to be right in the middle of it. And it's a big storm. So that's not so good. But, Ms. Leslie has found an RV park not too far away, so we plan to hunker down there. And we'll have plenty of supplies, and there's a generator and everything in case the power goes out. Don't worry. We'll be fine. I promise." He turned to look back at the church. What in the world made me tell her that, he wondered. I don't know a thing about snowstorms.

When he turned again towards Rachel, she smiled. "You're really a nice guy," she said. "No offense to Ms. Leslie and Liz, but I feel better knowing you're with us."

"Uh, huh," he mumbled. He didn't want to pretend to be something he wasn't.

"Do you have a girlfriend?" Rachel asked.

"No, uh, no. I don't. Do you? I mean, do you have a boyfriend?"

"Naw. I never had much time for a social life. I practically ran the RV park by myself. It was that or not eat. My parents stayed drunk or gone all the time. So, I've never really even had a date, much less a boyfriend." Rachel laughed a small, almost bitter laugh.

"Me either," said Reggie. "I mean, I, uh,….well, I've got a lot of baggage from my family too. I went to work when I was only thirteen. Had to lie about my age, but it was the only way to keep from starving. My dad left when I was four years old when my mother got breast cancer. Then Mom took to alcohol and drugs because she was sick. I grew up knowing that I'd have to take care of myself, and there just wasn't much time for dating or anything but work."

"I'm sorry."

"Me, too. I mean, I'm sorry about your situation, too. But hey, it looks like we turned out all right, huh? We got lucky hooking up with Ms. Leslie and them. Do you have any plans? What do you want to do? Where do you want to go?"

Rachel shrugged. "I've always dreamed of being on my own, and putting the past behind me. But I never got as far as making any real plans. I guess

I'll just have to figure it out as I go. Traveling with Ms. Leslie and Ms. Liz will give me some time to come up with something. At least we don't have to worry about food and shelter, huh?"

"Right," Reggie answered. He looked carefully at Rachel's face in the dim moonlight. She was staring at him, too. Hers was a young face, but her eyes, they seemed older. Like they had seen way too much for such a young girl. He felt an impulse to reach out and touch her cheek, but he didn't.

"We should be getting back," he stammered.

"Yeah, I guess."

Rachel called for Lulu and the big dog loped up behind them. She had burrs in her fur. There was no sign of Rosie.

"That cat might've wandered off again. Darlene said it was prone to run away."

They walked slowly back toward The Screamer, but halfway there, Rachel stopped. She reached out to grab Reggie's arm.

"Reggie, do you think we could be friends? I don't mean, like girlfriend or boyfriend, but just, well, just friends?"

Reggie's heart did a somersault.

"Sure. We can do that," he said. And maybe even the other later on, he thought to himself.

They made their way to the steps where Rosie lay curled up and waiting.

"I guess she's like us—figures she needs to stay a while and think things through before striking out on her own." Reggie smiled, and in the darkness, Rachel smiled back.

# Chapter 26

## Let's Stay Together

"Oh, there you are! I'm glad you're back," I said. The two looked more comfortable together than they had before. Again, I wondered. Wouldn't it be sweet if they fell in love? But, I pushed the thought away. "Reggie, we have some work to do."

Rachel joined Darlene on the couch, and Liz made her way to the bedroom to change. I led Reggie up front to turn on the radio. "Any news?" I whispered to him.

"Nope. No GPS, and No Ponderosa Man. But the storm's definitely headed our way, so I think we should leave early in the morning. We can't dump here, anyway, so that will save us some time. We should go gas up, buy groceries, and hit the road. If we make it to that park, tomorrow, we'll have a better chance of getting a spot. I bet every RV near here is headed to the same place."

"I hadn't thought of that," I said. "I need to go talk with Liz."

I stopped to mix us drinks and then headed to the bedroom.

"Here you go," I said as I handed the drink to her.

She looked at me suspiciously. "Okay, what's up?"

I sat on the bed and patted the space next to me. "Sit," I told her.

I explained the plans for weathering the storm out, and then I told her about the missing persons report that Reggie and I heard on the radio. "That's why Reggie stayed behind rather than join us for supper. And that's why I told Rachel to call herself Carol, you know, in case anyone at the church had heard the broadcast, too." When I finished, Liz's shoulders slumped.

"I think I need another drink," she said. "We'll have to tell Darlene that the homeless camp is out. Do you think we'll get arrested for kidnapping, Leslie?"

"I don't even want to think about that. But no, I don't. It's just inconvenient to have an alert out on Rachel and Reggie. If people recognize them, they're bound to think the worst of us. The sooner we get to that park and get hunkered down, the better off we're going to be."

Liz nodded in agreement. "Okay, let's make some coffee for Darlene, mix us another drink, and we'll just sit down and explain it all. She has to understand our situation. We did her church thing, so maybe she'll be satisfied with that." She sighed.

"What I want to know is how she became such a major force in our lives so soon? Who made her Queen?"

There was a slight pause, before we both answered, "*SHE* did, and *WE* did."

"Okay, so let's do this thing." We laughed together, and I reached for Liz's hand to pull her to her feet. Together, we made our way up front to talk with the others.

"Drinks all around?" Reggie asked.

"Yes, Liz and I could use another if you want to bartend. I'll make fresh coffee for Darlene, and Rachel can have a soft drink.

Reggie busied himself at the bar, while Liz and I sat down on the dinette benches to face Rachel and Darlene. Reggie soon joined us.

"So, there are some things you all should be aware of. Reggie, fill them in on the storm reports, please."

Reggie sat up straight in his seat, cleared his throat, and began. "The storm appears to be heading right toward us. Leslie and I have checked the map and the guidebook, and we found that the nearest RV park is called the Crossroads RV Park. We can hole up there and weather this storm, but the thing is, we need to head out first thing in the morning, gas up, get food, and hit the road. It's important we get there as soon as possible. It could fill up fast, and then, well, I don't really know what we'd do. It'll take us about forty minutes to get there. All this is good news, except…" he paused and looked directly at Darlene. "Except that it means we can't take any side trips."

Darlene slurped at her coffee. When she finally raised her head to look at us, she stated very calmly, "That sounds like a real responsible plan, son. And it makes sense. But, the thing is, that I have to go to that homeless camp. The Lord spoke to me tonight, and he put it on my heart that I was to go there for some reason. So, you all just gotta go a bit out of your way, drop me off, and head on to your park. I can get us there without any problem, I'm sure. Once you drop me off, you can forget about me and get on with your adventure. I won't be no more trouble to any of you. One less burden, you see?"

"Darlene, we can't just drop you off! This storm is nothing to fool around with. You need to stick with us, so you will be safe." I couldn't believe I was actually arguing with Darlene to stay with us.

"Yep, it is a serious storm. I know that. All the more reason for me to be dropped off at the camp maybe to help out. The Lord spoke to me, I told you. I don't know what He wants, but I've gotta go. You can't be planning on going against the Lord, now can you?" She stared hard at me.

I shook my head. "Okay, look. There's something else you should know. This afternoon, Reggie and I were listening to the weather report on the radio, and there was a missing person announcement."

Rachel and Darlene stared at me. "The missing people are Reggie and Rachel."

Rachel's face paled, and Darlene shifted uncomfortably in her seat.

"But there's nothing we can do about that right now. We're all tired and tense. Let's get some rest and we'll get up early and get on the move and figure out what we need to do about everything. We can discuss this over morning coffee."

Everyone nodded, but there was a heavy silence surrounding us. The anxiety of the coming storm was building. It had been a long day.

"Liz, I want to check the email one more time," I said.

I pulled up our mail server. The familiar tone indicating mail caused every head in the motor home to turn toward the computer. "It's from the guys," I said to Liz. She sat down beside me at the small desk. I double clicked the message. Bold type filled the monitor.

There were several minutes of absolute silence while we read. I turned to Liz who stared at the words with her mouth slightly open. Her eyes were huge in the glare from the screen.

Finally, she blurted out, "That's it? That's all they said? I can't believe this!"

"What? What did they say?" Darlene asked.

Liz read the brief message aloud.

"Huh, guess that puts you two in a different place, huh?" snorted Darlene.

"Darlene, I have a good mind to…" I rose from my chair, but Liz pulled my arm.

"Don't. Just leave it alone. This has Carl written all over it. I can hear him now, 'Let's let them wonder about us for awhile,' he probably said. The nerve of them!"

"We need to think carefully about a reply before we send one, Liz. Let's put this on hold for tonight, too."

I clicked off the computer and followed Reggie to the front of The Screamer. "Reggie," I whispered. "What do you think about dropping off Darlene tomorrow. Is it doable in our timetable?"

"I don't know. I'll check out the map again and talk with her in the morning. If it's close by like she says, it probably won't take too much extra time." He went back to climb the ladder to the bunk, but Rachel was already there along with Lulu. For a minute, he stared up at them. I wondered if he was going to try to join them. But he turned to grab a blanket and pillow from the closet and turned back to the cab. He reclined the seat as far back as he could and pulled the blanket up around his shoulders.

"Good night, Ms. Leslie," he said.

"Good night, Reggie. Thanks for all you've done. I'm glad you stayed on with us." I patted the top of his head and turned to go back to the bedroom. Darlene sprawled on the sofa, while Rosie purred on top of her chest.

I closed the bedroom door softly behind me. "Liz, we need to talk some more."

"No shit, Sherlock! That monster storm is headed straight for us. We could be arrested for kidnapping, and Darlene has taken control. Not to mention that we need to discuss that …that stupid email we just received from the guys. Please make me feel better, already!"

I flopped backwards onto the bed and stared up at the ceiling. "Liz, as far as the storm situation, I think we'll be okay. As for Darlene and the others, if it wasn't for the storm heading right at us, I think I could drop them all at the camp and never look back. I long for a 'Queen' week…just the two of us, traveling, listening to our music, seeing the country. But…"

"But that's not going to happen any time soon," Liz finished my sentence for me. "We've just gotta do what we gotta do. I'm okay leaving Darlene at the camp. I'd love to know her story, and I'll worry about her, but she's a grown woman. She knows the situation there, and she can pretty much take care of herself. But Reggie and Rachel, they're just kids. We can't just leave them on their own."

"You're right. I know. And tomorrow I need to call Mom again. And we'll have to answer that asinine email, too. We need to let everyone know we're safe. Let the guys play their little game. We'll give 'em just enough to say we're fine. Let 'em stew!"

I turned over on my side and pulled the bedspread up over my head. "I'm too tired to even put on my pajamas," I muttered into my pillow.

"Me, too," sighed Liz. She yawned loudly, stretched, and then slid under the spread beside me. "Good night."

# Chapter 27

## Build Me Up Buttercup

The smell of coffee and a muted conversation between Reggie and Darlene got my attention at 7:00 in the morning. Liz snored slightly beside me. I thought for a moment about what lay ahead of us that day. So many unknowns. Liz and I had run away to have some freedom. Now here we were, like prisoners in a motor home, facing a major winter storm. We had three other people and two animals in our care. Besides that, we had to face our families at some point.

I forced myself to sit up and reach for the cell phone.

"Mom?"

"Well, it's about time! We're worried sick about you girls. Have you even listened to a weather report? Do you know about the storm?"

"Yes, Mom, we know. We're fine. Our trip has just taken on a life of its own, and well, we've been busy."

"Busy? I thought the whole idea of this trip was to stop being so busy?"

"It was…is. It's just…oh Mom, just trust us, okay. We went last night to a church supper that Darlene insisted we go to, and we're still parked in the parking lot. Today we're heading out to an all-season RV Park to hunker down before the storm gets here. And we have another traveler with us. A young girl named Rachel. The problem is, there's a missing person report out on her and the computer guy we picked up."

"What? A missing person report? Leslie, have you lost your mind? You kidnapped two young people?"

"No, Mom, no. We did not kidnap them. They came of their own free will. And they're both of age. Oh, it's just too long a story to get into right now. Just know that we're okay. And Mom, I'll miss having Thanksgiving with you. I really will."

There was a moment of silence while both Mom and I fought back tears, and then Mom broke the silence.

"The least you can do is tell me where you are, Leslie."

"We're somewhere near a township called Buttercup Junction in the south-western hill country of Tennessee. We're heading for Memphis. There's an RV Park not too far from there where we'll wait out the storm. On our way there, we're going to drop Darlene off at a homeless camp. I'll email the guys today. Don't be worried if we don't call for a couple of days. The storm may affect the cell phone reception up here."

"Just be careful, Leslie. And please try to call as soon as you can. I love you."

"Love you, too, Mom. Bye."

I punched Liz. "Get up. We've got to get going." She groaned in response.

When we reached the kitchen, Rachel was just leaving to take Lulu out for a walk. Reggie was in a heated discussion with Darlene.

"You have to be sure about this, Darlene. We can't afford to get up in the back country and get lost."

"We ain't gonna get lost, Mr. Driver Boy. The camp is near here. It's not that far out of your way. I know what I'm doing."

"Yeah, right," he muttered.

"Okay, what's going on here? What's our plan?"

"Mr. Smarty pants Driver Boy here doesn't believe my calculations about the location of the homeless camp. So, I think you Queenies should put me out here and head on to your precious RV Park. I'll manage just fine on my own."

"No, Darlene, that won't work. I just wish I knew where the hell we are and where the hell we're going. If our GPS system was working, we'd know all of that."

"The problem is that it has been years since Darlene was up this way. The roads are all different now. There are interstates and highways instead of the dirt roads she remembers. We can't take the chance of getting lost," said Reggie.

"I'm telling you, I know where that camp is. I have instincts. More'n you have, buster. I can get us there."

Rachel made her way back inside with Lulu. "It's freezing out there this morning," she said. Lulu shook herself and trotted over to the sofa.

"Okay, let's vote. All in favor of dropping Darlene at the homeless camp, raise your hand." Everyone except Rachel raised a hand. Darlene seemed stunned.

"Rachel, it would be nice to have this a unanimous decision. What's the problem as you see it?"

Unaccustomed to being asked for an opinion, Rachel shuffled her feet and cleared her throat. She began haltingly, "It's not that I don't think we should drop her off. It's just that….well, I really like Darlene, and I just don't want her to leave us. I'm scared for her to be out in this storm." Tears rolled down her face, and she swiped at them.

"Oh, child," said Darlene reaching for her. "You are the sweetest thing. I 'preciate you caring and all, but like I said last night. The Lord has spoken to me. This is something I gotta do. I think He might want me to settle down there. Even if it is a homeless camp, it can be my permanent home. I don't know what He's got in mind. Besides, I can stay in touch somehow. It'll be fine. I promise."

Rachel hugged Darlene and sniffed loudly. "Okay, Darlene. If that's what you want. I'll vote for you. Let's go see this homeless camp of yours. I might as well get acquainted with 'em cause it may be that I'll have to make my home in one some day."

Reggie looked at Rachel with surprise. He started to say something, but caught himself and turned back to the front of the motor home.

I sat down at the desk and booted up the computer. Darlene sauntered by me.

"You gonna write your husband now?"

"Yes, Darlene, I am."

"About time. You still don't know how lucky you are." She made her way to the coffee pot.

"Okay, Liz. Let's get this done. I think we should stop worrying what to say and just say it. This isn't some delicate corporate deal. And we're not children who have to have permission from them. We're grown women. We're capable. We're deserving. We don't really have a beef with the guys per se. It's just the life we were living. So, Maybe Darlene is right. We are pretty lucky."

"Go for it, girlfriend," Liz said and took a seat beside me.

*Dear Bob, Carl, Rex, and Billy,*

*We are safe and we miss you, too. The trip has been quite interesting so far. It will be fun to tell you all about it when we return home. We don't know when that will be, but it won't be real long. After all, we've only been gone a few days now, and our journey has just begun. Please remember that none of this is about you guys. It's about us and dreams and hopes for the future.*

*We are watching the storm. It appears we'll be on the fringe of it, but we're heading for a safe camp today to wait out the storm. We'll stay in touch as long as we have email. Phone reception is not good here. Have a great Thanksgiving with Anne. We love you.*

*Leslie and Liz*

"How's that?" I asked.

"Perfect. Just enough info for now. Hit send and let's get on the road."

With that done, I turned to the others. "Let's ride, team!" I cried out. I put on my tiara and took the wheel. Reggie sat beside me with our maps spread across his knees. "Buckle up," I yelled to the others.

Reggie turned on the radio. "This is a weather alert. A winter storm warning has been issued for the entire state of Tennessee. Several inches of snow and high winds are expected. Blizzard conditions may affect the higher elevations with white out conditions possible. Travel is not advised, especially on back roads. Conditions will be severe by mid-afternoon in the southwestern part of the state. Seek shelter."

"Oh boy," I said. "I sure hope Darlene knows where we're going. There's no time to play around."

"I heard that," Darlene yelled at me. She stomped up behind me and parked herself in the co-captains seat right behind me.

"Darlene, you can't sit there. I feel like you're breathing down my neck."

"Tough! I ain't moving. You ain't gonna sit up here and bad mouth me and get us lost intentionally so you can blame me for it. I'm here and I'm staying here." She rose up to lean over me and crossed her arms across her chest.

158

"Darlene, sit!" I demanded, and remarkably, she did, but she sat leaning towards us in order to hear every word.

"Take a left," said Reggie.

"No, take a right," Darlene ordered.

Reggie and I looked at one another. I stopped The Screamer and turned to stare hard at Darlene. "This better be right Darlene. There's a lot at stake here, you know."

"I know what I know," was her answer.

Several miles down the road, we stopped at what looked like a gas station, though no lights were on, and I wasn't sure it had been open in a while.

"It looks like there's a light on in that cabin in the back. Let's go see if there's anyone there who can help us," Reggie said.

"Liz, I'm going to need some money…a lot, I think." She flipped through a book stored under the kitchen sink and handed me a handful of bills.

Reggie and I climbed out of The Screamer. We knocked on the door and behind it, heard a shuffling sound. A short wrinkled old man opened the door. At his side was a German Shepard. The dog growled deep in his throat.

I introduced Reggie and myself and explained that we needed gas.

"I'm Adams. This here is Christian, my dog." The Shepard continued to growl and inched his way carefully toward us. Finally the old man reached for the dog's collar and pulled. "It's okay, boy." The dog sat meekly at his side.

"You folks know about the storm headed this way?" Mr. Adams peered out toward The Screamer.

"Yes, sir, we do. That's why we need gas. We're trying to get to the Cross-roads RV Park to wait out the storm, but first we have to find a homeless camp that's near here. You see one of our friends traveling with us used to stay there, and she wants to go back there."

"Oh, I heard about that camp. I don't know as you ought to try to make it to that RV park either. Heard it shut down a while back, though. The storm's moving in fast. You're welcome to pull up out back here and hunker down with me and Christian."

"Thank you, Mr. Adams, that's very nice of you. But we really do need to try to make it to the RV park. By the way, do you sell any supplies at all?"

"Nope, not a one. What you looking for?"

"Well, I need some cigarettes for one thing."

"I can give you some of mine. They's home-rolled, but good. Why don't you take a few with you?" He reached behind him and then shoved a box filled with what looked like joints. I eyed the old man carefully, but silently convinced myself, that no, it wasn't likely he'd be rolling the funny stuff, though in our present predicament, part of me wished he did. I gave Adams a wad of money, about $100, to cover the gas and cigarettes. "Thanks Mr. Adams."

"You're welcome. Here's the key, boy. Go unlock that last pump to the right and get what you need."

Reggie and I made our way back to The Screamer and pulled up to the tank. It took several minutes to fill up, and while I did that, Reggie returned the key to Mr. Adams. When he got into The Screamer, he carried a large paper bag.

"What's that?" I asked.

Reggie blushed. "Well, I don't have any clean clothes, you know, so I asked Mr. Adams to lend me some. He put a few things in here for me."

I felt a bit ashamed. We had forgotten that Reggie didn't have a change of clothes, and I said a silent prayer of thanks for Mr. Adams' kind heart.

Reggie stored his bag of clothes, and we were soon back on the road.

It seemed there was an argument at every turn, literally. If Reggie said left, Darlene said right, and vice versa.

Finally, their bickering was interrupted by the CB.

"Come in, Queen Screamer…this is Ponderosa Man. What's your 1040?"

"Liz, come talk to Ray while I drive!" Liz hurried up front to switch places with Darlene. She leaned over the console to reach the CB.

"Hey P Man," she said. "How does it go with you?"

"Cut the small talk, Liz. Where the hell are you two?"

"Still on the road. We're going to an RV Park before the storm hits. How about you?"

"I had to take a detour from duty. My estranged daughter actually called and asked if I could be with her for some surgery she's having on her leg. So I went straight to the hospital in DC to be with her. It's been kind of strange. She never wanted me around before. But everything went okay. It's been good, in fact. But I've been off the road and out of touch for a few days now."

"10-4. Happy to hear she's doing well. Maybe you two can get closer now. We're heading to a homeless camp to drop off Darlene, you know, the lady we picked up. Then we're going to the RV park. We don't actually know where we are exactly though, because our GPS system is out. Anyway, all of this is too long a story for now. It's beginning to snow pretty hard already."

"You two are crazy. Don't mess around with this storm. It's not just a little snowstorm, you know. Where's this RV park, anyway? I don't think you need to be there tonight. You need to find a motel and sit it out."

"It's the Crossroads RV Park. Supposed to be open year-round, and it's not far from here."

"You two need to realize that year-round means that only if there is not a major blizzard coming. I'm in North Carolina right now, but I have a stop in Tennessee sometime this week depending on the weather. Look, just take my advice. Don't try for the park. Find a motel. And keep in touch."

"10-4 Ponderosa Man. We hear you."

"Here we go again. Somebody else doubting. I ain't never seen such doubting fools in my life." Darlene heaved herself up to get a soft drink from the refrigerator.

Liz made her way back to the sofa, and Reggie rustled the maps in his lap.

A few more miles down the road, and Darlene poked my shoulder.

"Turn left there on that dirt road."

"Are you…"

"Don't ask me that again. TURN LEFT." I turned left.

The narrow road was bordered by thick pines. The snow all but obliterated the ruts, and several times, I had to swerve to avoid low hanging branches that threatened to scrape The Screamer's side. The farther we rode, the thicker the forest and the dimmer the light. Snow blew in gusts, but Darlene insisted we keep going.

"You weren't expecting a neon sign, was you Queenie? Homeless camps don't usually have 'em. This time, you gotta trust old Darlene. I know what I know, and I'm telling you, this is the road."

# Chapter 28

## Chain of Fools

"You were saying?" Reggie smirked at Darlene. The road she had been so sure of had suddenly dead-ended. The snow swirled around us, blocking all but a few feet just ahead of the front bumper. There was nowhere to go but back.

"What are we going to do now?" asked Liz.

"We don't have a choice. We're going to have to turn around and find somewhere to park," I said. "Darlene will just have to wait to answer the Lord's call until after this storm."

"Don't be smart about the Lord, Queenie," Darlene sniffed and walked to the rear of The Screamer.

"Reggie, you take Lulu and scout around back behind us. We've got to find a safe place to turn around. I can't see a thing with all this snow falling."

"Sure," he said and turned. He seemed to be searching for someone, but there was no one besides Lulu to be seen. Darlene had shut herself in the bedroom, and Rachel had climbed up to the bunk to nap before we even turned off the interstate.

He bundled up and opened the door. Rosie followed them outside, but nearly jumped straight up in the air when her paws touched the wet snow. She didn't linger. She did her business and was back inside before Reggie closed the door.

"You know, I think I'll go out for a smoke, Liz. Why don't you come with me?"

She joined me just outside the door. We stood and stared at the snow and the woods all around us. We couldn't see Reggie or Lulu.

"What's going to happen next?" Liz asked.

"Well, let's just hope we have enough booze and coffee to get us through. Don't worry. We'll be out of here and be heading back to civilization in no time."

We stared off into the whiteness. The trees stood like giant white sculptures against a white velvet carpet. "It is beautiful, isn't it?" Liz whispered, as if in awe.

"I used to think so. Back when I was snug and warm in my living room in front of a fireplace and looking out at it."

"Are you saying you're ready to go back?

"No. I'm not saying that at all. It's just that…well, we're in a precarious position here. I just hope we can get The Screamer out."

Liz's eyes grew wide and round. Reggie and Lulu trudged up from the rear of The Screamer. "It's gonna be a tight squeeze to turn her around, Ms. Leslie. Should I try it?"

"No, but thanks. If The Screamer's going to get bummed up, then I should be the one responsible." I walked to the rear to take a look myself, and then trudged back up to the door.

"Might as well give it a try," I said, and we all went back inside.

"I'll take the flashlight and go stand behind you. Maybe I can guide you back." Reggie snatched the light and headed back out into the cold. Liz took the passenger seat. She reached over and placed my tiara on my head. Then put hers on.

"We can do this," she said and smiled.

Slowly, I inched The Screamer back. I could vaguely see Reggie swinging the flashlight, guiding me on. Lulu whined. There was no sound from Darlene or Rachel. Inch by inch I turned through the tight three-point turn.

"One more to go," I said. I opened the window and yelled for Reggie to come back inside. I eased my foot off the brake and pressed the accelerator. The Screamer groaned and then shot backward. I had forgotten to switch the gear into Drive. A strange scraping noise rose from the rear of the RV and slowly, the whole backside sank.

"Reggie, did you see a ditch or anything back there?"

"No M'am, but you know, the snow's covered everything, so it's hard to tell what's what exactly. Let me go look."

We sat silently waiting until he returned.

"It's a ditch all right. Our back wheels are in it. I'm not sure we can get it out."

I laid my head down on the steering wheel. "It's not his fault, Leslie," Liz whispered. I nodded. It wasn't anybody's fault but my own for listening to a crazy old woman and her instincts, I thought. I allowed myself two minutes of sulking, and then I straightened in my seat.

"Well, here goes the old college try!" I began to alternate the gears between reverse and drive trying to rock The Screamer out of the ditch. It felt as if we were sinking deeper.

Reggie came up behind me. "I'm so sorry, Ms. Leslie. I should have looked better. It's all my fault."

"Look, Reggie," I said. "Shit happens. Let's not place blame. The good news is that we have gas, power, a generator, and each other. What say we take a break, eat something, and then we'll try again?"

He grinned slowly. Liz and I plundered the cabinets for something to offer for lunch while Reggie raided the bar. He mixed a strong vodka and sat down to nurse it and his downtrodden mood. Darlene moseyed out of the bedroom, and Rachel climbed down from the bunk and took a seat very close to Reggie on the sofa.

"What's the problem? Why are we stopping here and why am I now walking uphill?" Darlene asked.

I had to laugh. Getting angry wasn't going to help anything. "Sit," I ordered and pulled Liz over to join us. "I'm calling another pow-wow," I said. They all looked at me as if I had lost my mind.

I stood before this motley group and reached up to straighten my tiara. Funny, how a silly little crown can command such awe, I joked to myself.

"We have a little predicament," I said. ""We seemed to have backed our way into a ditch. So, it looks like we'll be stuck here for a while, unless we can figure out some way to get the rear end of the motor home up, or unless someone comes along to find us. Which, by the way, has a snowball's chance in hell of happening."

Liz giggled.

"So, let us take a breather. It IS Thanksgiving, after all. Food is called for. We'll eat, we'll feel better. We'll get a fresh perspective on the situation. And then we'll figure out what's next."

I looked dead on at each of them. "Are you with me, team?"

One by one they nodded, and I realized that, in spite of the circumstances, I was very grateful for each and everyone on board The Screamer at that moment.

After a feast of popcorn, baloney, and Ritz crackers, Reggie and I made our way to the cab to try out the GPS system again. Darlene and Rosie retired to the bedroom again, while Liz and Rachel dozed sitting up on the sofa with Lulu at their feet.

Reggie and I sat staring out into the blizzard. "You're awfully quiet, Reg. Are you okay?"

"I'm fine. Just thinking about life and how funny it works out sometimes."

"What do you mean?

"Well, like, I never would have dreamed I'd be spending Thanksgiving like this, with people like you all." He ducked his head.

"What do you mean people like us?"

"Oh, you know, good people. Not like at home. Not like all the other Thanksgivings I had." He opened up to share part of his past as he had with Rachel earlier. "In spite of all that, I was lucky that I got on with a computer company, and I was good at it. I saved up enough money to move out and take some night classes at the technical college. And I got the job at Circuit City. I was doing okay, not really hoping for much more. Not expecting life to get any better. For some of us, it just doesn't work that way, you know. I figured I was one of 'em.

But then I met you ladies, and Darlene, and, well, Rachel. And I realize what I've missed all this time. And I guess it's made me sort of start hoping for something more than I've had in the past. I really would like that, you know. And well, I guess I really like Rachel, a lot, too. I didn't expect to like her. But I do." He looked up at me then with sad heavy eyes.

I couldn't help but brush my hand across his forehead and smooth back the hair that strayed into his eyes.

"You know, Reggie. This could be a real turning point in your life. I think you should try and put the past behind you. Start fresh. Give this new life a chance. And I think you should take it slow and easy with Rachel. She's not had it easy either. Just leave yourself open for what lies ahead. And hope, Reggie. That's the thing. Never settle for anything. You deserve….we ALL deserve better than settling."

He grinned up at me.

"Okay, let's go take a look around outside. There must be something we can do." We grabbed our coats and headed out into the storm again.

After surveying our position carefully, I turned to Reggie. "Let's gather up some limbs and branches and try building up the ditch under the wheels. Maybe we can drag some of those larger limbs over and make sort of a bridge. If we can get them lodged under the tires and up onto the ditch bank, we may just be able to get her out."

Between the two of us, we dragged limb after limb to the ditch until we had filled in as much under the tires as we could. Then we hauled two larger limbs over and wedged them as far under the tires as we could.

"Okay, let's give this a try." I led the way back inside, but this time, I let Reggie take the wheel. "I'll get everyone to come up front. It might help a little to have some of the weight off the rear."

Darlene grumbled when I woke her, but after I explained what we were doing, she followed me to the front of The Screamer. Even Lulu crouched close to the console.

We all held our breath as Reggie started the engine and began the slow and steady back and forward move I had tried before. The Screamer groaned. The tires spun. Branches and limbs cracked and spun from underneath the tires. It was like a war raged outside. After several tries, The Screamer's tires finally dug in tighter, and there was no more rocking to be done.

I began to laugh—the kind of laughter that caused tears to flow and shoulders to shake. Soon, Liz caught it, and then Reggie and Rachel. Last of all Darlene joined in. Lulu barked, and Rosie slunk under the sofa.

"I don't know when I've laughed so much," I said, trying to get control of myself.

"Me either," said Liz. She spilled a bowl of popcorn across the carpet and began picking the kernels up one by one.

"Well, what do we do now?" asked Reggie.

"We could string popcorn garlands," said Liz.

"What?" Darlene was incredulous.

"Well, we've got to do something to keep our spirits up. I say, we go out there and find a Christmas tree. We can decorate it with popcorn garland. We've got enough popcorn to feed a ….a …a homeless camp!" At that, we all burst into laughter again. Even Darlene gave in to it.

After several minutes, Reggie stood and grabbed his coat. "Okay, Rachel and I will go find a Christmas tree. We might as well make this a real celebration!" They called to Lulu and went out into the snow.

It was a while before the two young people and Lulu returned. Reggie dragged a small pine behind them and brought it inside. We finagled a prop for it and stood it on the table. Liz began to drape the string of popcorn she had made around and through the limbs. Rachel dug into her backpack and pulled out a red wool scarf. She tied this into a big bow and placed it on top of the tree. Liz tossed a box of costume jewelry to Darlene and told her to hang some on the smaller limbs. Pretty soon, we had a fully decorated, leaning Christmas tree. Liz lit two candles on either side of the tree and dimmed the lights. We all stepped back. Rachel sighed, and Reggie came up behind her and draped his arm across her shoulder.

"I think it's beautiful," Rachel whispered.

"Prettiest one I've ever seen," Reggie agreed. "Course, I've never really had a tree of my own before."

"You had a right good idea, here, Queenies." Darlene said to Liz. "Now all we need is a little music, and we'll have Christmas right here."

Liz cut her eyes at me and grinned. I stood up and straightened my tiara.

"Ready?" I waved my arms in the air and belted out the first line:

*Oh! We ain't got a barrel of money*

Liz joined in:

*Maybe we're ragged and funny*

Darlene, Reggie, and Rachel looked at us, then at each other. "Why not," said Reggie, and they joined in:

*But we'll travel along*
*Singing a song*
*Side by side.*


By the time we finished three full verses, I had no doubt that it was the best Thanksgiving I had ever had.

# Thanksgiving
# at Home…

# Chapter 29

## Cry to Me

Before leaving for Thanksgiving dinner at Anne's house, Bob checked his computer. There was a message from Leslie and Liz. That he actually had received a response to his email so soon caused him to hold his breath. He reread the important parts: *We are safe and we miss you. None of this is about you guys. Headed for a safe camp location to ride out the storm. We love you.*

At least they're safe, he thought. But we still don't know where they are. Why the secrecy? Why all this drama? He shut down the computer and packed it in the carrying case so he could show the email to everyone at Anne's.

Anne greeted him, not with a "hello," but with, "You need a stiff drink."

"How'd you guess?" He asked, smiling.

She fixed the drink and handed it to him. "Happy Thanksgiving, Bob."

"To you, too," he answered and took a large gulp of his drink.

Anne led the way to the den where Billy, Rex, and Carl lounged.

"It doesn't feel like Thanksgiving with the girls not here, does it?" Anne asked.

"No, but here we are, so we might as well make the best of it I suppose. It doesn't sound as if they'll be home any time soon. Take a look at the email I got this morning." Bob booted up the computer and pulled up the email from the girls. Four sets of eyes devoured the words.

"Well, that's informative," Carl smirked. "Must have taken them days to write all that. And so much detail…my, my."

"Ah, come on Carl," Billy said. "Chill out some. At least they're safe, and they seem to be taking the storm warnings seriously. Even if we don't know exactly where they are, we know that much, at least."

"Precisely, the problem, son," Carl retorted. "We DON"T have a clue where they are. And this storm's nothing to play around with. Some reports say it will be life threatening in some areas. I vote for an APB and full track-down." He emptied his glass and rose to fix another drink.

"Life-threatening?" Anne repeated. She reread the message. Her daughter would be out in that, she thought. "Look guys. I was all for the girls having some time to just get away, but none of us knew about the storm when they left. It was right not to go after them at first, but now, well, this storm has me worried. I think it's time to take some action. I vote with Carl this time. Let's start the ball rolling. We can even help with the hunt. It beats sitting here doing nothing but listening to the storm warnings." She looked at each of the men.

"Okay. I give in. I think you're right. We should try to find them. But let's not go off half-cocked. Carl, call your buddy. See what he recommends."

"You got it!" Carl pulled out his cell phone and dialed the police station. Two rings later, he asked to speak to his friend.

"I'm sorry; Sergeant Wilson is off today. Is there someone else who can help you? Is this an emergency?" The receptionist was all business.

"Yes, it is, but I need to speak to Larry. Give me his home number."

"I'm sorry, sir, but I cannot give out an officer's home number. Sergeant Baker will be happy to speak with you."

"Forget it!" Carl shouted and snapped his cell phone shut.

"Carl, what's going on?" Anne asked.

"Larry's off, and they won't give me his home number. But, I know where he lives, so we'll just ride over there." He rose from the sofa to go.

"Wait," said Anne. "First, let's eat. I've cooked all this food, and we're going to be hungry no matter what. Another hour won't matter one way or the other. We'll eat, and then you can go find your friend."

Carl opened his mouth to object, but the boys backed Anne.

"Yeah, Carl, we're starved. Let's eat, first. It's not like anyone's dying."

Carl grunted, but followed the others to the food Anne had laid out.

"All the traditionals, I see, " Bob said eyeing the spread before them. Everyone took a seat and Anne said Grace. For a few minutes, there was only the sound of plates being filled and passed.

"Hey, Dad," Rex said. "We'll need to take a picture of Mom and Liz with us to the police. They'll have to have one."

"Good point," said Bob. "I'm sure there's more than one of the two of them at the house. All those so-called 'Queen Scrapbooks' she's kept are probably full of 'em. We'll go by the house before we go to Larry's."

"Scrapbooks?" asked Carl. "Liz never mentioned any scrapbooks to me. Are there some big-time secrets in there that I'm not supposed to know about?" He looked around the table.

"Yeah, right, Carl. Big-time secrets. Get over it, man. I haven't seen inside of them either. I'm sure it's just girl stuff…you know how they save everything from movie ticket stubs to dead flowers. That's all it is. No big deal." Bob's voice sounded less sure than he had intended.

"Wait. I have the perfect picture right here. Leslie gave it to me last year. It was taken when she and Liz did their Glamour Shot thing. I have quite a collection of those pictures! I'll go get it." Anne left the table and soon returned with the photo.

"Here. It's a great picture of them both."

Carl examined the photo. He looked up at Anne with a scowl on his face. "They're wearing those stupid tiaras on their heads. We can't use this. The police will think they're just two loonies and won't do a thing. We need something else."

"Carl," replied Anne, "whether you like the tiaras or not is not the point. It's a perfect photo of both. It's fairly recent, and besides, the girls wear those tiaras a lot as sort of a private joke, and I'd bet they've been wearing them on this trip. If they have, whoever has seen them, will remember. The tiaras can turn out to be a big help here."

"Anne's right," offered Bob. "I think we should go with this picture." He held it out to the boys, who both nodded in agreement.

"All right, already! We'll go with this, even if it IS embarrassing as hell. What's Larry going to think of my wife? I can hear him now telling the guys at the poker club." Carl threw down his napkin.

"Anne, when you talked with Leslie, did she give any hints about their location?" Bob asked.

"They did say they were heading to Memphis to an RV Park and had just come through some place called Buttercup Junction." Anne answered, and then smiled. "Okay, then. Let's finish up here, so you guys can get going." Anne began cutting huge slices of pumpkin pie.

# Stand by Me…

# Chapter 30

## I Will Survive

Decorating the Christmas tree had taken our minds off the storm and being stuck for awhile, but after my calls on the CB went unanswered and the radio gave off nothing but static, the realization that we were indeed stuck in the middle of nowhere, finally hit home hard. Reggie and Rachel had gone out with the animals again, so I called Liz up front.

"Liz, we're really in a mess. We have absolutely no service on the cell phones, so the computer is our only means of communication. I don't want to think about this, but well, we may have to contact the guys and tell them our situation. What do you think?"

"I think I need another drink before I answer that one," she said. "We've got to consider the safety of these young people first. So, maybe we better pull Darlene in on this conversation."

"I'm not believing you just suggested that, but at this point, I suppose you're right. She knows the area, or at least she used to. So, go ahead."

"Darlene? Come up here a minute please. We need your advice."

"My advice? You two want advice from ME? I can't believe what I'm hearing."

"Me either," I muttered.

"But now, I heard what you just said about contacting your husbands, and far be it from me to give out marital advice, but I for one wouldn't want to be in your shoes and have to call them to rescue me after I ran away like you two did."

"Gee, thanks, Darlene. Can you rub it in a little more?"

"Lookie here, Queen Leslie. You got your own self into all this. It's not…"

"What? YOU are the one who gave us these stupid directions to nowheresville."

"I see my instincts were a little off, but that don't mean I'm wrong about everything. Why don't we just wait until those two young uns come back and we'll all sit down and talk it over? They're old enough to help out. Besides, they're a part of this mess, too. Might as well be as informed as we are."

Liz made her drink and Darlene sipped another cup of coffee while I studied the road map. I never was good at maps, and these back roads could confuse even a seasoned traveler. At last, Reggie and Rachel returned, stomping snow from their shoes and leaving wet shoe prints across the carpet. Lulu made it to the sofa and shook off a small rainstorm. Rosie was content to curl up and lick her paws dry.

"Come here, you two. We got some decision making to work out," Darlene said.

When we were all seated around the dinette, I explained our lack of communication and the possibility of calling the men for help. "I know they'd come, but are we jumping the gun here? What do you think?" I looked at Reggie and Rachel.

"Look, y'all have become like family to me," Reggie began. "And I have to take some of the blame for our situation, so I'm probably not the best one to offer an opinion. I want all of us to be safe. It's a bad storm, for sure, but we've only been stuck here this one day, and maybe, we're jumping the gun about calling for help. What do you think, Rachel?" Reggie turned to her and slipped his arm around her shoulder, as if to encourage her to speak up.

"Well, I feel like y'all are family, too. And I trusted you from the beginning to take me in, so I'm not likely to start untrusting you now. I'm not afraid, and like Reggie said, this is just our first day. Why don't we wait it out until tomorrow and then decide?"

I turned to Darlene. "Okay, Road Queen, what's your vote?"

Darlene walked to the window and raised the blind. She stared out at the whiteness for a minute and then turned back to us. "It's all my fault. I know that. And it's a problem, for sure, but I know just about where we are if not exactly, and I think we're pretty safe here. The thing is, I've been in a whole lot tougher situations, so being stuck our here in all this pretty snow with you all don't seem so dangerous to me." She smiled a half smile and then continued. "Even though I scolded you two Queenies about being so ungrateful and leaving home like you did, a part of me understands why you did it." She paused and looked out the window again. "And why you HAD to do it. So, whatever you decide is what I'll be living with."

By the time she finished, Liz had tears in her eyes. "Okay, so I guess it's up to Liz and me. What do you think, Liz?"

She stared from face to face and then looked at me. "For what started out to be just a fun little adventure trip has turned into one of the best things that has ever happened in my life. I miss my son, and I even miss grumpy old Carl, too, but the truth is, right now, I just don't want to bring them into this. I feel like I've found a whole new family with y'all, and I don't want that ended so soon. I say we just hang tight until later tomorrow."

She turned toward me, and I knew what we had to do. "Well, I never dreamed our little adventure would turn out like this, but...." I looked at each face around the table. "I'm really glad it did. So, for now, we wait it out."

There were big smiles around the table as if the wind and snow that roared and swirled around The Screamer didn't exist at all. Reggie and I got busy in the kitchen making more popcorn while Darlene and Rachel settled down with their books. Liz made her way back to the bedroom and returned a few minutes later with a box dripping with costume jewelry and, of all things, two rhinestone tiaras sat on top.

"Where'd you get those?" I asked.

"I just remembered that I stashed two extras in with the rest of the Queen jewelry, just in case we lost ours. But, now I have a better idea." She placed the box carefully on the table and pulled the tiaras out of the box. Then she proceeded to literally march over to the sofa and crown Darlene and Rachel. "I pronounce you official Queens!"

Rachel blushed. "It's so beautiful! Thank you."

Darlene bit her cheeks to keep from smiling. Her only verbal response was a half giggle, half grunt. She looked back at her book as if nothing extraordinary had happened, but I knew by the way she straightened her back and held her head, that she was pleased. Maybe we'll get her story, yet, I thought.

"What about me?" Reggie laughed.

"Oh, I have something for you all right." Liz returned to the box and rummaged through the strings of pearls, rhinestones, and glitter. She dug to the bottom, pulling out a rhinestone crusted elastic headband. This she slipped over Reggie's head like a crown.

"And you will be our Mighty King," she said.

The whole lot of us guffawed at Reggie in the sparkling bling. Even Lulu barked.

When the noise settled down, I faced the group one more time. "There's one more thing, folks. We need to conserve as much water as possible, so I guess we'll have to make do with sponge baths and make use of Mother Nature's privy."

"Huh?" asked Reggie and Rachel together.

"I mean, that we'll have to do our 'business' outside in the woods. We can't be flushing the toilet and using up the water. Besides, we can't dump the boxes here."

"Don't bother me none," said Darlene.

The others nodded approval.

"I do think we should go outside in two's for safety reasons. Reggie can take Lulu with him; Liz and I will go together, and Darlene and Rachel can pair up."

Darlene glared at me.

"Nobody's going to look, Darlene!" I turned away from her and continued, "We can cover our shoes with plastic garbage bags. That will help keep us a little drier. And if we pull the bags up high and tie them around our thighs, our pants will stay dry as well."

They all stared at me as if I had lost my mind. It was obvious that keeping their shoes and pants dry wasn't an issue for them.

"Just a suggestion, gang." I huffed. "Come on, Reggie. Let's finish cooking up this Thanksgiving feast. We've got pretzels and green olives for hors d'oeuvres, and gourmet chicken noodle soup for our entrée!"

"Cheers!" shouted Darlene, raising her coffee cup in salute, and the rest of us answered with a boisterous, "Happy Thanksgiving!"

# Leaving Home…

# Chapter 31

## So Very Hard to Go

The men piled into Bob's Buick and Carl gave directions to Larry's house. Billy and Rex sat quietly in the back seat.

"I hope your friend Larry won't mind us barging in on his Thanksgiving dinner," said Bob.

"Naw. Larry's a great guy. Besides, it's not our fault. The blame goes directly to Liz and Leslie. Larry knows how women can be. Hey, turn right at that next street."

Bob followed Carl's directions and they soon pulled up to a house glowing with lights. Several cars filled the driveway.

"Oh, man. It looks like they've got a big family thing going on here. Are you sure this will be okay with him?"

"Relax. It'll be fine." Carl left the car and made his way to the front door.

Bob could see a tall man standing at the door, but he couldn't hear what Carl was saying to him. But soon, Carl called for Bob and the boys to join him.

After the introductions, Larry invited them inside. They heard laughter and voices from the back of the house.

Bob cleared his throat. "Larry, we apologize for barging in on your holiday like this, but it is sort of an emergency, and Carl seems to think you're the man we need to help us out."

"No problem. We've already eaten, and I was needing a little diversion from all the family stories, know what I mean?" Larry grinned. "So, what's up?"

Carl and Bob told Larry the whole runaway story and voiced their concerns about safety with the pending storm. Larry listened quietly, and when they were finished, he rubbed the back of his head before speaking.

"That's some story, guys. And I'd love to help you out, but we have some complications here. Technically, the women aren't missing persons, so we can't file a report and we can't send out an APB either. In fact, the law would look at them as having left their husbands of their own free wills. You've had contact with them, and because of this storm, every available officer will be out on the roads to deal with vehicle accidents and injuries and such. I don't really know what I can do to help you at this point. Have they asked you to come get them or mentioned any kind of danger?"

"No, they haven't," said Carl. "But we know that they DON'T know how to deal with a storm like the one coming straight toward us. They don't have any experience with RV's or blizzards. I wouldn't want either of them driving a car in this storm, much less a motor home."

"And you don't know precisely where they are?" asked Larry.

Bob answered, "Nope, only that they told Leslie's mom they were headed toward Memphis, and they had just left a place called Buttercup Junction."

"Well, that's like hunting a needle in a haystack, guys. I'm sorry, but at this point, without an SOS from them, there's not much I can do for you."

Bob and Carl looked at each other and shook their heads. "We appreciate your time, Larry." Bob said. He reached to shake Larry's hand. "If we hear anything specific, we'll get back with you. I guess for now, we'll have to just sit and wait and hope for the best."

"That would be my advice," Larry said. "Chances are, they've found a safe RV park and are settled in one place. They should be fine if that's the case. And I wouldn't advice it, but if you two decide to go looking for them, stay in touch with me. If you get a lead somewhere, I can always contact the local law enforcement office at that location and maybe get you some help that way. I wish I could do more."

The men shook hands again, and Carl and Bob returned to the car.

"I guess we're back to square one, here," Carl sighed, climbing back into the car. Bob cranked the car, and immediately, the radio station broadcast more storm warnings.

"I say we go find them," Carl blurted out. "What about you two?" He turned to the boys in the rear seat.

Rex answered first. "Part of me says yeah, let's do it, and then the other part of me says we should just leave 'em alone. If we just knew what they really wanted, it would make it easier. I think it's important to do what THEY want us to do."

"Me, too," agreed Billy. I don't want to spoil their trip for them, but I am worried about this storm." He looked at the older men in front.

"To hell with what they want. I say we go get them." Carl said.

"Okay, let's stay calm. I can take off some time from work. The boys are on holiday, now, but they'll have to go back to school on Monday. What about you Carl? Can you take a few extra days?"

"I've got some leave days built up—about a week, so it shouldn't be a problem."

"Okay, then. You and I will hit the road. The boys can check on Anne while we're gone, and we'll keep in touch with her so she won't worry. Let's go back to Anne's and fill her in and we'll map out a plan."

They drove in silence for a while. Then Bob pulled over to the side of the road and turned to Carl. "I just had a great idea. I think we should rent an RV. That way we can get into campgrounds where the girls might have been. There's probably an RV sales lot open this afternoon. They always have holiday specials going on, and lots of people travel on holidays and need to stop in for repairs and whatnot. How about if we go take a look around? We can leave this afternoon if we can find something. The sooner, the better with that storm coming. What do you think?"

Carl turned to Bob and stared. Over the last few days, his face had grown taut and strained with worry, but now it began to relax. "I think that's a plan, man!" He held up his hand for a high five.

Back at Anne's house, they filled her in on the decisions and worked up an email to send to the girls.

"We can't give ourselves away, now. It would be better to surprise them. That way, they won't fuss and try to talk us out of coming. Hell, they act so crazy sometimes, they might just pick up and leave wherever they are and run again. So let's think this through."

After several drafts, everyone agreed on the following:

*Dear Leslie and Liz,*

*We miss you a whole bunch. Seems like you've been gone forever, and we're counting on you coming back soon. We are trying to honor your space and time out, but we are very worried about the weather forecast and hope you are prepared wherever you are. It would ease our minds if you'd tell us where that is, so we don't worry so much.*

*Love, Bob, Carl, Billy, and Rex*

Anne approved, and all that was left was to hit the send button and then the road.

"Would you like to do the honors, Carl?" Bob asked pointing to the computer.

"Absolutely!" Carl said and grabbed for the mouse. In less than a second, their message was soaring through cyber space.

# Chapter 32

## Hit the Road, Jack

Bob and Carl searched the newspaper ads for RV sales places. Not all of them advertised rentals, but Danny's RV World did.

"Let's call to be sure they're open today," Bob suggested.

A half hour later, they pulled into Danny's RV World. Stretched before them were hundreds of different models of campers, RV's, and buses. Danny, himself, strolled up to greet them.

"You the ones that called about the rental?" He asked, turning his head just slightly to spit a wad of tobacco from his mouth.

"That's right," said Bob. "We're going to need something for about a week. There's just the two of us, so we don't need anything big."

Danny looked them up and down. "I see," he said.

Bob blushed red, but Carl was clearly steamed. "It's not what you think, man. "Our wives left a few days for some time out, and we thought we might use the time to go to the bowl game in Jacksonville."

"Oh," said Danny, looking relieved. "I have to admit, I did wonder. It's strange to get just two men wanting a rental. Most of my customers are families, you see. Except for that weirdo woman that came in last week. She was wearing this crown on her head, and I knew right away, something wasn't right with her. She didn't buy anything either after all the time I took up with her. So, for what you've got planned, you won't need anything really big. Most of the rental units come with a queen bedroom and a sofa pullout bed. Will that work for you?"

"Sure, sure," Bob answered. "There's just a couple of things we really need, and that's a large TV, high speed Internet service, and a CB radio set-up. Do you have anything like that in the smaller units?"

"Hmmm, well, the small units don't usually have all that stuff, but Big Daddy back there in the corner has all the bells and whistles. It's larger than you need and costs more, but it's got all the frills. Come on in, and take a look at it."

Bob whispered to Carl as they followed Danny to the rear of the lot. "That weird woman he mentioned had to be either Leslie or Liz. Who else would be wearing a crown on her head? But since she didn't buy the RV here, there's no need for him to know we know her."

They stopped in front of a huge bus. It looked like Darth Vader on wheels, black and silver, hulking. The name "Plane to Catch" was painted on the front.

Carl and Bob went inside with Danny to check it out.

"Man, oh Man! Look at this!" Carl gave a low, shrill whistle.

"We didn't have *this* in mind, but it's certainly impressive. I'll bet this baby has seen some fun times."

"You are oh, so right!" snickered Danny. "If these walls could talk! But I won't—talk that is." He winked at the men as if there were some kind of conspiracy going on and not the innocent bowl game they had claimed.

"Just take a look around. See here: cherry cabinets, crown moldings on the ceiling, halogen lighting, dimmers, wall sconces, imported tile flooring, lush carpet."

Wow! Leslie would love this, Bob thought. He ran his hand over the wood cabinets. Carl took a seat on the black leather sofa, holding the remote control.

"Let's take it," he said to Bob.

Bob looked around again at the posh cabin.

"Yeah, let's take it," he said softly.

"Right this way, then. We'll do the paperwork, and you'll be on your way in no time." Danny led them back outside and over to the office. He pulled out a rental agreement and began filling in blanks. "By the way," he said, "The Big Daddy is my personal unit. I only rent him out for special trips!" He winked at Bob and Carl again.

"When do you want to pick it up?"

"Now," said Bob.

Danny looked stunned for a moment, but quickly recovered. He coughed and cleared his throat before speaking. "In that case, it'll cost another fifty dollars to put a rush on the prep. It'll be ready in about an hour. We'll store your car back in the garage."

Bob and Carl signed the rental agreement and an insurance agreement. Bob wrote out a check to Danny to cover the week's rental and security deposit. Carl then wrote one for half that amount to give to Bob. Meanwhile, Danny called his service man to come gas up the unit and get it ready for the road.

"Oh, the CB handle is the same as the name: Plane to Catch. And the operations handbook is in the console."

After they completed the paperwork, Bob and Carl left to pick up some clothes and groceries. They returned in a little over an hour. Big Daddy sat shining in the front lot. Bob traded his car keys for the RV keys and he and Carl headed for the unit.

They stowed their gear and then headed for the cab.

"I'm driving first," Carl said. "I can't wait to feel this baby on the road."

Bob laughed as he climbed into the passenger seat. "I never in my life thought we'd be together in an RV under these circumstances. And in spite of what the girls have put us through, this is actually exciting." He grinned as he adjusted the leather seat.

Carl revved the engine. "Ready?"

"Ready!" Bob answered. Carl eased up to the highway and stopped. He looked both ways, and then turned to Bob. "Which way are we going?"

Bob laughed. "West, remember. Toward the mountains, toward Tennessee. Toward the biggest snowstorm this area has seen in years!"

Carl made a left and headed for I-40.

Bob busied himself with the cell phone. "I'll call Anne and the boys and let them know we're on our way. They can reach us by phone or email as long as we have reception. I'll also give them the CB handle just in case of an emergency and the other two don't work."

There were few cars on the road at this hour on Thanksgiving Day. A few truckers zoomed past them and the occasional RV headed the other way. The men made a game of who could read out the RV names first.

"I think we should change this baby's name from 'Plane to Catch' to 'Bitches to Catch,'" joked Carl.

Bob couldn't help but laugh. Carl had a biting sense of humor and he was really in his element now behind the steering wheel of Big Daddy.

"How about trying out the CB, Bob? Danny said the Truckers' Channel is 19. Let's tune in and see what they're saying."

Bob fiddled with the CB and soon the cab was filled with static, and then with gruff, deep voices.

"Peterbilt Blue, this is The Wanderer. Do you read?"

"10-4 Wanderer. This is Peterbilt Blue. What you got on I-40?"

"I-10 is shut down. I'm heading for the Pit over near Nashville. Same story over here on the parking lot. Detours all over the Smokies."

"Sounds bad. Thanks. Over and out."

"Over and out."

"Looks like we are in for quite a trip," said Carl. "I wonder how this baby handles snow and ice?"

"I guess we'll find out soon enough," Bob said and settled back into his seat.

"Hey, maybe later when we're closer to Tennessee, we should introduce ourselves over the CB, and see if anyone has seen the girls. What do you think?"

Bob yawned. "Sure, later. Right now, put the pedal to the metal and let's get moving. Maybe we can outrun the storm and find them before it hits."

Carl shifted gears and blared the horn. Both men laughed as they headed toward the setting sun.

# This is Your Life…

# Chapter 33

## The Love I Lost

Liz and I had eaten most of the peanut butter crackers and plowed through the olives and two more vodkas. The snow continued to whirl outside the window, but inside The Screamer, we were snug. Rachel and Reggie talked quietly while cuddled together on the sofa under a throw with Lulu and Rosie snug beside them. Darlene had retired to the bedroom for some "shut-eye" as she put it.

I logged onto the computer to check the weather report again. Same story. Storm worsening, still heading straight toward us. I hope the vodka holds out, I thought. I decided to try the CB channel, but it crackled off and on. I caught phrases like Turkey Day Emergency, a Spanish driver by the name of a La Banda, and Mud Duck, which indicated poor signal. I also learned that an Interstate was closed, but not which one. My guess was that it was I-40. I even tried to raise Ponderosa Man, but with no luck so I gave up. I used this quiet time to scan some pages in my RV Dunce book. I learned the generator information could be crucial for us, and silently sent a Thank You out to Della for the foresight of giving us the book.

The falling snow proved to be mesmerizing. One thought kept circling in my head. I had to be the strong one. No matter how bad things got, I had to stay calm. There was always the email to the guys if we had to do it, but for now, I'd do my best to maintain calm.

Darlene stumbled from the rear. "What's going on? What's everybody doing?"

"Nothing. Everything's the same. I just checked the weather. Looks like we're here for the long haul. So, how about if we play a game? It's sort of like that TV game show 'This is Your Life.'"

"Oh, the one where you tell about your life to perfect strangers?" Darlene asked.

"Well, sort of. We aren't exactly strangers, Darlene. What would it hurt to share a little of yourself with us?" I looked around the group. The vodka made me feel more confident and less afraid.

No one answered. "Okay," I said. "Liz, how about a little sing-a-long. Maybe that'll loosen up everybody."

She thought for a minute and then began slowly and quietly,
"Show….show….show….
Show me the way to go home…
I'm tired and I wanna go to bed.
Well, I had me a drink about an hour ago
And it went right to my head."

She stopped and giggled. Then began again, louder and stronger. Reggie joined in followed by Rachel and me. Finally, Darlene stood and belted out the final lines. We were all amazed at her voice.

"Darlene! That was magnificent! You're quite a singer!" Rachel exclaimed.

"I've done my share," she muttered and sat back down. "Besides, that's a great song. Makes anybody sound good."

"You're right, Darlene, it is a great song," I said. I didn't add that Liz and I usually sang it only when we were feeling really good after a few drinks, which evidently was now. No need to advertise it, I thought as I stumbled over my own foot going back to the cab.

"Reggie, how about come up here for a minute, will you?"

Reggie came forward and took the passenger seat. "I'm going to let the engine run for just a bit to charge up the batteries. I tried the CB earlier, but only got broken pieces of conversation. From what I can tell, the interstate is closed now, which doesn't matter to us cause we're stuck here for now, but the thing is we have to be careful not to use too much fuel because the generator won't run when the fuel is less than a fourth of the tank. The tank holds 65 gallons, and we filled up at Mr. Adams' place. The owner's manual says the generator uses about a half gallon of gas per hour, so we need to keep track. We've got about fifty gallons left."

Reggie nodded solemnly. "Do you think the holding tanks are okay?"

"The water supply in the holding tank should still be ample, since we aren't using it for anything other than drinking and washing hands. Still," I warned, "we've got to keep track of all this. We can't afford to be without the generator. We'll freeze to death out here. We'll have to run the engine every so often to keep the batteries charged so The Screamer will be warm since there's no electrical power, but we do have to be careful to conserve our fuel."

"I hadn't thought about all of that stuff before, Ms. Leslie. There's a lot more to owning a motor home than just travel and fun. How do you know all this stuff, anyway? Things could get pretty bad, huh?"

"I read it in the RV Dunce book," I said and smiled at him. "But, let's stay positive. And keep this between you and me. I don't want to upset the others. Just help me keep track okay?"

"Yes, M'am."

I went to the dinette. "How about Thanksgiving dinner? Anybody hungry?"

Reggie joined me to spoon up the chicken noodle soup. I opened another box of crackers and poured them into a bowl. "Here, you go. Take this to the table." I handed him the crackers. We gathered around the table and said Grace again. The soup was warming and filled the cabin with a comforting smell. I scooped a bit of it over the top of Lulu and Rosie's food too. They deserved a Thanksgiving treat.

When the table was cleared, Darlene leaned back against the seat and rubbed her stomach. "That was a mighty good dinner, Leslie."

Shocked, I barely stuttered out a thank you, but her kind words brought tears to my eyes. What was wrong with me, I wondered? Was I going to fall apart right here in front of all of them? No, I couldn't do that. I realized I was worried. Here I had all these people stuck in the middle of the woods in a snowstorm and I had no idea how in the world we would get ourselves out of this mess. I felt like the walls were literally closing in tighter by the minute. We had no hookups, no plug ins, and now wedged between the pine trees, no pop out. It was all my fault. I had forced Liz to come. She'd have never done this on her own. And I was the one who dragged Reggie into this. Granted, Liz had been the one to champion Darlene and Rachel, but I should have known better than to take all this on.  What if something happened to one of them?  To all of them?   I mentally shook myself and got up to put on some music.  I chose Aretha Franklin's "Another Night" and slowly swayed to the music all alone, and then I felt Liz come up behind me.  She grabbed my hand and twirled me around, forcing me to follow.  We danced as best as we could in the tight inclined quarters while the others laughed.  Sometimes, all it takes is a really good song to change your outlook, I thought.

Lulu barked happily at us.

"Hey, I just had a brilliant idea," said Darlene.  "We can send Lulu for help.  Saint Bernard's are raised and trained as search dogs, you know.  They have this special way of sniffing out danger.  And they'll go find help when somebody needs it."

"And your point is?"  I asked.

"Don't you see?  If the homeless camp isn't far, Lulu could find it.  We could send a note and tie it around her neck."

"But what if she got lost and didn't come back?  What if she died out there in the storm?" Rachel looked distressed.

"Well, it was just a thought," sniffed Darlene, stumbling back to the sofa.

"And a good one, even though that kind of rescue only happens in the movies," I reassured her.  "Besides, Rachel's right. And, Lulu's not our dog.  How would I tell Beulah that we sent her dog out in this storm to freeze to death?  Tomorrow we'll reconsider our options.  For now, I vote for another drink."

# Chapter 34

## Heard It Through the Grapevine

After everyone settled down again, I brought up the idea of the game again. I was determined to get Darlene to talk some about herself.

"Okay, let's play the game," I said.

Everyone, except Darlene nodded. "Liz, another round of drinks for us, please. Reggie, you get the peanuts, cheese, and pretzels."

While they were busy, I explained how the game worked. Looking directly at Darlene, I said, "Now in this game, we ALL have to answer questions about our lives. It's sort of a way of reminiscing about our past and it will help us get to know each other better. But first, the Oath of Secrecy!" I held up the cheese knife that Reggie placed on the table. Rachel's eyes grew large, and Darlene's bottom lipped poked out.

"Just kidding, you guys," I laughed. "But seriously, what is said here, stays here, agreed?" They all nodded yes, but Darlene sat stone-faced.

"Darlene? Either you're with us or not. Which will it be?"

"All right! You Queenies are the nosiest people I ever did see. You go ahead."

"We need a bottle to spin since we don't have any dice. Reggie, bring over that empty vodka bottle." Liz said.

After we were all settled, Liz spun the bottle. We watched silently as it spun round and round, and then slowed to a stop, pointing directly at Darlene.

"I ain't going first. Uh, uh. No way. Might as well throw me out in the storm." She crossed her arms in front of her chest and shook her head.

"Okay, I'll take your turn," I said. "Ask me a question. After I answer, everyone gets to comment or ask another question for more information. Got it?"

"In that case, I'll ask the first question, Ms. Queenies." Darlene said.

"Go ahead." I sat back in my seat and readied myself."

"Now, truth to swear: What was the REAL reason you ran away and left your nice home and husband?" asked Darlene.

I should have expected it, but I didn't. I found that I couldn't answer right away.

So I stalled for a bit of time. "I, quite honestly, can't remember at this minute, Darlene. But it had a lot to do with my job, all that corporate crap. All that society mess. Keeping up with everything and everybody. I just wanted a different life, that's all. I wanted to see other places. Meet new people. Find a new way to BE." I paused for a moment to gather my thoughts. Then I looked at each person around that table. "And I have to say, that I'm learning quite a lot from you all. I did have a good life, plenty of money, nice things. But I woke up one day and felt like, well, I don't need all this anymore. My life felt empty.

"Liz and I had talked forever about doing something like this. But it was always sort of a joke, you know. When things would go wrong, we'd call each other up and say, 'This is www.queenmotorhome.com calling.' That's why that code is on The Screamer. A motor home sort of represented freedom to me. It's a way to simplify. You can't take all that stuff with you 'cause there's not room." I smiled. "It was a dream. A really, really good dream, that's what it was. And when I got the chance to make it come true, I took it. That's all."

"Do you love your husband?" asked Rachel.

"Oh yes, very much. And I really do miss him, but I NEEDED to do this. Bob wasn't ready for it. I don't know if he'll ever be ready. He's a very caring, nice man, and…." I lowered my vodka-laced voice and pretended to whisper so that Reggie couldn't hear. "He's really good in bed!"

Darlene, Rachel and Liz broke out in hoots. Reggie blushed.

"Will you ever go back to him? I mean, if we get out of here and you're able to get back on the road. What will you do? Keep going or go back?" asked Reggie.

"First of all, we WILL get out of here, okay? Now, I can't speak for Liz, but I intend to keep moving on. I do think I'll make more regular contact with Bob and my son. That's only fair. But yes, I'll keep going."

"What have you learned on this trip so far?" asked Darlene.

I thought for a moment before answering. "That's a loaded question, Darlene. And I could answer it with a lot of information, but I can't tell all my secrets in one night!" I laughed. "But seriously, so far, I've learned that strangers on the road can be some of the nicest people to know. And that it's really easy to care for them, especially those who have had it harder in life than I have. I feel filled up inside, now. Before, I always felt sort of empty. You know? And I've learned that it's important to me to try to make a difference in other lives. To simplify my answer, I'd have to say that I've learned that it's important to give back, and I'm ready to do that."

"Okay, that's enough from you for now. Spend that bottle again," demanded Liz.

This time the bottle pointed to Reggie. He repeated much of what he had shared with us earlier about his life. But then he added something new. "I think it says it all when you remember that the missing person report on the radio was filed by my boss and friends at work—not my family."

"That report worried me too," Rachel said, reaching to touch his arm. "My parents can only want one thing: me back to work for them. But I do need to confess something. I'm not eighteen. I will be in just two days, though." She added hurriedly when she saw the looks of dismay on my and Liz's faces.

"I knew you wouldn't take me in if I was underage, and I really, really needed to get away from there. I'm so grateful that you did bring me along. I'd rather die out here in the snowstorm than go back to the way I was living back there. You just don't understand what it's like. The drinking, the cussing, and I couldn't ever get any sleep because I was afraid some nights, my step dad would…." She stopped and choked back her tears. Reggie reached for her and drew her closer to him.

"I'm sorry. I just want you to know that I can't go back. Besides," she looked up at Reggie, "I think I've fallen in love." Reggie blushed and kissed her tear stained cheek.

Liz and Darlene all but blubbered, and I had difficulty keeping my temper under control…if ONLY I could get my hands on her parents, I'd, I'd…… I didn't know what I'd do, but it wouldn't be nice, that's for sure.

"Rachel, don't you worry. You won't be going back to them. You can go with me, and I'll take care of everything. You won't have to worry about your step dad again, I promise." Darlene reached to pat Rachel's shoulder.

"Darlene, if the police find her here with us, it's Liz and me who will be in real trouble, not you."

"Shush up, now! I meant what I said. By the time anybody finds you, me and Rachel will be well on our way. Reggie can come, too," Darlene looked directly at him.

"You bet, I would," he answered. "Rachel and I are in love and we want to move on once we get out of here. You've all been great to us, but we need to make our own way. I don't know where we'll go just yet, but we'll get it all straight with the authorities after we're married. And we'll keep in touch with you, too."

There didn't seem to be much to say after that. Liz broke the silence by spinning the bottle one more time. It twirled around and finally stopped dead on at Darlene.

"Well?" I asked.

She muttered something under her breath, but finally looked up at me and said, "Go ahead. Ask your question."

"How did you get to be homeless, Darlene?"

"That's a long story. I don't know if I can answer it all in one night. But I'll hit the high points. She straightened herself in the seat and cleared her throat.

"I'm sixty-five years old or close to that, now. About twenty years ago, I was somebody else in Nashville. I've lost my identity since then. Me and Les, my partner and manager, went to Music City with nothing but the clothes on our backs. I loved to sing, and we were determined to make it in Nashville. We finally got a break. Had an audition. They loved me, and me and Les recorded all kinds of songs. We had a good life. The recording studio even assigned a special manager person to take care of everything for us.

"Trouble is, he took extra care of us in the areas of alcohol and drugs. While I was recording at the studio, Les would be hanging out with other musicians. When I was home, he wasn't. We never got to see each other.

"But several of my songs hit the Top 40. And then I had an album. It sold millions of copies, and the money was rolling in. They wanted me to keep right on singing and recording, and I did. But it got harder and harder to get there in the mornings. Les introduced me to the snort drug, and I started using and abusing, and then I started to crash.

"But even high, my singing was good, really good. I just couldn't get to work on time or finish on time, and sometimes I didn't show up at all. Les, he was always high. You couldn't talk to him. He couldn't sleep. We got to be totally different people from what we started out. Eventually, the studio canned me. Then the money ran out. I hit rock bottom and finally woke up one day. I quit the drugs, quit the drinking. Haven't had a drink since. But we got kicked out of the apartment, and there wasn't no way to change things. I remember holding that eviction notice and staring over at Les, passed out on the couch, and I thought, I can't live like this no more. So, I left. I filled up my backpack, and started walking.

"I have one tape with me for safekeeping. Ain't played it in years, but I hold on to it. It reminds me of some better times.

"In a way, I've been happier on the road than in that studio especially with all those party people around and all that drug business. I missed Les at first. Still do, sometimes. But lonely as it's been, my life on the road has been right interesting. And at least I'm sober. I ain't never been hungry or too cold." Darlene stopped to catch her breath. She hadn't realized that she'd cried while talking. But we had, and we all cried silently right along with her.

In an effort to lighten the mood, Liz chimed in with another question: "What was your stage name, Darlene."

"Ain't telling you that, Ms. Queenie."

"Well, then, what was your top hit back then?"

"Darlene hesitated, but finally answered. "Oh, I don't know about the top hit, but my favorite and Les', too, was 'Close to You.' Wrote it while we was higher than kites one night, but it was good, and it was a hit!"

"But why do you want to be a homeless person, Darlene? Don't you have any family left?" Rachel asked.

"You mean, why would I want to live the way I live? Ha! I'll tell you why: 'cause on the road, I can be myself, not somebody else, or what somebody wants me to be...just me. I can see the world. I meet plenty of nice folks and animals, too. I had my fame and fortune. And it's all gone now. That ain't what lasts in this life. What I've found on the inside of me out here on the road, that's what lasts. Besides, I still sing to myself sometimes. And God and all his creatures are the best audience there is."

"Darlene," interrupted Liz. "You mentioned a granddaughter that you haven't seen in years. What happened with her?"

"Seems my granddaughter only love me for the fame and fortune, if you get my drift. Her mom, my daughter, got into drink and drugs herself along about the time my granddaughter got out of high school. I used to send them money and pretty things all the time, but once I lost it all, they didn't want nothing else to do with me. My grand, she'd be about thirty years old now. I don't' have no idea where she is or if she's got a family or nothing. She just quit on me when I quit on myself."

"What's her name, Darlene?" Asked Rachel.

"Mary Sue." Darlene choked up and then pretended to cough to cover it up.

"Why did that lady at the church ask you about working in the administrative office at the recording studio?" I asked.

"That was just a lie, I told. Didn't want people to know the truth about my music. When they recognized me at church, I made it sound like I had wanted to work in the office. It was a way to stop some of the rumors."

Darlene closed her eyes. She looked weary.

"Well, I think we've had a great time tonight," I said. "But it's getting late, and I think we should all try to get some sleep. Reggie and I will take turns starting the engine every so often during the night. The rest of you, go on to bed. Darlene, you take the bedroom. Liz and Rachel can share the sofa bed. I'll make do with the passenger seat. It reclines nicely."

"Well, now, that's nice of you," said Darlene. "I thank you." She turned to walk to the bedroom, but stopped at the door and turned around to face me. "I thank you for everything." Then she closed the door.

# On the Road Again…

.

# Chapter 35

## Farther Up the Road

"What's with that trucker? He's been riding our tail for miles, now," Carl grumbled to Bob. No sooner than he got the words out of his mouth, the truck pulled alongside them. As big as the RV was, the truck still dwarfed it.

Just as Carl turned to look at it, the CB crackled.

"Hey there cute boys…this is Peterbilt Blue Brenda Babe. Brenda Babe here. What's up with 'Plane to Catch' and where are you headed in this weather?"

"Bob, looky there. It's a woman driving that rig." Bob leaned forward to look, but all he could see were the passenger door and window.

"She thinks we're cute?" Bob chuckled. "Let's talk to her." He grabbed the CB.

"Go ahead, Brenda Babe. This is 'Plane to Catch.' Talk to us."

"Do you hotties know there's a major storm coming in? You don't want to be furloughed out here all alone when it hits."

"Ten-four, we got the news.  Making plans to hunker down.  But for now, we're starved.  Where's some good eating along this route?"  Bob grinned over at Carl and winked.  He liked this trucking deal.

"The Joint's just up the road. Follow me."

"Ten-four," Bob replied.  Brenda Babe pulled ahead, laying on her horn as she cut back into the right hand lane.

"Man, I can't believe this.  We're actually going to meet a strange woman—a trucker, and have grub at The Joint.  Sounds like a country music song."  Carl laughed.

"I could get used to this, my friend.  We've got plenty of space and you can move it anytime and anywhere you want.  What else do you need?"  Bob looked around the cab and then behind him to the spacious living space of the bus. "You know, I think I'm beginning to understand what Leslie meant about our lives.  Back home we've got 4000 square feet and we actually use about a fifth of that."  He looked thoughtful as he rubbed the leather on the seat arm where he sat.

"Hey, I didn't mean to get you going," said Carl.  "Remember, we just want our wives back."

"Yeah, I know.  I miss Leslie like crazy.  I don't have much of a life without her."

"I've tried to compromise about this little escapade of hers.  I know her too well, and I just know I had to honor her wishes if I ever stood a chance of getting her to come home.  But now, I'm worried about her safety, and that's a whole new ballgame, you know?"  He looked at over at Carl.

"Well, Liz and I don't seem to have the relationship you and Leslie have, but I sure as hell do miss her.  We spar all the time, but underneath that, well…."  Carl's words drifted to a halt.

"Hey, look, Brenda Babe's pulling off at this exit.  The Joint must be right up the way here."  The guys concentrated on following the big rig ahead of them and soon, pulled into a parking lot full mostly of eighteen-wheelers and a few other RV's.

Brenda stepped out of her rig and stood waiting for them.  Her bleached blonde hair, tasseled suede jacket, blue jeans, and cowgirl boots making her look ten years younger than her actual age.

"Ready, guys?" she called to them and motioned for them to join her.

Carl looked at Bob who nodded, and they followed like two ducklings after their mama. At the door, she stopped to introduce herself and get their names as well.  Then the three entered and found seats at the bar.  Brenda Babe ordered a double scotch on the rocks and the guys ordered beers.

"You know, Brenda, we hear all kinds of tales about psychos on the road, so we were surprised when you contacted us on the CB." Bob was curious about this woman who seemed so relaxed and friendly around two complete strangers.

"Oh, I can recognize 'green' from a long way away, and you're definitely green," she answered. "Besides, with this storm coming our way, it's unusual to see RV's roaming around. They usually hunker down immediately and stay put until it blows over. So, just your being on the road right now was a signal. What gives? What in the world has you two out in all this?"

Bob reached into his coat pocket and pulled out a photo. He passed it over to Brenda. "Well, it's a long story, but these two are the reason." He proceeded to tell the story of the two runaway wives. Brenda listened quietly and then looked at the photo she held again. She handed it back to Bob.

"Can't say I've seen these two. Are they queens, or princesses or something?"

"They call themselves Queens, sort of a private joke, I guess. They've been playing around with those tiaras and dreams of traveling for years, now. And it seems now, they've decided it's time to live out their fantasies."

"Say, we can ask around in here if anyone's seen them. What are they driving? Tilly over there remembers everybody that comes in The Joint." She took the photo from Bob and motioned for Tilly to join them at their end of the bar.

"Seen these two in here, lately, Tilly?" she asked. Tilly stared at the photo and then frowned. "Matter of fact, I have. Just a few nights ago, wearing crowns on their heads. The regulars were having a ball with that. Never seen girls wearing crowns in here." Tilly smirked. "As I remember, they had a run in with a trucker that night, too."

"Run in?" Shouted Carl. "What do you mean? What happened?" Carl left his bar stool and leaned into Tilly's face.

"Relax, cowboy," she said, pushing him back to his stool. "They didn't get hurt or arrested or anything. A run in is just…well, it just means there was some action here and everyone took notice for a few minutes."

"What kind of action?" Carl demanded. "One of those girls is my wife!"

"Carl, calm down and quit jumping to conclusions. Go ahead Ms. Tilly." Bob kept his hand firmly on Carl's shoulder.

"Oh, it was probably nothing. Your girls didn't provoke it. This regular trucker that hangs out here was making moves on one of the girls on the dance floor, so we had a little skirmish and they left. Didn't see 'em again."

"If it was night time, they must have been staying pretty close. Do you know where they were staying? Is there any place nearby where they'd park a motor home?"

Tilly shook her head. "I don't ask questions, and I don't get in other people's business. Sorry. But, you two might better find a place to hunker down for the night with this storm coming. Might try Beulah's place just over that way." She pointed up the road and to the west, and then walked away.

Bob and Carl stared into their drinks.

"Look guys, sounds like it was innocent enough. But I get the feeling you two aren't telling me the whole story. Maybe they're trucker wanna bees, and I can understand them wanting to travel, be in charge of their own lives, have some adventure, and maybe get away from a rocky marriage. Those are some of the same reasons I came to be trucker myself."

Carl shook his head, dismayed at the idea that Liz might next take up driving eighteen-wheelers across country. "I need some sleep, Bob. I'm beat. Let's go find some place to park for the night. Then we can come back here to eat."

"You're right, Carl. Better to get a fresh start in the morning. Say, Brenda, will you keep an eye out for the girls. You just might run across them. You could call us on the CB and let us know. Or, here, take our email address and cell phone numbers. Contact us any way you can if you have news. We'd appreciate any help at all."

"I'll keep an eye out for 'The Queens'". Brenda smiled and wrote her handle and cell phone number on a napkin which she passed over to Bob. "But you two best be careful. Some of the roads are closing, and you might not get through. You don't want to get stranded on the interstate in this storm."

"Thanks, Brenda Babe." Bob said. "We'll keep in touch."

The guys made their way back to their RV and climbed in. Signs guided them to the Cozy Run RV Park. The park was dark with only a small trailer out front at the entrance showing a light.

"Guess we need to try that. It must be the office," Carl said. The men made their way to the trailer door and knocked. A heavyset woman with grayish hair answered.

"Yeah? I'm Beulah. What can I do for you?"

Bob introduced himself and Carl and pointed to the Big Daddy Bus. "We need a place to stay the night, M'am. Tilly down at The Joint recommended your place."

"I might be able to accommodate you. But first, what's your story? I like to know a little about my guests. Can't be too careful these days."

She looked at both men carefully.

"Sure, we understand," said Bob. He pulled the photo of Leslie and Liz from his pocket and held it out to her. "Actually, it's a long story, but bottom line is that we're looking for our wives. They took off in a motor home a few days ago, and now we're worried about them getting stranded in this storm. Have you seen them?"

Beulah looked at the picture and then folded her arms behind her. "You say these two are your wives, huh? Well, you best come inside and tell me your story, long or not." She did not return the photo to Bob.

Bob and Carl looked at one another, but realized they had no other choice in the matter. They stepped inside Beulah's trailer.

"Take a seat, fellas, and commence to talking," she ordered them.

They told their story, each taking a turn to fill in gaps, explain, justify. When they'd finished, they stared at Beulah. "We just want to bring them home safe, that's all. To be honest, we were against this trip of theirs at first, but now that we've had some time to think things through and we're getting on the road ourselves, we understand better what the girls were after when they left. Honest, Miss Beulah, we just want to find them and make sure they're safe."

Beulah nodded and held out the photo to Bob. "Those Queenie Girls were here, all right. Real amateurs, for sure. Had more trouble with them the two nights they were here than I've had all year long."

"Trouble? What do you mean?" Carl was nearly standing.

"Oh, minor stuff, really. It's just that they were so green, that's all. I really liked them after a while. In fact, I'm kinda missing 'em, and missing my baby Lulu, too. She went with 'em when they left."

"They took your baby?" Bob and Carl all but shouted.

"Yep, my baby—Saint Bernard." Beulah smiled. "Gotcha, huh, fellas?" She chuckled. "I gave 'em Lulu to take with them. She likes to travel and she took a liking to those two Queenies. I think she's missed traveling since my husband died. So, I thought it'd be a nice change for her. They'll return her when they come back this way."

"So, do you know where they were headed?"

"Not exactly. But you two might as well park here for the night—on the house. Get a fresh start in the morning." Beulah coughed hoarsely into an old handkerchief. She had been sick for days now, and seemed to be getting worse.

"Thanks, Beulah. But we don't expect to stay for free." Bob handed her a twenty. "Are the hookups working?"

"Yep, haven't closed up those right next to the entrance. Take your pick." She coughed again, a deep, strangled cough.

The men left and Beulah locked up behind them. She couldn't help but chuckle to herself. Those Queenies were really in for a surprise, now, she thought. "But isn't it nice that those guys missed their wives," she commented out loud. "I sure miss Joe. I sure do." Beulah made her way back to the sofa and pulled the quilt around her feverish body. She settled in for the night.

# Chapter 36

## Think What You're Doing to Me

After doing the hookups and plugins, Bob and Carl walked back to The Joint and took a booth in the bar area. The place was rocking since most truckers had stopped for dinner or for the night. The bar seats were full, and country music blared from the jukebox. Tilly greeted them with a smile and welcomed them back.

"What can I get you, boys?"

"A double scotch," said Bob.

"A tap beer for me," added Carl. "What's for supper?"

Tilly recited the special, and the men ordered. She rushed off to the next table of noisy truckers, and Bob faced Carl across the booth.

"That Beulah was nice. But she sounds sick. That's a bad cough she's sporting. I wonder if that's why she sent her dog with the girls?"

"Who knows? If they had thought she was sick, you know Liz would have insisted on nursing her. That's just the way she is: Mother Earth to everybody!" Carl shook his head sadly.

"You're missing her, aren't you?" Bob asked.

Carl nodded. "When we were dating, she used to love to come to little joints like this and dance. I always like the no frills scene myself. Seems they're friendlier, or something. Not like those silver flashy places we go to be seen in back home."

"I know what you mean," Bob answered. "Maybe that's also part of the road lure and leaving the pretend world as Leslie said."

Tilly arrived with their cheeseburger plates. "You know, I been thinking," she said. "There's a lot of folks here tonight. I could ask around about your wives. Maybe some of these regulars have come across them. I'll be sure not to ask the one trouble maker that was involved in that little incident, though."

"Is that son of a bitch here?" asked Carl, already starting to rise from his seat.

"Carl, settle down," said Bob. "We can't afford to get slammed in jail tonight for fighting. Let's let Tilly handle this. She knows these people. They're more likely to tell her something than us." He handed the photo to Tilly, and she slipped it in her apron pocket and left.

The guys dove into their cheeseburgers. "Everybody's staring at us," commented Carl with his mouth full.

"Oh, it's probably because we stand out. Look at our designer clothes. And like Brenda said, Green stands out."

Tilly returned with another round of drinks. "The guy sitting at the end of the bar bought these drinks and wants to know if he can join you. He may know something."

"Bob and Carl looked over at the bar and motioned for the guy to join them. He brought his beer and held out his hand. "I'm Ray, but most folks know me as Ponderosa Man. "I'm a trucker, and I know those two queens you're looking for. They're Leslie and Liz."

Carl's face burned red, and he stood up to face Ray. "What do you mean you 'know' them?"

"Sit down, Carl. You are such a hot head. Let's hear Ray out." He stretched out his hand and shook Ray's. "Nice to meet you, Ray. I'm Bob, Leslie's husband, and this fool here is Carl, who belongs to Liz." He moved over on the booth seat to make room for Ray to sit, but Ray grabbed a chair from another table and slid it up to the end of the booth table. Carl watched Ray with suspicion.

"Believe me, I didn't mean anything by the comment of 'knowing' them. I met 'em on the road. In fact, told them about the park just up the road where they could camp out their first night. What can I tell you?"

Bob relayed their story once again. "We're just worried about them getting stranded in this storm."

Ray nodded his head. "Yep, I'd be worried, too. I knew they were amateurs right off." He smiled and chuckled under his breath and then told his own story of meeting the Queens. "I guess I saw myself as a road brother to them or something. So many things can happen out here on the open road, and they both seem like real nice ladies to me. Smart, too. And pretty," He grinned over at Carl. "You two are lucky guys. But the good news is I think I can help you a bit. I've got their CB handle. That's how we've been communicating. They were supposed to call me if they needed help, but I got a little sidetracked back home with my daughter, and I haven't had recent contact with them."

"Well, what's their handle?" Carl demanded.

"The Silver Queen Screamer," Ray replied. "They seemed happy enough. Just out for a little adventure. But, like I said, I haven't heard from them in a couple of days. Their location must be remote. Makes radio contact tough. The only real clue I have as to where they're headed is kinda broad, at best. They mentioned heading toward western Tennessee towards Arkansas. And they said something about having gone to visit a black church. Then they were going on to a homeless camp."

"I can't believe this," Carl muttered. "For Pete's sake, wouldn't they realize that a handle called the Silver Queen Screamer would be asking for trouble? And why would they go to a black church service and a homeless camp? What kind of adventure is that?"

Ray decided not to say much more. He kept his knowledge of the homeless woman and other passengers to himself.

"I guess I haven't been much help, huh?" Ray asked, searching their faces for any clues as to what the two men were really thinking.

"Actually, you have been. It just reassures us that we need to find them and fast. The girls mentioned to Leslie's mom that they were near a place called Buttercup Junction. Does that ring a bell with you?"

"Well, I can probably figure it out. Let me get on the emergency CB channel and make contact with some truckers. If anyone is familiar with the place, it'll be them. Where are you staying tonight, by the way?"

"Up the road at Beulah's park," answered Bob.

"Oh, good place. You'll be okay there."

"You know her, too? She said the girls stayed with her for a couple of days, and she sent her dog Lulu with them. She seems real nice, but lonely, and she sounds like she's really sick."

Ray looked troubled and called Tilly over to the table. "When's the last time you saw or talked to Beulah?" he asked her.

"Probably a week or so. Why?" replied Tilly.

"Just asking. Think I'll go over and check on her tonight. These guys say she might be real sick."

Bob and Carl nodded in agreement.

"So, is it okay if I walk back to her place with you two? Then I'll get on the CB and do some checking for you. We can find out about the roads and the weather, too."

The men nodded and rose to return to Beulah's.

The one dim light still glowed in her window. Ray rapped sharply on the door, and they could hear Beulah shuffling slowly to the door.

"What on earth are you doing here?" she asked, and then coughed and reached out a hand to steady herself against the doorjamb.

He hugged her tight and then stood back from her to look closely at her face. "I came to check on you, old woman. Your new friends here thought you might be sick, and Tilly hasn't seen you in a week or more, so let me check you out." He pushed his way inside Beulah's trailer. Bob and Carl followed.

Ray felt Beulah's forehead. "That cough sounds horrible, and you've got a fever. What are you taking? Have you seen a doctor?"

"No, and I don't want to," answered Beulah. "Well now, ain't it nice all you Queen boys have met up!" She gave them a weak smile and coughed again.

"Seriously, Beulah. You might better see a doctor," Ray insisted.

"Tell you what. I've been thinking since those two showed up tonight. I think I better go with them to find those girls and Lulu. I ain't gonna see no doctor, but I will ride in that big rig with you. Besides old Beulah just might be ready for some Queen Road Adventure, herself."

Ray studied her face, and then sighed. "Okay woman, you talked me into it. I guess I better go along with these two and I'll take you along so I can keep an eye out on your health. You are one stubborn lady." He turned to Bob and Carl. "Does this all suit with you, two? Beulah and I can tag along and help you track the Queens. It might be helpful to have some more hands around, you know?"

Bob and Carl looked at each other and then back at Ray.

"We'd appreciate any help you can offer, Ray," conceded Carl. "For now, I say we hit the sack and we'll meet up early in the morning."

"That's a plan. See you at seven in the morning. We'll meet at The Joint," replied Ray. The men shook hands while Beulah looked on smiling and nodding as if she had thought of the idea herself.

The guys stumbled out and down the road to Big Daddy.

"We need to call Anne and fill her in on our progress and whereabouts. Tomorrow's going to be a long day on the road, I think." Bob said. Carl agreed.

As soon as they were inside they checked for email messages from the girls, but the screen was empty.

# S. O. S....

# Chapter 37

## You're Gonna Miss My Loving

After Darlene went to bed, I motioned for Liz to join me up front. We got comfortable in the two seats and pulled two blankets around our legs to ward off the chill that was seeping into The Screamer. I'd have to crank her up again, soon, if we were going to be able to stand the night.

"Liz, do you realize who Darlene is?" I whispered.

"No, should I?"

"Think about it: her time frame, all that good music coming out of it. I just can't think of her name. I think we have a living, breathing music star on board with us! And it just might come in handy soon. I wish we could get her to sing again. Maybe we'd recognize the voice if she sang one of her old songs. What do you think?"

"I don't know, Leslie. That's not likely to happen. You know how stubborn Darlene is, and she just clams up any time we mention her past. Except for that story she told during the game, we know very little about her." Liz stared at my fallen face.

"Of course, we can try, but things are getting tense between all of us stuck in this motor home together. Must be mobile cabin fever setting in, and we're all going to get it bad by tomorrow night if we don't get out of here."

"I know. Just keep the faith, Liz. We'll get out. You'll see." I turned and started the engine to warm us up a bit. "Mixed Up Shook Up Girl" played softly on the radio.

After humming along for a while, I grabbed Liz's hand and said, "Let's see if we have an email from the guys."

Sure enough, there was email from them. For some reason, I was excited. Why? I didn't know, but there it was. "Liz, it looks as if they sent it tonight."

"Well, they were all to go to Anne's for dinner, so she probably made them write to us," Liz said.

I enlarged the email and read it aloud:

*Dear Leslie and Liz and Moms,*

*We miss you a whole bunch. Seems like you've been gone forever, and we're counting on you coming back soon. We are trying to honor your space and time-out, but we are very worried about the weather forecast and hope you are prepared wherever you are. It would ease our minds if you'd tell us where that is, so we don't worry so much.*

*Love, Bob, Carl, Billy, and Rex*

"Well, that was comforting, I guess," said Liz.

"What do you mean?"

"I guess it means that they are trying to honor our request to let us go, which is what we wanted. And I guess it means they still love us. But honestly, Leslie, why aren't they trying to find us in the Big Ass Storm?"

"Because they know we can take care of ourselves. And it's great that they're honoring our wishes. We'll be all right. Okay?"

Rachel and Reggie moved past us on their way to the cab section, and Liz never answered me. But I knew she was worried. So was I, but I wasn't about to admit it, yet.

"Should we respond to the email?" Liz asked.

"Oh, I don't know." I hesitated. "No, I guess not. I think we should wait until morning. I don't know what we should say at this point anyway, and I don't want to tell them about our predicament. Not yet. So let's just sleep on it, okay?"

"Suits me," said Liz.

"Come sit by me. Let's surf the net for a while. It's early yet."

"I knew it was a mistake to let you buy this computer. Now you want me to get addicted to it, too. But, because we're stuck here, and I'm bored beyond belief, I'll give it a try."

The lights in The Screamer dimmed a bit.

"Reggie, did you see the lights dim? Are there any signs of power loss up front?"

"Looks like our coach battery may be dying. That's not a good sign."

The lights dimmed again. "You know, I ran the engine several times today to keep the batteries charged, but maybe it's time to switch over to generator power just to be safe. Reggie, bundle up and come outside with me. We can flip the generator on, and we won't have to worry about losing power tonight."

We wrapped ourselves head to foot in several layers, even using several of Liz's scarves to protect our faces and plastic garbage bags over our legs and shoes. Then I grabbed a flashlight, and we headed out the door.

The wind howled around us, and snow blew almost sideways against the motor home. Reggie and I held hands and inched our way around the front of The Screamer trying to get our bearings, as we sought out the generator.

With The Screamer sloped down in the ditch, it was difficult to open the panel. Finally Reggie pulled the panel door open and flipped the switch while I held the flashlight. Even with the whiteness of the snow, the flashlight barely penetrated the darkness between our bodies and the panel. We were like islands surrounded by a deep, dark, and angry sea.

"This storm will probably be one for the history books in the South. It's already almost up to our thighs!"

We reversed our steps, still clinging to the sides and made our way slowly back to Liz and Rachel who stood at the door holding a flashlight to lead us back.

Back inside, all seemed fine. But I kept thinking about the fuel tank quota, and wondering how long it would be before we reached that perilous quarter tank and the generator would go off. In normal circumstances, that quarter tank of gas would get you where you needed to be to get more gas. But hell, we couldn't go anywhere. So, the question that roamed around in my head was if it came down to it, did we cut the generator in hopes of driving out of here before we froze to death, or did we use the fuel to stay warm for as long as we could.

I pulled out my dunce book and opened it to the generator section. I had to laugh out loud at myself because right here inside The Screamer was a switch that turned the generator on. We hadn't needed to go outside to do that, after all.

"Liz, is there any coffee left?"

"Just a bit, but we'll need that for morning."

"Okay, that leaves the field open for more booze. It's a good thing we don't have to ration that!" I fixed another drink and went back to the computer.

"Liz, let's go online and see if we can find the names of some of Darlene's songs. Maybe we can find her stage name, too. Reggie, come here. Can you do this?" I explained what we wanted and he changed places with me. Soon the four of us were huddled tightly together staring at the screen as if the storm raging outside were only a dream.

"Oh, oh, I think it's coming back to me! I'm thinking that name is Miriam Langley," I said. The others stared at me.

"Huh?" Reggie said.

"I think Miriam Langley is the stage name of the singer so popular when Darlene was singing. Let's look her up."

Reggie played around with several sites and then said, "Bingo! Here's the oldies site that should tell us all we need to know. But I don't see that name here."

He clicked a few more tabs. "Wait, I found the song that Darlene mentioned, 'Close to You.' Let's play it."

The music swept out of the computer and filled the cabin. "Shhh! Turn it down. I don't want to wake up Darlene."

"That's Darlene," Rachel said. "No doubt about it. Let's see if we can find some old pictures, Reggie."

Reggie clicked on more sites, and eventually came up with an album cover. There in the center decked out in sequins was a younger Darlene. We were all awed.

"Man, she could make a comeback," said Liz. "She's awesome."

"Yes, she could," I said. "She's the real Queen after all. I think we need to talk to her about this tomorrow. It's a sin to waste all that talent. She's still young enough to go back. Look at Ella Fitzgerald. She sang until she died!"

"Are there more songs?" Rachel asked.

"Apparently not. Looks like she had just the one big one."

"No, that's not right," I interrupted. "She mentioned writing several songs and recording a lot of them. We'll look up more later. For now, just for fun, let's do a search for Queen sites and see what comes up."

"Oh yeah," said Liz. "I'm sure there'll be an RV site for Queens, and we'll find other fools just like ourselves stuck in the woods in this storm. Ha! Why I'm sure we'll find out that this happens to people all the time!" Liz yawned.

Reggie hit a few keys, and list after list of sites referring to "Queens" popped up.

"Liz, take a look at this!" I said nudging her shoulder. She was almost asleep in her seat.

"Look, there's our Queen City of Charlotte, North Carolina. And there's the musical group called Queen—hey, they wrote that hit 'Love of My Life.' And look, there's a Queen.com dating service, Queen of Fine Foods and of Course Queen Latifah and the Queen of England. The list goes on for pages!"

"Oh, oh, there's Queen for a Day! We could purchase videos of the old shows. Reggie, click there to see a preview." I was so excited I could hardly keep from nudging Reggie right out of his seat and taking over the computer myself.

When Jack Bailey appeared on the screen, Liz came wide-awake. "Look at him! Look at those clothes and hairstyles." She giggled out loud. "Oh, and there, see, there's the old guy advertising Dog and Cat Yummies by Hartz in the bright orange box. Oh my, and there's something I hated for my mother to give me: ExLax! It'll fix you up all right."

"This brings back so many memories," I sighed. "Look at the little show girls in their red velvet outfits. And there's Jean Cagney who always came on to describe the prize wardrobe and the Sarah Coventry jewelry!"

We watched the preview show almost without blinking. I think Reggie and Rachel were as surprised by my and Liz's excitement as we were about the old show.

"That's the one, there. She'll win. That Vivian lady from Oaklahoma. She has seven kids and all she wants is a diaper service and a short vacation. Look at those horn-rimmed glasses on the one from Minnesota, would you! She wants new bedroom furniture! They all look so scared of the camera, and you know, none of them asked for anything huge. They chose simple things, but they usually ended up getting quite a haul! Remember Liz?"

Liz was holding her sides and trying to smother her loud guffaws. "Look! Look at that applause meter. Remember that? When I was a kid, I used to think the people watching at home could actually make the meter move! What a hoot!"

"Oh, I was right. The lady with all the kids wins. Told you." We all leaned closer to the screen to catch the list of prizes. Reggie read the list out loud for us: "Westinghouse pots and pans, lunch at the Brown Derby Restaurant (where the stars go) a sewing machine, a new Amana refrigerator stocked with frozen TV dinners, and a floor polisher."

"Wow, that's a lot of stuff. Not what I'd want to win, but I guess for women like them, it was a real haul. I wonder why they don't still do this show. Seems like a good way to help out others," Rachel said.

"You are so right, Rachel, it was a good concept. "We'll have to come back to this site for more entertainment later. Let's go back and find other queen sites."

Reggie hit the back button, and the list scrolled before us again. "Okay, Queens," said Reggie all flustered, "we played your game of 'This is Your Life,' now it's time for the 'True Confessions' game. Leslie and I talked the other night about setting up a website, and I did, but there wasn't anything on it. So, a couple of nights ago when I couldn't sleep, I went in and set up a little information on the site. It was sort of a game for me, and hopefully would turn into a nice surprise for you. So, here it is!" He clicked on another site and Liz and I responded together, "Oh my God! It's us! Look: www.queenmotorhome. com! What did you post on it?"

"Not much really. See, I plugged in this little blog: *Coming soon: The tale of two beautiful Queen Runaway Women who had to get away from it all. No more spoiled husbands! No more corporate offices! No more society games! No more having to do what others EXPECT you to do! Instead, it's all about moving forward, being in control of your own destiny, meeting new friends, and having a little adventure. In short, we're getting a REAL life!*"

"I also added and activated a 'Contact Us' selection menu, where people can send you brief messages in emails directly to the site."

Liz was overcome, and I halfway expected her to make up some quip about how this was really going to break my promise about no technology, but instead, she sat grinning like a child on Christmas morning .

"Well, let's open them up, and see what's what, " I said. Staring at the list of emails that popped up, I told Reggie to double-click the first message, and I thought briefly of Pandora's box.

# Chapter 38

## On the Radio

"Who's Winston?" Reggie asked.

"It's from Winston?  Oh, read it, hurry." Liz exclaimed.

Reggie gave her a puzzled look but began to read the email out loud:

*Hey there Queen Leslie and Queen Liz,*

*Just wondering where you are.  Tried your mobile phone several times, but had no reception.  We hope you are safe.  Ronnie, Kenny, and I were goofing around on the net and typed in Queens, and VOILA! There you were!  We were so excited to find your website up and running.  You can email us at 3bees@ttt.com.  We're still traveling, too, but not in your style.  Right now, we're in Nashville waiting out the* storm.

"I can't believe this!" I said. "Who would have thought that the first guys we met on the road would come back into our lives via our Queen website!"

"Well, I'll ask again, who are they?" Reggie said.

"They showed up at our campsite the very first night and crashed our planned Queen party at the RV Park. They were tired and hungry and ended up staying overnight with us. They even fixed our first breakfast on the road."

"It was terrific, too." Liz added. "Let's email them and tell them our situation. They might be able to come get us."

"I doubt that they'll come riding up on a white horse to save us, Liz. But we will email them later. Right now, I'm curious about the other messages. Reggie, open another one," I said.

"Okay. Sure sounds like you two have a lot of stories to tell about your road trip. And here Rachel and I thought we were the most exciting things to happen to you!" Reggie laughed. "Okay, here's one from Mary Rucker in Saint Cloud, Illinois. She says:

> I went on line to check out Queen sites and found yours. Are you really traveling around the country in a motor home? I would love to be doing that right now myself! I hate my life, and my husband. I really need to get out of here before he really hurts me again. Please contact me and help me if you can. Mary.

"Oh," said Liz, "that's so sad to think someone is living like that. But why would she think that we could help her? I wouldn't know where to start except to say 'RUN, WOMAN, RUN!' This could potentially be real trouble, and I don't think we should get involved here," she said shaking her head. "Let's try another one."

Reggie clicked up number two.

> Dear Queens, I have always wanted to run away in a big and beautiful camper. Can I come with you? Contact me about your whereabouts.

"Yeah, right," I quipped. "Like we're going to tell a perfect stranger where we are and invite 'em aboard! Delete that one, Reggie. Let's go to number three."

> Dear Queens, Are you really Queens? Have you ever seen the Queen for a Day Show from the 50's? That was a cool show. I think they should bring it back. There are a lot of women who could benefit from it these days, if you know what I mean.

"Now that's really too weird since we just watched the show clip. Go to the next one."

*Hello Queens, want some action? Me and my boys are willing and able. Tell me where you are and we'll be right over.*

"Pervert," said Liz. "But I guess that's to be expected, huh? But it is fascinating what people will write over the internet. Leslie, I think I'm becoming a convert for technology."

*How does one become a Queen? I don't mean the real kind like the Queen of England or anything. I would just like to feel like a Queen once in a while. My life is about a zero right now. I'd love a motor home like you Queens have, but there's no money for that. I wish you could help me.*

"Y'all had enough?" asked Reggie. "There's plenty more."

"No, that's enough for tonight. I think we need to just think about some of these. It's awful to have people asking for help and not knowing if it's a real cry or just some hoax. And some of these are downright scary."

"You're right about that," Liz agreed.

Darlene stumbled from the bedroom rubbing her eyes and yawning. "What are all y'all talking and laughing so for out here. Have we been rescued?"

I whispered to the others, "Don't tell her about finding her on the internet." I looked back at Darlene and said, "I'm so glad you're awake. Darlene. You need to help us figure out what to do about some of these messages, here."

She made her way to the computer, and Rachel stood up so that Darlene could have her seat. Reggie explained to Darlene how the website got started and then pulled up the blogs and emails. Darlene leaned close to the monitor to read them slowly.

"Humphf!" she said, after reading several. "Can't understand why you two who are supposed to be so smart are so dimwitted when it comes to figuring out your purpose in life. Why it's right here in front of you in black and white. I don't think the Good Lord can make it any plainer for you."

"What are you talking about Darlene?" I asked, already wishing I hadn't asked her to read them and preparing myself mentally for her next verbal attack on our ingratitude.

"Just think about it. Queen for a Day. Wanna' Be Queens, helpless women who want to be you, and women who think you two got the answers and can help them. Remember our conversation about how you two are just selfish Prima Donna's leaving perfectly good husbands and homes? Well, I didn't say so outright, but the truth is this is the stage of life when you ought to be out helping others. And cupcakes, I think right here on this computer is opportunity knocking. The chance to make something useful out of your lives!"

"What are you running on about now, Darlene? Honestly, sometimes I can't understand anything you say." I leaned back against the seat back and glared at her.

"I ain't running on about nothing. I got a good idea, but it's late, so we'll talk about it in the morning. Maybe you'll dream up some ideas of your own while you're sleeping tonight." She stood, stretched, and yawned. "Goodnight everybody." She stopped to lift Rosie from the sofa and carried her back to our bedroom, and Lulu followed.

"That woman is going to drive me crazy!" I grumbled. "But I'm too tired to try and figure out what she meant about our purpose in life. Let's go to sleep."

Liz and I made a bed on the sofa pullout while Rachel climbed to the top bunk. Reggie hit the light switch and made his way to the front to recline in the passenger seat.

"Liz," I whispered. "Say your prayers. I'm praying for our generator to hold up and that the snow stops. You do the same."

"Okay," she yawned. "Good night."

" Night. I love you, Liz."

"Love you, too, Les."

I turned on my back and propped my head up higher on the pillow. With the blinds across from me raised, I stared out at the whiteness of the storm. Snow still fell, sometime in heavy gusts, but for now, it was like a gently, soothing rain. The drip, drip of water and snow falling from the tree branches became a lullaby and before long, the only sounds besides those of Mother Nature were Darlene's snoring from one end of the motor home to Reggie's coming from the other end.

# Chapter 39

## Stay…Just a Little bit Longer

Reggie and Rachel made the last of the coffee in the morning. Liz and I rose slowly from the sofa sleepers and made our way to the table. We had cold Granola cereal, no milk, and a few slices of bread left. Spirits were low.

"Where's Darlene?" I asked.

"She hasn't surfaced yet," replied Liz. "And the animals really need to go outside. I'm surprised Lulu hasn't raised a ruckus by now."

"I'll go check on her," I said and rose to make my way to the bedroom door. I tapped lightly and eased the door open. Darlene was cocooned in a quilt with Lulu and Rosie curled next to her. The room was colder that the front of the motor home, and outside, snow continued to fall.

"Darlene?" I called softly.

"Okay, okay. I'm getting up," she grumbled. "Give me some space."

I shut the door and returned to the table with Rosie and Lulu in tow. "Reggie, the animals need to go out. It looks like the snow is almost to the top of the front cab now, so we'll have to keep them nearby. When you get back, the rest of us will take our turns outside."

He bundled up again in layers and opened the cabin door. Snow had piled up around the door, so he had to shovel a path out using a kitchen pot.

Finally, he called to Lulu who lumbered out completely oblivious to the cold and wetness outside her snug bed. Rosie was a different story, though.

"I'll get her. You go ahead and take Lulu," I called to Reggie. The two of them romped down the path and were soon hidden by the snowdrifts and trees of the forest.

Rosie spit and spat when I put her down in the snow, but she did her business, pawed at the snow to cover it, and then yowled loudly to be let back inside.

"I'm going out now," I called. "Liz, come on with me. Let's get this over with."

Liz waddled over to the door in the layers of sweaters and coats she had piled on. "I'm not sure I can get these damn clothes off to go to the bathroom," she complained.

"Oh, come on. We'll manage."

I reached for the digging pot and handed her one as well. "We'll have to dig us a garden path. But not toward the back. I don't want to step in any big dog shit." It was clear from Liz's complaints and my grumbling that the day was going downhill for sure.

We dug and dug and dug, piling snow on either side of the narrow walk we carved out of the drifts. A clump of wild holly bushes provided the perfect screen for the ladies room, but just as Liz had worried, it took an incredibly long time to get undressed enough to use the damn thing.

Thirty minutes later, we made our way back inside The Screamer. Reggie and Lulu had already unwrapped, and Rachel and Darlene stood waiting on Liz and me for their trek.

"Hold on tight to her," Liz whispered to Rachel. "We don't want her to fall out there." Rachel nodded. Liz stood at the door and watched them go.

When everyone had returned and shed the heavy wear, I asked them to take seats on the sofa. "We need to have another team emergency meeting," I began. "Reggie and I will try the radio again, but honestly, it's not likely that it's working. We've got to shift to emergency mode thinking now. Any ideas other than contacting the guys? I'm not ready to yell Uncle to them yet, if at all."

"Like I said before, we could send Lulu out to find help. I know that homeless camp is somewhere around here," suggested Darlene. Lulu barked at the mention of her name as if she understood Darlene's words. "Maybe old Les is still hanging out there. Not that I want him to find me here, but for your sakes, he may our nearest hope."

"Oh, no," said Liz. "We can't send Lulu out in that storm. She's not even our dog! What if she didn't come back? How would we ever face Beulah and tell her we had lost her beautiful doggie?"

"Well, honestly, Liz, Darlene may be right for once. I think Lulu would come back. But we'd have to fix a message of some sort like they do in the movies. We could tie it around her neck. Everybody think. What can we use to hold the message?" I replied.

"A soup can would work. Maybe there's a can of soup left in the cabinet. We can slit holes in the top, drain the can, and put a message inside—like people put messages in bottles, only ours would be more original: Message in a Can." Darlene chuckled at her own joke.

"Anyway, we can tie the can around Lulu's collar and send her off. She's a smart dog. She'll find somebody, and she'll bring them back here to us, too." Darlene folded her arms across her chest and sat back, proud of herself.

"Reggie and I'll try the CB one more time," I said to no one in particular. Darlene's plan could wait a few more minutes while we tried a few more traditional SOS attempts. But we had no luck with the CB or the regular radio for news. Too much static and no real reception.

"Okay everybody," I said. "I guess Plan Lulu has to go into effect. We have no other options. Darlene's plan sounds crazy, but the truth is, it's our only hope right now. Liz, get the soup can ready. Darlene, you write out our message."

In no time, our plan was ready to go into action.

"How does this sound?" asked Darlene.

*Les,*

*It's been a long time, very long, but I'm thinking and hoping that you are still at the camp. As for me, I've been traveling with friends, good friends—no drugs or alcohol in years. I was hoping to make it to the camp to see you. We stopped at the Praise the Lord Congregational Church for a Thanksgiving Eve supper, and left there to find the camp, but it seems we took a wrong turn somewhere (I think we're within just a few miles of the camp) and we ended up stuck in a ditch and trapped in the storm.*

*This dog's name is Lulu, and we have sent her to find help. We are in a camper named The Silver Queen Screamer, but are half buried in snow at this point. Our CB is out and so are the mobile phones. If Lulu finds you, try to find a trucker somewhere who will let you use the CB and contact a guy named Ponderosa Man. He's a road friend of ours and will come to help us.*

*Please take care of Lulu until we are rescued.*

*Darlene*

*P.S. She likes saltines.*

"Why Darlene," I teased, "I do believe you are still in love with Les. Why don't you tell him?"

Her answer was a haughty snort aimed in my direction as she plodded back to the bedroom.

"I think that's a beautiful letter, Darlene," sighed Rachel.

"Okay, let's launch Lulu," I said. The four of us bundled up and took Lulu outside where Reggie threaded her collar through the holes in the ends of the can. We slipped the note inside and then added a note taped to the outside that said "SOS! NOTE INSIDE."

"I think somebody will notice that, don't you?" Liz asked.

"Let's hope so," I answered.

"Wait," yelled Darlene. She stuck her head outside the door and dangled a red silk handkerchief at me. "Let her smell this and take it with her. Lulu might be able to find Les's scent from it and tail him better. It's an old handkerchief of Les' that I held on to for some fool reason." She cut her eyes toward me. "See here? That's his initials. He'll recognize them and know that this is not a joke. He'll know it came right from me."

"Great idea, Darlene," grinned Reggie who proceeded to rub the scarf over Lulu's nose and then tied it to her collar. The big dog sneezed twice and then sniffed at it again.

"Oh, and give her these, too." Darlene held out a handful of saltines to feed Lulu.

"Ready?" Reggie asked. We all nodded, afraid to say goodbye to Lulu, not wanting to think that we might not ever see her again. Reggie trudged down his snow path and Lulu followed right behind him, her tail up in the air. We watched them for as long as we dared, then turned and moped our way back inside.

Before long, Reggie returned alone.

"Now, don't start crying, y'all. I had a good talk to Lulu. She's a smart dog. She'll find help. And she'll come back to us safe and sound. You wait and see," said Reggie. We all sniffed, and he swiped at his nose with the sleeve of his jacket.

"Okay, enough moping. We did what we had to do. Let's get busy. I seem to remember Darlene that you had an idea last night that you were to share with us this morning….something about my and Liz's purpose in life?"

"I do at that," she answered. "But let's pull up a few more of them computer messages first. Then I'll tell you all about it."

# Heading Out…

# Chapter 40

## Ain't No Mountain High Enough

"Wow!" exclaimed Beulah as she climbed into the Big Daddy with Bob and Carl. "Now this beats what the Queens are sporting. Their's was pretty modest."

Bob and Carl looked at each other, a little embarrassed. "Well, Beulah, this was the only rental available that had what we needed," explained Bob. "By the way, how are you feeling, this morning?"

Beulah nodded her head up and down. "I'm okay. Don't worry yourselves about me. I'm ready to ride."

A few minutes later, they pulled into the parking lot at The Joint. Ray stood outside by his rig. "Let's get some breakfast and discuss our plans. Then we need to hit the road. The weather reports are far from good. Most of my trucker friends have been turned around or turned around on their own because of the storm. I sure hope those wives of yours checked into a motel like I suggested."

"Well, it's more likely they stuck to their own plans, whatever those were," Carl grumbled. "Those are two stubborn women!"

"Yep, they are," agreed Beulah. "But I like that kind of spirit. I actually envied them a bit, and a part of me wanted to take off down the road right along with them."

The Joint was overflowing with truckers and other travelers who had given up roads because of the storm forecast. The group found a table and placed their orders. Bob looked directly at Beulah and said quietly, "Whatever plan the girls decided on, I just hope they're safe. I think Carl and I are just now realizing how very worried we have been and how much we really do love our wives." He glanced at Carl who ducked his head shyly.

"Okay," said Ponderosa Man. "Now we're here in eastern Tennessee and the last we heard, they were headed for the western part of the state. With some of the main highways that way already blocked off, we'll have to take some back roads, but I think we can make it through. My rig will limit which roads I can take, you know. And just for the record, how are your snow and ice driving skills?" He looked at Carl and Bob.

The fact that they didn't answer told him what he needed to know.

"Did you find out about Buttercup Junction?" Bob asked.

"I know the general area it's in—about half way between Nashville and Memphis, so unless they've moved a great distance, the worst of the storm won't hit them. There's not much there except an old black church, a few small farms, and up the road a bit, there's a homeless camp," said Ray.

Bob and Carl nodded solemnly. The waitress brought their food, and the group ate in relative silence until they were finished. Ray pushed his plate to the center of the table and leaned back in his chair balancing on its two rear legs. "I'll take the lead in my rig. Beulah can ride with me. We'll take it slow. That bus of yours will fishtail in a second if you aren't careful, so don't get to playing any road warrior games or running any races, okay?" Once again the two guys nodded like young boys taking direction from their scoutmaster.

"Tilly, how about fix up a few meals to go for us. We'll need something for lunch and maybe something for supper, too."

"I got just the things you'll need," she said and busied herself piling various foods into styrofoam containers. When they were full-to-bulging, she loaded them in two large plastic garbage bags and lugged them to the table. "Here you go. This ought to keep for a while, anyway."

"Thanks, Tilly. Well folks, I think we're ready. By the way, I'll need your CB handle, Bob," said Ray.

234

"Sure, it's 'Plane to Catch', and I remember yours for sure, Ponderosa Man." He grinned at his new friend.

With that, they walked outside and climbed into their rigs. Ponderosa's big red rig took the lead. "Stay tuned to Channel 19," he yelled from his window.

They were barely on the interstate when the CB crackled.

"Hey, Green Babies, this is Peterbilt Blue Brenda Babe. Come in."

"Brenda Babe!" Bob responded, grinning that he was feeling very comfortable chatting on the CB now. "How are you?"

"The better question is how are you two? Found your girls, yet?"

"Nope, but we've got a good plan now and some help."

Their conversation was interrupted by another voice. "Come in Peterbilt Blue Brenda Babe. This is Ponderosa Man. What are you up to and what's your ten-forty?

"I'm right behind these two greenhorns. Are you the help they've got?"

"Ten-four. That's me. And I've got Beulah with me, too."

"Well, sounds like a real party caravan. I'd be happy to join in and help out where I can, if you can stand more company. Besides, my curiosity is killing me."

"That would be terrific, Brenda Babe!" Broke in Bob. "We can use all the help we can get."

"Sounds like a plan, man. I'm right behind you. Over and out," she replied.

Ponderosa Man broke in again. "We've got to make a quick stop at the Mason Dixon Truck Stop. Beulah needs some medicine."

"What's wrong with Beulah?" Brenda asked.

There was a scratching fumbling sound and then Beulah's voice came through loud and croaky. "It's just a cold. This one's just making too much of a few sniffles."

"I see," replied Brenda. "At any rate, you can still take the meds. They'll do you good. Now don't grumble or you might be put out on the side of the road and miss out on all the fun!"

"Oh, and greenies," she continued. "When we find those queens of yours, I want me one of those crowns like they wear."

"Absolutely, Brenda Babe. You're the Trucker Queen and you'll certainly have a crown of your own when all this is over."

While Bob chatted on the CB, Carl had tuned into a football game and drove with one eye on the road, and one on the television screen mounted in the dash.

"Touchdown!" He yelled suddenly. The Big Daddy rocked from side to side as he swerved to get it back on the road.

"Hey, Carl!" Bob yelled. "Keep both eyes on the road. I think this is a design flaw when manufacturers put a television up front with the driver, so you can watch and drive at the same time. That's about as safe as drinking and driving."

"Sorry," yelled Carl in the general direction of the CB.

"I'll call Anne and fill her in," he said to Carl.

"Yeah, you do that," was Carl's absent-minded reply, still eyeing the television screen. Bob made his way to the back of the bus to place the call. When Anne answered, he explained briefly what they had learned so far, and where they were now headed.

"For goodness sakes, don't you two get into a mess in the weather, now," she advised. "And don't worry. You're doing the right thing going after them. Just be careful, Bob."

Ray pulled the rig into the Mason Dixon truck stop. Carl and Bob parked just beside him, and Brenda closed in on them from the rear.

"No need for y'all to get out," called Ray. "I'll get what Beulah needs and be out in a less than five minutes."

And he was good for his word. He tossed the brown sack of medicines over to Beulah and ground the rig into gear. The interstate was virtually empty, and the rigs made good time until about an hour on the west side of Nashville where they ran into snow. Flashing lights swirled up ahead between two highway patrol cars pulled onto the shoulder. The caravan slowed down as the officers motioned for them to stop.

Bob and Carl watched as Ponderosa Man talked with the officers, occasionally pointing back at them and at Brenda. The officers stared but then nodded and waved us all on.

"Come in Plane to Catch and Peterbilt Blue Brenda Babe."

"We're here. Go ahead." Brenda Babe answered.

"The Smokies waved us on by because I told them we have a sick person on board and we had to make it to the Yardstick Truck Stop about thirty miles up the road. There's another road block about ten miles past that, so we may have to give it up then."

"You're not serious," exclaimed Carl.

"No man, I'm not gonna give up unless these roads get impassable. I'm thinking of another plan as we speak. Stay cool!" Ray answered.

# Crazy...

# Chapter 41

## We Will Rock You

Darlene sat staring at Liz and me and laughed out loud. "You two Queenies sure do have a way of stirring things up or getting in a fix. I can't believe how many women out there want to be like you and they don't even know you. If they did, well, they might think twice." She chuckled deep in her throat.

"Very funny, Darlene," I said. "We didn't ask for any of this. And the smart thing for us to do would be to forget all of this weird stuff and concentrate on surviving this storm, but I have to admit I am intrigued and curious as to why all of this is happening to us. All Liz and I wanted was a little freedom and adventure."

"I know why it's happening," Darlene said with her face suddenly serious and thoughtful. "You two got a calling, as we say."

"A calling?" Liz asked.

"Yeah, it's like you're destined to do something that you wouldn't ever in your wildest dreams figure on doing. It's a purpose in life."

"So, what Old Wise One do you see as our calling?" I smirked.

"Helping out others."

Darlene's comment was dead serious, and the silence that followed it filled the motor home as all eyes turned to Liz and me.

"Us?" I asked incredulously. "A calling sounds like some kind of ministry. You'll have to help me out on this one, Darlene."

"Well, it could be a ministry of sorts. You could even call it a Queen ministry." She chuckled at herself. "I'm just thinking that you two can possibly help others. You know, people who aren't as strong and set up so good in life as you two are. What would be wrong with helping them out instead of letting 'em just sit around and dream their lives through you and your adventures. All you gotta do is give 'em a little encouragement. Sometimes, that's all it takes."

"I don't know, Darlene," Liz said. "What do we possibly have to offer? Maybe if we survive this storm, we could offer motor home survival suggestions or something." She half-chuckled, then stopped.

Rachel spoke up suddenly. "But look what you two did for all of us. You set out to have an adventure, met us, the wonderful people we are," she paused and smiled shyly at Reggie. "And everything changed because of that. Our lives changed, just like yours."

"You're right about that," I said.

"Yeah, that's right, but there's more to this than you all are seeing," said Darlene.

"Well, would you share that wisdom, Oh Great One, please?" I asked her.

Darlene pulled herself up straight in the seat and folded her hands in her lap before she replied. "I think, that you might start up some kind of club. A Queen Club, and put it on the radio, maybe. There used to be some doctor woman named Laura on the air…a psychologist, I think. I sometime thought she was kind of short with the girls that called in, and maybe that's the way it should be, but you know, you could go back to the days of Queen for a Day and figure a way to help people out. Might make some money at it, too. People are just dying to hear some sort of encouragement from somebody. Why, these people writing you now, they just want to be you even though they don't know you from Adam or Eve. I think you ought to think about it. We're gonna get out of here, and then it'll be your time to give something back." She looked directly at Liz and me.

"What about you Darlene? What about making a change in your life?" I asked.

"I don't know 'bout that. I ain't got that particular calling, I don't think. But I would feel a part of what you two are doing, if you was to take my advice. As for me, I can just go back to the bridge and live right on there. I was happy enough. Hadn't thought of living any other way 'til you two grabbed me off the road."

"I think Darlene's got a good idea, here. A Queen Radio Station might just work. You could do like those talk shows and have people call in and tell about their problems, and maybe you could call on other people to help solve some of their problems or just help 'em reach their dreams." Liz commented.

"Maybe you could get businesses and other professionals to donate money or things to help out," said Reggie, seemingly caught up in all this dreaming.

"Yeah, and you could have a contest and whoever won each week for the best story, would get a tiara, too," piped in Rachel. Everyone laughed at that.

"You know, you might just have a workable idea here," I exclaimed, surprised at myself for taking any of this seriously. "Maybe it's the storm affecting my brain or something, but I have a college buddy who owns a radio station, and he just might be willing to help out. It couldn't hurt to email him and ask, I guess. Hell, we could even give EVERYONE who called in a tiara, and then have one big weekly prize."

"Yeah, we'd have a Queen network in no time at all," said Liz.

"Okay, everybody, let's give this a rest for a bit. Darlene, I have to admit, you've made me start thinking. Thanks." Darlene didn't acknowledge my comment, but I knew she was pleased with herself by the way she reached up to straighten her tiara, which she hadn't removed even to sleep.

"I'm starving," said Reggie. What do we have to eat?"

"Half a box of Lorna Doone cookies, some dry cereal, and a little bit of peanut butter. No sodas, coffee, and only a dribble of milk. Plenty of water, though." Rachel answered with a smile.

Darlene leaned forward. "I happen to have two cans of Vienna sausages and some saltines stashed in my backpack." She looked around as if expecting us to beg.

"Being on the road teaches you to think ahead, you know. I ain't had a privileged life like some." She cut her eyes at me. "But, I can share, too. And when that's gone, we can make snow ice cream. Any of you every done that before?"

"Snow ice cream?" Reggie looked downright excited. "I never heard of that."

"Well, you don't know what you're missing, son," replied Darlene. "I'll fix you some right after we dine." She shuffled back to the bedroom and returned with her food offerings.

Liz looked curiously at the shriveled Vienna's on her plate. I saw her smile, and then bite the inside of her mouth as if trying to stop words from coming out. I knew I was thinking the same thing: that they looked like shriveled penises, but I didn't dare say it out loud. Reggie would have died of embarrassment.

We ate in silence until the last of the sausages were gone. Darlene wrapped up the remaining saltines in plastic wrap and tucked them back in her pocket. "I'll save these for Lulu when she gets back," she said.

"I sure hope she's okay," commented Reggie. " I miss her. And Rosie's perched up there in cab like she's watching for her."

"Lulu is fine, I'm sure," Darlene nodded. "We'll see her soon."

Liz and Rachel cleared the table while Reggie and I tried again for contact on the CB, but there was no reception. The snow continued to swirl, but it did seem to have slowed a bit.

I called to the others, "It looks like the snow is easing up a bit. Maybe the worst is over and we'll get out of here soon."

Reggie returned to the table and started a game of Scrabble with Rachel. I sat with Liz and Darlene still thinking about Darlene's idea for a radio show. I had to admit that I liked it. I liked it a lot, and my friend Brent just might be willing to help out.

"Darlene, how about singing for us. Last night after you went to sleep, we were playing around on the computer and looked up some of your old songs. The only one listed at that site was "Close to You," but there must be hundreds more. Would you sing that one for us? Please?" I pretended to kneel in front of her, and she laughed.

"I don't sing no more," she said.

"Oh, come on Darlene. Do it for me and Reggie," begged Rachel.

"Yeah, it could be sort of like mine and Rachel's song from now on," he said and hugged Rachel.

"Well, I guess I could do it for you two young 'uns," she said, and began. She started softly, but soon closed her eyes and belted out the lyrics as if she was on a Broadway stage. We were all awed, and there was a distinct, telling pause before we burst into applause and cheers. That woman could sing.

Darlene simply got up and walked to the bedroom and closed the door.

"I've got chill bumps," said Liz. Her eyes shone.

"Me, too," said Rachel.

"She's got a gift, all right," said Reggie. "Which she has obviously decided to waste and not use anymore."

"We'll have to work on that, won't we, gang?" I asked. They all agreed.

"I'm telling you, she's the real Miriam Langley."

I went to the computer and logged on to do a search for my friend Brent, but frustration set in, so I called Reggie over to help out. He left Liz and Rachel at the table and came to join me.

"I'm estimating that we have enough fuel in the tank to run the generator until late tomorrow afternoon," I whispered. "After that, I don't know what we'll do."

# Chapter 42

## Another Night Without You

Reggie and I stayed at the computer for a while. While he didn't know a lot about radio frequencies and broadcasting, he knew more than I, so we fumbled our way through some search engines together.

"I think the best thing to do is email your radio friend," suggested Reggie. "I'm sure he can tell you everything you need to know."

"If you're emailing Brent, how about email the guys, too?" Liz called to me.

"I thought we had decided to wait until tomorrow," I said, giving her my firm look.

"Well, I've been thinking. The storm might quit, but it could be days before anyone found us back here. I don't know. Maybe I'm just having second thoughts now."

"I know you're all worried. I am, too. But let's just give it until tomorrow, okay? Something's bound to break, or we'll know exactly what we have to do when the time is right. Let's stick to our Lulu plan. Is that okay with everybody?"

They all agreed.

"We're all in this together, for sure," Liz said, and I knew she remained hesitant.

I turned back to the computer. Reggie had located his business email address, so I began typing.

*Brent Baby,*

*Long time no talk to. A lot has been happening. Actually I've been out of town for a bit doing some research, which brings me to our last discussion about your radio station. You mentioned the remote possibility that you might add a talk show section and that maybe I should be the host. Well, Brent, I think I've got an idea for that. Don't laugh! I'm serious. Let's talk.*

*Leslie*

I sent the message before I could talk myself out of it.

"Reggie, pull up some more email from the Queen's site. Somebody get Darlene back out here."

Rachel and Liz piled on coats to take a bathroom break and grabbed two cooking pots to take with them. "We'll bring some snow back to make the snow ice cream, too." Liz said as they stumbled out into the storm.

When the girls returned, Darlene made the snow ice cream, less vanilla flavoring, and we devoured it. It was the one time in the last few days when we all felt full.

I went back to the computer and began reading some of the emails and finding lines such as: *Tell me how you did it. Come get me. I'll be your slave. I hate my life. I want to run away. Can you please help me? Do you like girls or boys?*

"It's amazing. There are the few weirdo messages, but for the most part, these emails are cries for help. These people just need someone to listen to them and help them." I said. "The more I read here, the more I think our idea might work."

"Whose idea?" Darlene quipped.

"Well, yours originally, but we added some to it, you know," I smiled at her. "I think basing it on the old 'Queen for A Day' show just might work. We could offer prizes like a spa weekend, a pink boa, and a scepter! Maybe we could even vote once or twice a year and choose a Queen to receive a motor home all her own."

"We'd have to find somebody to donate that, Leslie," interjected Liz.

"Oh, I know, but hey, maybe even Della and Lerline would pitch in. Who knows how many people might want to contribute. It's a worthy cause, after all."

"You're right. I'm beginning to visualize it all, myself. Maybe you can start brainstorming about potential contributors after you talk with Brent."

"Hey, you know what? You might even be able to take the show on the road a couple of times a year. You know, choose a town and go to it and do the show from there." Reggie said.

"Everyone can have a part in this if they want to," I said, staring intently at Darlene, who ignored me.

"Well, for now, I think I just want to go home." Liz sighed.

We all turned to stare at her. Her face was strained and circles under her eyes darkened her complexion. Her lips quivered.

"I'm sorry, Liz. I've made a mess of things, I know. Our adventure just sort of took on a life of its own. But I promise you, we'll get out of this mess. And we'll go home for a while and get this radio show organized and you'll see, it will all work out just fine." I reached over to pat her arm. "Well, let's put this conversation on hold for a bit. I say we email Winston and his friends. After all, they're a part of this journey, too."

*Dear Winston, Ronnie and Kenny,*

*A lot has happened on our trip since we started out. Long story short, we took a little detour and are now stuck in a ditch and five feet of snow in the woods on the southwestern side of Nashville. We are somewhere near a place called Buttercup Junction and supposedly (and I stress that word) near a homeless camp. We've got some more friends with us as well, but I'll save those stories for another time. For now, we're okay. I hope we'll all get to meet again soon. We've got some great ideas for our website, and I know you guys can help us out. Can't wait to tell you all about it.*

*Love, Leslie and Liz*

"They sound like a real interesting bunch." Rachel said.

"Yeah, I think you'd all like them very much," I replied.

"Okay, how 'bout a little poker game, folks. I've got toothpicks galore, and they're burning a whole in my pocket wanting to get spent," laughed Darlene.

Reggie and Rachel pulled out a deck of cards to play with Darlene, but Liz and I made drinks and took them to the bedroom and closed the door.

"Leslie, I'm sorry about my comment back there. It's not that I really want to go home, I'm just tired. And I do want to go home, but I don't. Does that make any sense?"

I hugged my best friend close. "I understand. And I promise, everything will work out fine. I've been the one pushing this on us. And frankly, I'm tired too. I guess I'm tired of being the strong one at home, and trying to be strong for everyone here." My voice cracked, and I swiped at the tears that started down my cheeks. "Geez, I don't know where all that came from. I must be REALLY tired. What I mean is that, we are going to get out of this. Don't you worry."

"Leslie, you don't have to be the strong one all the time. You're not responsible for this situation. Besides, I think if you let go a bit, Darlene might just pick up the slack. That's what she did when she came up with the idea for the talk show. Maybe that's what she needs...to feel like she can be strong and contribute something valuable."

"I don't know about letting Darlene take control..." I was interrupted by Reggie's voice calling out to me. "Hey Leslie, you've got mail."

Liz and I rushed to the computer.

*Hey there, Queenies of the Road!*

*We think we might be pretty near to where you are so we are coming to the rescue. The weather looks bad, but we're going to head out tonight anyway. Hope to find you early tomorrow.*

*Love, Winston and Company*

"Oh, no," I sighed. "Now we've got them out in this storm. And even if they do find us, where will we put them? The Screamer is full already."

"Tell them to come, Leslie," Liz said, her voice rising in excitement. "They'll find us for sure. Tell them as much as you can about where we are. We'll find room if it comes down to that, but maybe they can get us out of here."

The look on Liz's face left me no choice, and I emailed them our SOS reply with as much direction as the five of us could come up with, remembering landmarks and such to help guide them to us.

There was another email in the cue. This one from Brent.

*My Dear Leslie,*

*Where the hell are you? I'm not crazy enough to believe that research shit, but you are crazy enough that this idea of yours for a talk show just might work. We can do a pilot test here in the studio. I'm excited about talking to you more about this. Call and we'll do a meeting.*

*Love, Brent*

"We're making progress people!" I called out. "Darlene, what do you think?"

"I think I've given you a new lease on life, is what I think." She smiled at me, meaning it. "My toes are wiggling. And that means the storm is almost past us. I have a feeling deep down that Lulu will find Les, and that all will be well."

"Well, I for one, am beat," sighed Liz. "I say we go to bed."

"You're right, Liz. It's been a long day. Tomorrow is bound to look better."

"Oh, it will be. I told you I feel it deep down," said Darlene.

"Are you some kind of psychic, Darlene?" Reggie asked, and she answered with a smile.

# The Rescuers...

# Chapter 43

## Fly Robin Fly

The blue lights swirled in Winston's rearview mirror.

"Oh, man. I hope they don't smell that weed we just lit up." The boys immediately rolled all the windows down and fanned the air. Winston pulled to the side of the road and watched as the officer pulled in behind him and strode cautiously up to the car door.

"Where you boys off to tonight in this kind of weather?" he asked.

"We're going to rescue some friends of ours who are stuck in the snow, Officer." Winston spoke slowly and carefully, afraid of giving away his buzz.

"Just where are these friends stuck, son?"

"Somewhere close to Buttercup Junction in southwestern Tennessee," replied Winston. Ronnie and Kenny remained quiet, but nodded and smiled as they stared at the officer.

"Never heard of it. So, try again. What are you boys up to?"

"Honestly, sir. We're not up to anything but trying to help our friends."

The officer bent low to look in at Ronnie and Kenny, and then straightened up to his full height placing his hands on his hips. "Uh,huh. And are your friends gay like you?" he smirked.

"No, sir, they're not. They call themselves Queens, sir, and they wear tiaras, and they could be real Queens, but they're not gay. No sir."

"You bunch are real fruitcakes, you know that? But I guess I better let you pass. No sense wasting my time with you nuts when there are real emergencies out there to care of. Now go on your way and get off the road. And don't be pulling any tricks along the way, you hear me?"

"Yes, sir. I mean, No sir. We won't."

The officer strode back to his cruiser, cut the lights and squealed out onto the highway racing ahead of the boys.

"Whew! He was a real nice guy, huh?" Ronnie commented.

"Yeah, real nice. But at least he let us go without too much hassle. Let's get out of here and find Leslie and Liz."

# Chapter 44

## Desperado

The stalled train sat on the tracks on the right side of the camp by the bridge. The storm had brought everything to a standstill. Fortunately, for Les and his homeless friends, one of the cars was empty and worked just fine to ward off at least some of the cold. Five of them huddled together, as unidentifiable as piles of laundry with their layered clothes and worn out blankets covering their bodies.

Les stirred from his nap. "Lyle, did you hear something. Sounds like something scratching on the door there."

"I ain't heard a thing, but then, I'm most deaf anyway." Lyle grinned.

Les struggled to his feet when he heard the next bump and then sharp scraping sounds. " Guys, everybody up. Come help me with this door. Somebody wants in."

The five of them pushed and pulled until the door finally slid open. Outside, the world was entirely white, but the wind seemed to have died down a bit.

"I don't see nothin'," said Lyle. "You must've been dreaming or something." He turned to go back to his nap, but the whining stopped him in his tracks.

"Who's there?" Les yelled. "Show yourself." Gradually his eyes adjusted to the glare of the snow and suddenly, he saw her. A huge monster of a beast standing just below the car.

"Hey, it's a dog. A really big dog. Seems like it wants inside. I bet she's most frozen by now."

Lyle peered over Les's shoulder. "Well, I'll be. That there's one of them Saint Bernard dogs. They live up at the North Pole. She ain't gonna freeze out there, no way."

The big dog whined again and raised one paw to scratch at the metal car again.

"Look, poor thing. One of its eyes is frozen shut. Let's get her up here and see if we can do something for her. She'll be blind if she stays out there much longer."

Les and Lyle eased their way off the edge of the train car and landed with soft thumps in the deep snow beside Lulu. She sat still but whined again, just to let them know she was aware. Slowly, the two men made their way up to her side, crooning, "Nice doggie. Poor doggie. Come on now, ol' Les and Lyle gonna help you up out of this mess."

When Les reached out a hand to pat her head, Lulu turned quickly and sniffed at him. Up one side of his coat and down the other she breathed in the scent of him, and then sat back and barked once.

"Huh! Ain't that peculiar. Seems like she was smelling me like she had found just what she wanted. Look, there's one of them canister things tied round her neck." He reached under Lulu's chin and slid the can around so that he could see it more clearly. "Damn, this is a soup can. And it's got a message on it. "SOS! NOTE INSIDE." Let's get this dog up there in the car and see what's what here."

They heaved and strained and finally managed to get Lulu's front legs up into the rail car. Then Les bent and placed his shoulders beneath her rear and pushed her up. The other men in the car pulled, and soon all of them were safely in the relative warmth of the train car again.

Les took an old flannel shirt from his bag and ran it up and down Lulu's body, drying some of the sleet and snow that had accumulated on her coat. She sat perfectly still, and when he finished, she eased herself down on to the floor and immediately went to sleep.

"Guess she got lost in the storm. She's gotta belong to somebody, cause she looks all clean and cared for, 'cept for what the storm's done to her coat and eyes." Les ran his hands down her body feeling for any broken bones, but finding none, soon sat back on his haunches and looked at his friends.

"I say we gather around her to try to keep her and us a little warmer. We'll tend to that can in the morning when there's light to read whatever is inside it."

By dawn, the men were awake and stomping their feet to get the blood circulating better. They each pulled a meager meal from their coat pockets and began nibbling. Lulu was the last to rise. She stood and stretched herself, then sniffed the circle of men, turning until she located Les again.

"Damn, if she don't seem like she was looking for me, the way she keeps zeroing in on my scent." Les said. He bent to rub her ears and held out a saltine for her to eat.

"Probably won't like it," he muttered, and then chuckled as Lulu gobbled down the cracker and licked her lips wanting more. "Well, it's a dog after my own tastes, I see." Les grinned and handed her two more crackers.

Remembering the note, he bent to pull the can around her neck closer to his face to see what the note said. "Says 'S.O.S. NOTE INSIDE.' And look, there's a scarf tied around that collar too."

He pulled the scarf loose and examined it carefully. "This is my scarf. How the hell did this dog get my scarf? And what's up with all this?" He loosened the can from the collar and shook it until the message floated out and down to the car floor.

He picked up the folded paper and made his way to the sliding car door where he held the note up to the light coming through the crack. The others watched him as Lulu calmly bathed first one paw and then the other and swiped at her eyes.

"What's it say?" Lyle asked.

Les shook his head and refolded the note. Then he put it carefully in his pants pocket. For a minute there was silence, except for Lulu's licking. Les stared out into the cold whiteness of the countryside.

"Friends, meet Lulu." He pointed to her and her ears perked up at the sound of her name. "Seems like Lulu here was sent on a mission to find me."

"Huh?" the men asked almost in unison.

"Yep, this note, it's for me. It's from...well, it's from a woman I thought I'd never hear from again. And she needs help. I gotta go find a trucker."

"What you mean, find a trucker? What kind of help this woman need and why would she send a dog out to find you in this weather?"

"I need to find a trucker with a CB and radio another trucker by the name of 'Ponderosa Man' and then tell him where Darlene is. She and some friends are stuck in a ditch and trapped in the storm somewhere near here. She was trying to make her way to the camp when they took a wrong turn. I wonder what she was coming here for? I wonder if she was coming back for me?" Les shook his head and then turned to gather his things. "Well, guys. I gotta go find me a trucker. If any of you want to come along, I'd be grateful."

Lyle didn't hesitate. He packed away his blanket and grabbed his sack. "I'm ready, my friend." The two men and Lulu jumped from the car and walked slowly through the snow toward the highway.

They arrived at a truck stop a little after lunch and saw only one rig in the lot, but no one near it. While Lyle waited outside with Lulu, Les went inside where people stared, but he wasn't bothered by that. He knew he looked the part of a homeless bum. He couldn't help that, but he was on a mission. A mission to help his long lost Darlene. And nothing or nobody was going to stop him. But there was no help in sight.

Outside again, he turned to Lyle. "Look, there's a trucker just pulling in." He strode determinedly toward the driver as he climbed from the cab.

"Excuse me, sir, but I wonder if you could help me? We're not here for a handout, sir. I just need a hand, so to speak. You see this big dog here? Well, she walked around in that snow and sleet all night with a message in this can here." Les pointed to Lulu who sat quietly at his side.

"It seems some people are in trouble and need help. They're stuck in a motor home out in the storm, and this dog came to get them some help. Only, I need a CB radio to get the help they need."

The trucker eyed Les warily, but continued to listen.

"Here, you can read it for yourself. Take a look there what it says do." Les handed the note to the trucker who read silently.

"Mmmm. Ponderosa Man? Seems like I've heard that handle before. Well, I guess it'd be okay for you to try. After all, that looks like a mighty fine dog and I'd hate to think I wasn't helping out somebody who was really in need. By the way, my handle is Eagle One." He motioned for Les to go to the other side of the cab and climb in. Then he climbed up and reached for the CB. They tried repeatedly to raise an answer.

"This weather's got most everybody holed up somewhere off the road. I don't know what to tell you to do now. But it seems the weather might be clearing a little, so we'll try again in a bit. I need to go get some lunch. How 'bout you? You hungry?"

Les shook his head. "No, but thanks. We'll just wait out here 'til you get back. There's a bunch of folks out back here with a trash can fire. We'll huddle up there 'til you come back."

256

The trucker went inside and Les, Lyle and Lulu made their way to the back of the truck stop and joined the bedraggled group of men hunched over a small cook fire. A big pot of soup boiled on the makeshift grill.

"The restaurant people gave us this here soup. There's plenty if you want some," an old woman said to Les. Lulu went right up to the fire and sniffed loudly. "Looks like your dog is hungry too. She's a big one, that one."

Les smiled and bent to dig out his one plastic bowl from this pack. He and Lyle joined the others in the circle, while Lulu sat just behind Les. When everyone had eaten, Les took the leftovers and poured into his own bowl and placed it before Lulu. The big dog lapped at it greedily. Full and warmed a bit by the hot food, the small crowd curled up around the trash can fire and dozed. Lulu curled herself around Les's back.

"Want to tell me about this Darlene?" Lyle asked.

"Oh, buddy, that's a long, sad story, that one. But if you really want to hear it, I'll tell it." Lyle nodded. And while those around the fire napped and Lulu snored loudly, Les spun his tale of lost love. "And that ain't the worst of it, either. I ruined her career. I did. It was all my fault. And I ain't never forgiven myself for it."

"That's some story, man, " said Lyle. "Is that what put you on the road?"

"That and the drugs and booze. And then the Lord, he came after me. I gave up the bad habits years ago. Hell, I couldn't afford it anyway, and I was afraid to use the shit they sell on the streets around here. So, I got straight. Actually, I ain't had such a bad life out here. It's simple. No complications." He stretched his legs out and yawned.

"Is that what you want, Les? You want this life?"

"If you'd have asked me that this time yesterday, I'd of said, 'sure, it's what I want.' But now, with this dog bringing that message from Darlene, all those old feelings are stirring. And well, I guess I ain't so different from any man. We all like to dream and think we can turn things around."

"Do you still love her?" Lyle asked.

"I have always loved her," Les replied.

# Chapter 45

## You Thrill Me

Bob and Carl parked behind Ray in the back lot of the Yardstick Truck Stop. They headed inside to eat and talk over their plans. Beulah seated herself at one end of the table and Ray took the other end. Brenda, Bob, and Carl took the side chairs.

"Beulah, you look like you're feeling better," commented Ray. "Being on the road must be good for you, huh?"

She grinned. "Nothing like a road trip to perk up the spirit," she said.

They ordered lunch and began making plans.

"I think we need to make some transportation switches," said Ray. "When we hit the deep stuff on the roads, the trailers will start to jack-knife, so Brenda and I will need to leave our trailers here. The Big Daddy rig is much safer as long as you don't stomp the brakes and make him fishtail. I'll take the lead with my Bobtail, and Brenda can drive you two in the Big Daddy. If we can make good time, we just might reach the girls by tomorrow afternoon at the latest. That is, if we can find them."

"Sounds like a good plan," Bob said.

"You mean, I gotta have a woman drive me around?" quipped Carl. But his grin softened what could have been misunderstood.

"We won't have much choice about where to stay, so I think we had better park in a mall or office complex lot and just bundle up in the Big Daddy. You've got all the comforts of home, anyway." Ray laughed.

"Okay, sure. Everybody can stay with us." Bob replied.

"I've mapped out a route in my head and I'll explain it before we get back on the road. If we spot a road block, I'll radio you to stay close behind me and we'll blaze right through." Ray looked determined.

"Sounds like a real Rockford Files highway chase scene, Ray," Brenda laughed.

They ate lunch hurriedly and returned to the lot. Ray and Brenda unhooked their trailers, and Brenda climbed right into the driver's seat of the Big Daddy. "I can't wait to steer this baby, guys. You've got all the bells and whistles on this rig. And I hope, plenty of scotch for later. I think we're gonna need fortifying tonight!"

Farther down the highway, visibility decreased. A strong wind blew the white powder in swirls across the pavement.

"Come in Plane to Catch. This is Ponderosa Man. We've got action up ahead."

"Go ahead P man," said Brenda.

"The block's made up of small construction horses, no barrels or concrete from what I can tell from here. We shouldn't have a problem, but let's speed up a bit and give the Smokies a warning with our horns and flashers. Remember, no brakes or that Big Daddy will fishtail on you."

"Ready when you are," replied Brenda. "Hang on, Boys! We're shooting the chase scene here. Yeah man! This is going to fun!"

Carl had lost interest in the football game. He sat behind Bob looking a little green as the Big Daddy picked up speed on the icy road. "Oh, man, if the boys could see us now!" he said.

"Yeah, they'd probably think we're crazier than Leslie and Liz," Bob chuckled.

Ray pushed on with his horn blaring. Brenda Babe rode his back bumper as tight as she could. The patrolmen, dressed up like Eskimos, jumped out of their cars, waving them down with flashers, and Ray's cab jostled as it sprayed snow on them as well as the windshield of Plane to Catch. Parts of the wooden horses flew to the side of the road. One bounced off Big Daddy's hood, barely missing the windshield. Finally, a mile past the roadblock, Ray slowed and radioed Big Daddy.

"Okay, Brenda Babe. You can back off just a bit, but do not, repeat do not hit your brakes. I have to keep my Bobtail floored to plow through this stuff. You just stay in the tracks. We're in for about a thirty minute ride to get to the next exit."

"Ten-four," replied Brenda. "Say, I really like your style, Ponderosa Man. What are you doing tonight? Have a date?"

"Just Beulah, you, and me and the Greenies, of course," laughed Ray. "Beulah says you'll have to fight her for me."

"How's she holding up on the ride?"

"Beulah's a real trooper," replied Ray and you could hear the smile in his voice.

"What about the cops? Won't they follow us?" Bob asked, mentally trying to figure out how many charges they'd be written up on.

"Are you kidding?" Brenda replied. "They aren't going anywhere and couldn't get there if they wanted to. They'll probably call in a report, but they've got their hands full with accidents and other things. We'll be okay."

They rode in silence for a while, and then Bob reached over to find some music on the radio. But what they found was another thing altogether.

"Reports just in of a renegade truck and RV traveling west on I-40, near exit 34, ignoring road condition warnings and roadblocks. Use caution if encountered."

Brenda laughed out loud. "We're on the news, boys. And they can't come get us! I love this gig."

She radioed Ray to fill him in on the report and they decided to avoid the major exit they had planned to take and move farther west on the outskirts of Nashville.

Thirty miles later, Bob and Carl sat white knuckled while Brenda steered the Big Daddy behind Ray's rig off the interstate and onto the exit. At the top of the ramp, Ray took a sharp right onto a frontage road. Ahead was the abandoned manufacturing plant he had mentioned earlier as a place to spend the night. No one would look for them there.

Easing the Big Daddy into the snow blanketed lot, Brenda came to a stop directly behind Ray's rig. Beulah and Ray grinned and trudged back to the Big Daddy.

"I tell you one thing, Ponderosa Man. That was the most exciting thing I've done since I last had sex. In fact, it was better than sex!" Brenda exclaimed.

The men laughed and Beulah blushed slightly. Carl met them with a tray of drinks, and the five settled down on the leather seats to talk over the day's adventures.

Here we are, thought Bob, with these perfect strangers and we're actually having a great time in the middle of a snowstorm and being wanted by the police! I wonder if this is what Leslie meant about a new kind of life. He chuckled to himself, not being able to imagine his wife in any circumstance similar to this.

Supper and more drinks left the group weary.

"You ladies can share the bedroom," Bob offered, and Brenda rose but paused to flirt with Ray on her way there. But Beulah hesitated. "I'm not sure I want to share a bed with that woman! She's a handful!" She giggled and watched as Ray blushed.

"Well, then, you take the pull out here, and we'll put Ray on that one over there. Carl and I can sleep up front. We've both become accustomed to sleeping in our recliners since the girls left."

With everyone settled, the interior of Big Daddy quieted down. But the calm was disrupted by the jangling of Carl's cell phone.

"Maybe it's the girls," said Bob.

Carl checked his caller ID. "No, it's Larry, my friend the cop. Remember him? God, surely he couldn't have heard about us busting through that road block back there!"

He turned his back to Bob and answered the phone.

"Oh, hi, Larry. How are you?"

"The question is, how are you guys?" Larry said. "Any word on the wayward wives? And is there anything I can do for you guys?"

"Oh, well, we're fine. We decided to hit the road and find the girls before that storm comes in. We've got a good lead as to where they're camping." Carl swallowed hard. "I appreciate your calling, though, buddy."

Larry must have added more to the conversation because Carl looked a little pale as he turned back to Bob.

"Why'd you make out like everything's so great?" Bob asked.

"Because, if we get arrested for this crazy ride, he'll be our only hope for rescue. I didn't want to risk making him suspicious of us already. He did say that we should watch the roads and the Tennessee cops. They're hard tails, he says."

Bob turned to face Carl in the dim light of the cab. "Well, this just gets better and better, doesn't it? Here we are, camping out in a playboy RV with three strangers in the middle of a snow storm. Leslie and Liz will never believe all this, and neither will Larry. And now you've lied to a cop. Ain't this some fun?" Bob said sarcastically.

"You've got that right, buddy-roo." Carl answered.

# On the Edge…

# Chapter 46

## If You Don't Know Me By Now

I woke early the next morning to find Darlene at the computer while Reggie and Rachel slept soundly in the top bunk. So much for chaperoning, I thought.

"Darlene, what are you doing? I didn't know you knew how to use a computer."

I went to stand beside her.

"I didn't. But I couldn't sleep, and Reggie was up, too, so he showed me a trick or two. I've been having a grand old time with this thing. Goes to show you can teach an old dog new tricks, huh?" She chuckled.

"What have you been doing?"

"Oh, just checking out some of those other Queen sites. Reggie helped me pull up some more clips from the Queen for a Day show and we watched those. I think that idea of ours for the radio show just might be the thing. Nobody else seems to be doing it. Reggie and Rachel and I made a few notes last night, sort of what you corporate types would call a business plan, I guess." Darlene looked smug.

"I can't believe…" I began, but Liz interrupted me.

"What's up in paradise this morning, Queenies?" she quipped.

"Come over here. You're not going to believe what this woman has done now." I pointed to Darlene.

Liz looked hesitant, expecting me to be upset over another of Darlene's comments.

"Darlene's turned into a computer guru overnight. She's even made out some business plans for our radio show."

Liz skimmed the notes I held out to her, and then, in surprise, she looked from Darlene to me.

"Well, I never thought…." she began, and then stopped.

"Oh, she's just pulling your leg, Liz," Darlene sniffed. "And poking some fun at me at the same time, I 'spect. Those are just some thoughts the kids and I worked up. Nothing big. And I have no intention of becoming hooked up with you Queenies for the rest of my life, that's for sure."

"It looks like a good plan," Liz commented.

"But it's not that simple, Liz," I said. "If we decide to do this thing, we have to go back to …well, to that life we just left, and I'm not sure I'm ready to do that just yet."

"But that's the whole point," Darlene said. "You're missing the whole thing, Queenies. You girls talked about your other lives being so bad, empty, and wanting to leave all that behind, but you know what? You two don't really know anything. This idea could be great. It could give you just what you been wishing for…something meaningful to work at, to fill up your time with, instead of all that corporate and society stuff. And taking the show on the road will still give you girls a chance for new adventures." Darlene leaned over to point to her notes.

"You may be onto something, Darlene," I said. "But it's hard to let go of a dream that Liz and I have shared for years. And you make me feel guilty for holding fast to it."

"No reason for guilt, girlie. It's just reality. You wanted to escape the normal right? So you did, and you ended up here with us, which you did not count on. And by pure accident you finally found yourselves and your purpose in life. It's simple, the way I see it."

"But what do we know about counseling women with real problems? We aren't qualified to do that." Liz interjected.

"No, you ain't. But picture the Queen for a Day show. Do they counsel anybody? No, they don't. They just listen, applaud and then give 'em prizes. That's it.

And that's all you got to do. Besides, that's what most people want and need anyway...just somebody to listen, applaud, and pay 'em a little respect once in a while."

"What makes you think you two are the only ones with dreams of getting in a motor home and driving off into the sunset? Think what might happen if you took some poor old soul out of her day-to-day drudgery and sent her and her husband on a little motor home trip. Might just save a marriage. Never can tell." Darlene straightened her back and held her head high, proud of her reasoning.

Rachel and Reggie joined us and looked at me with questions in their eyes. I was forced to admit that Darlene was on to something. "But this is going to take a lot of work. We'll have to find sponsors, and..."

"But your friend Brent already said he'd help...or at least he said he was interested in hearing more about it," added Reggie.

"And I know we can surely approach Della and Lerline about this. I'm getting way into this," Liz said. "I feel like we really can make a difference."

"Well, since Darlene here has made out the plan I think she should be required to help us out with implementing it." I said. "What do you say to that, Ms. Road Queen? You want to arrange our lives, but what happens when yours gets turned around along with ours?" I looked at her expectantly.

Darlene hesitated and then answered slowly. "I didn't say I wouldn't help out. Besides, that's not the problem to deal with right now. I was just thinking about Lulu. I wonder if she's found the camp by now. Or Les."

"You're right, Darlene. Damn, twice already this morning." I grinned.

"Course, I'm right, Queenies. This whole situation has brought up a lot of thoughts about how we all have lived. And I been thinking about it a lot. You know, it felt real nice to sing the other night. I ain't sung in a long, long time. And just like you two, I ain't been so good at using my gifts either. So, we all got some deciding to do."

"You could make a comeback, Darlene," Reggie said. Rachel grinned her agreement.

"I don't know about no comeback. But still, there might be something I can do."

We ate a meager breakfast of dry cereal and peanut butter. Then Liz and I forced Rosie out into the snow for her morning constitutional. She spit and hissed, but finally obliged us, and we let her back inside. We stomped around The Screamer on both sides as far as we could, somehow hoping a miracle had occurred overnight and the whole back end was free and clear of the ditch, so we could be on our way. But it wasn't.

Liz sat down on a fallen branch and stretched her legs out in front of her.

"I think Darlene's right, Leslie," she said. "We've just begun finding ourselves and those people in there, those stowaways we picked up, have taught us a whole lot about life and living. I think we should go for it. We need to email the guys and tell them to come and get us."

"You aren't serious?" I said.

"Oh yes, I am," she replied, and threw a snowball at me.

Back inside, we began to make plans.

"Okay, we need something like those little yellow flag things you see in people's yards out on the main road so maybe somebody will notice us." Liz suggested.

"We don't have any little yellow flag things," I answered. "But maybe we can make an S.O.S. out of something." I looked around the cabin.

"I know what we can use," said Darlene.

"What?"

"Colored undies would sure get the attention. Surely you Queenies have some in every color. They'll show up good against all that snow."

We all gaped at her. "Colored undies?" I repeated. "Well, I never...I... that's perfect, Darlene!" Liz, go get all of our colored underwear except for one spare. Reggie, you go out and find us some tree limbs we can tie them to."

"Put 'em out quick. I got a feeling Lulu's on the trail." Darlene rubbed her knee.

"Oh, a feeling, huh?" I said.

"Yep, this time in my knee. And you should have more faith, Ms.Queenies."

"Whatever," I replied, determined not to argue with her at this point.

Reggie knocked at the door and motioned for us to join him outside. We began tying the underwear garments to the branches.

"Oh, maybe not these," said Liz holding up a pair of delicate red lace ones. "These are my special favorites." She reached to take them back, but Reggie snatched them away.

"Oh, no, you don't Ms. Liz. These are just the ones we need out there on the road," he grinned.

When the undies were all tied to the branches, Reggie trudged off toward the highway to plant our flags. He was to line the road on both sides of the dirt road we were on, so that any vehicle passing by would notice.

"Okay, Liz. Let's go do the dirty deed." I said pulling at her sleeve.

"What do you mean?" she asked.

"Email the guys that we're coming home."

# Chapter 47

## Mister Sandman, Bring Me a Dream

*Dear Bob and Carl,*

*We are safe and should be heading back home in a few days. The storm did hold up our trip, but we made out just fine. We've learned a lot on the road and can't wait to share it all with you. We miss and love you. Please call Anne and the boys to fill them in.*

*Love, Leslie and Liz*

I hit the send button, and it was done.

"Well, it isn't entirely honest, but that's all they need to know for now. We'll work out the rest later." I reassured Liz. "Now, one more email to send."

*Dear Brent,*

*Will call next week for a lunch meeting about the radio show. I am SO excited. I think I've finally found out what I want to be when I grow up."*

*Leslie*

"Isn't it amazing how much two little emails can change your entire life?" I asked Liz, not really expecting an answer. She didn't, but her face told me she agreed.

Reggie stomped his feet at the door and came inside shivering. "Okay, the roads are lined with your undies. If that doesn't catch somebody's attention, nothing will!" he said. He stripped his coat and plastic bags away and sat down to cuddle with Rachel.

"By the way. Rachel and I have been talking. We think we might better head back home…but together. We want to get married. Rachel's going to contact her folks and I'll go back to work at Circuit City. We aren't giving up on the idea of adventure, but right now, we think we just want to get married, and maybe start a family. That's pretty adventurous, wouldn't you say?" He grinned at all of us.

There were hugs and kisses all around, and if any of us felt the slightest doubt about the relationship working, we kept it to ourselves. This was a morning to be positive. The afternoon held only the shadowy possibilities of cold and hunger. Our fuel was running low.

"What about you Darlene?" Liz asked.

"I don't know yet. "I haven't been excited about anything in over twenty years like I am about this show of yours. I want to wait until Lulu comes back and then decide."

There was a moment's silence and then I had to ask, "But what if she doesn't come back, Darlene?"

"She'll be back," she said stubbornly.

We spent the next few hours talking about the radio show and our futures. We brainstormed about road shows, contests, and grand prizes.

"Oh, and we need to answer those emails," I reminded them. "They'll be good contacts when we're up and running. But of course, some of those won't get an answer," I smiled.

"Right, those from the Casanovas of the web. Can you believe some people?" Liz laughed.

"Okay, so we can send out replies and tell them to stay tuned to the web site www.queenmotorhome.com. and that special plans are underway. Reggie can help us list some of the features we might want on the website, so when we get home, we'll have a head start on some of this."

Reggie came over and took a seat in front of the keyboard while Liz and I dictated ideas to him. Rachel helped out as well, but Darlene remained very quiet.

"You okay, Darlene?" Liz asked.

"Just thinking," she said. "I'm just sitting here thinking how happy I am right now, this minute. I don't have a dime to my name and I'm stuck in a snow storm in the woods, but I have found friends...some really good friends, and I just..." she sniffed. "I just think maybe there might be a chance to start over again." She wiped at her eyes and there was nothing to do but get up and share a group hug.

When we settled back down, Liz asked, "Darlene, whether you come with us or not, can Rosie come with me?"

Darlene reached over to pet the cat curled in Liz's lap. "Sure, honey. She can be the station mascot. But you'll have to promise to get her a pearl collar and maybe a tiny little tiara all her own."

Our laughter was interrupted by an announcement on the radio. "Middle, western and Southwestern Tennessee residents are digging out from what has been called the storm of the century. It will take days for travel to return to normal. There are numerous reports of power outages. One homeless man was found frozen to death somewhere near Buttercup Junction. The highway patrol reports that most citizens heeded warnings to stay home, so injuries and deaths were at a minimum. There was one report of a renegade truck and RV bus that busted through a road block on I-40, but neither vehicle has been seen since."

"God, don't let that homeless man be Les," Darlene prayed out loud.

"Don't jump to conclusions, Darlene," Reggie told her. "We don't even know if he's still in these parts."

She nodded and turned to stare out the window again, searching the whiteness for a sign of Lulu.

"I wonder what happened to that crazy trucker and RV driver?" Reggie asked.

"Who knows? Can you believe some people? Who'd be fool enough to drive like that in all this snow and sleet? Anyway, that reminds me. While we're on generator mode, let's try Ponderosa Man again," I suggested. But there was no response.

Liz and I left for a brief walk outside.

"You know, we'll probably lose all power very shortly, Liz," I told her. "If Lulu doesn't show by late afternoon, we'll have to go to Plan B."

"And what is Plan B?" Liz asked.

I thought for a moment before I answered. "Well, that would be our big S.O.S. to the guys. But without power, it doesn't matter what the plan is." I shrugged and walked ahead of her through the snow seeking out the patches of sunlight that spilt through the dense canopy of trees. It was going to be a long afternoon.

Rescue Rendezvous…

# Chapter 48

## Only the Lonely

Les, Lyle, and Lulu made their way back through the snow to the train car for the night, but returned in the cold to the truck stop the next morning. They saw the huge American Flag splayed on the rig's grill and right off, knew that Eagle One was still there. He invited them into the cab to try their S.O.S. call again.

The Big Daddy crew woke up to the smells of a great breakfast cooked by Ms. Beulah herself. Brenda stumbled out of the bedroom in an oversized flannel shirt that made it obvious she wore nothing but panties beneath it. The men pretended not to notice.

After eating, Ray grabbed another cup of coffee and went out to check on his rig.

"I'll be back in a few minutes. I'm going to radio some trucker buddies and see what's happening up the road before we start out."

Static filled most of the airwaves, but one name broke through: Eagle One. Ray listened and suddenly realized that Eagle One was calling Ponderosa Man.

"Eagle one, this is Ponderosa Man. Don't think I know your handle."

"Ponderosa Man, there's a fellow by the name of Les who needs to talk to you. I'll put him on."

"Hello Mr. Ponderosa Man?"

"Yeah, that's me."

"My name is Les and I have a dog here with me called Lulu. She showed up the other night at the homeless camp where I stay nearly frozen to death, and she had a soup can around her neck. There was a message in it that said my old girlfriend is trapped in a camper in the snowstorm with some people. Their names are Leslie and Liz, Reggie and Rachel. The note said to contact you and call for help."

"My God, man! I'm on the road searching for that bunch right now. And you've got Lulu with you? What's your location, Les?"

"I'm at the Hwy. 309 truck stop about three miles from the camp," Les responded.

"Okay, buddy. Tell you what. I'm heading your way. It'll take me a while, but with any luck, I should be at the truck stop in about four hours depending on road conditions. Can you meet there then and bring Lulu?"

"Les says that's a ten-four, Ponderosa Man. I'm stuck right here myself, so I'll be around. Just holler if you need me."

"Eagle One, what's the news on road conditions out your way?"

"Several truckers here said the storm took a sharp turn to the northeast, so we missed the worst of it. Got plenty of snow, but very little ice. If you go a little south and then cut back to the northwest, the roads won't be too bad."

"Ten-four. We're on our way. And thanks Eagle One."

Ray rushed back to the Big Daddy and all but shouted the news.

"My Lulu has saved the day! What a great dog she is. I just knew sending her with those Queenies was the thing to do," Beulah sighed.

"Okay folks. Let's load up and hit the back roads. Les and Lulu will meet us at the truck stop in about four hours. There's no time to waste."

Traveling the back roads was rough and slow, but as the group made their way to the Southern Connector, conditions improved and they moved faster. Brenda drove and Ray took the passenger seat intending to take over when she tired.

"So how long have you been on the road, Brenda?" Ray asked.

"Too long, most would say," she replied. "After a bad first marriage, I took to trucking as a way to see the world and have a little adventure. But these have been a tough seven years, and there are lots of times when I think about quitting and settling down—you now, starting a family. How about you?"

Ponderosa Man paused before he answered. "I'm going on twenty years in the business. My ex-wife didn't like me being away from home so much, and she eventually turned my daughter against me. We didn't speak for a long time until recently. She had some surgery and called me to come to her. We're trying to mend things, now."

"You got something going on with those Queenie girls?" Brenda whispered.

"Hell, no! I met them by pure accident, and I took it on myself to be a road buddy. They needed somebody to look out for them. Those two are greenies for sure."

"So, you're not in a relationship?

"Yes'm, I am—going steady with my truck." Ray laughed and Brenda joined in.

Beulah entertained Bob and Carl with her life story. They were fascinated, but when they asked about Liz and Leslie's adventures in the park, Beulah refused to talk. "That's their story to tell you when they're good and ready. I ain't breaking no trust."

"I'll tell you this, though. Those two got a taste for some adventure right now, but they'll be back home. You'll see. Just be nice to 'em, give 'em some space, and it'll all come round right in the end."
"Well thanks for the advice Beulah. I think you're right. I think we're all about ready to make some serious changes. I know I am."

"Speaking of the girls, Carl, let's check the email. We need to contact the boys and Anne."

They logged on to the computer and found the email Leslie and Liz sent earlier.

"Can you believe those two? Telling us they are safe and heading home soon, when they've put a Saint Bernard out in the storm to search for help."

"They're too stubborn and stoic to ask for help from us. And you know what, that's not a good thing. We must have really messed up handling a lot of things if they don't even want to call us when they're needing help. I just hope they really are safe." Bob shook his head sadly, and Carl stared at the computer screen.

"Wonder what made them decide to come back home?" Carl finally asked.

"Who knows? Who cares, as long as they do it? I just want to get to them and make sure they're safe. I know I wouldn't want to be stranded in all this mess." Bob made his way up to the cab where Ray was radioing Eagle One to let him know the CB handle for Big Daddy.

"Ten-four, Ponderosa Man. I got that handle written down: Plane to Catch. Keep

it steady. Over and out."

Carl called from the back. "Hey Bob. There's an email for you from somebody named Mark Pringle."

Bob hurried back to the computer.

"Who is he?" Carl asked.

Bob hesitated and then spoke. "He's a business broker. I asked him to research companies for a buy-out. I've done a lot of thinking since Leslie's been away, and I've decided to get out like she did. I'm looking to sell the company. Leslie's right. We are in a rut, and I plan to fix it as soon as possible."

Bob read the email through and then turned to Carl grinning. "Watch this, buddy." He said as he hit reply and typed in the word SELL!

# Chapter 49

## What does it Take?

"Hey guys!" said Eagle One. "As long as we have to wait here for Ponderosa Man, we might as well get a hot breakfast. My treat."

"We better not," replied Les.

"Why, you're hungry, aren't you?" Eagle One asked.

"Yeah, we're hungry. Always hungry," said Les. "But those folks might not want us in there." He motioned toward the restaurant.

"Too bad for them," said Eagle One as he climbed out of the cab and slapped both Les and Lyle on the shoulder. "We're going for breakfast." The three of them managed to lift Lulu into the cab where she'd be safe and warm and then strode toward the restaurant door.

Stares greeted them, but no one made comments. Eagle One shepherded his little group to the counter where they all sat down. "Get whatever you want, guys." he said.

The three men ate quietly and listened to the murmur of voices around them. Rumors bounced from one booth to the other. Top on the list was the story of a renegade trucker and an RV bursting through roadblocks. Eagle One grinned to himself, but he couldn't help but wonder what in the world he had gotten himself into.

Down the road, Ray pulled into a gas station that seemed deserted, but there was a small building at the back that appeared to be living quarters. He wanted to check it out. Brenda Babe was right on his heels. Bob handed Ray a photo of Leslie and Liz to take with them just in case someone answered the door.

Sure enough, a scruffy old man shuffled his way to answer their knock.

"Sorry to bother you sir," said Ray, "but can you tell us if we're anywhere close to Buttercup Junction?"

"Yep, you are. You're in it," grinned the old fellow.

"We are!" Brenda exclaimed. "We didn't see any signs anywhere, so we thought we might be totally lost."

"Nope, you ain't lost. There's signs around, but the snow's probably covered them. What can I do for you?" He and Christian, who growled, peered around the two strangers at his door and stared at the huge RV parked in front of his station.

Ray and Brenda introduced themselves and explained that they were looking for some friends who just might have come this way. "Here's a photo of them. Do you think you've seen them in the last few days?" Ray asked.

The old fellow held the photo up close to his face and then began to chuckle. "I know this one. She was here looking for gas and supplies. Had a young fella' with her. The other one could have been in the camper they was driving, I guess. That was just before the storm blew in."

"Do you know where they were headed?" Brenda asked.

"They said something about a homeless camp and an RV Park. Both are nearby, but I told 'em I wasn't sure the RV Park was still there."

"Thanks, Mr. Adams. You've been a big help. Can you give us some directions toward a truck stop on Hwy. 309?"

"Go down this road about three miles and take the cut to the right. Then about ten miles later you'll come out just a ways from the intersection with Highway 309. You take a left and it should be just a little down the road there. By the way, what's all the fuss about getting to that homeless camp anyway?"

"Just wanting to help out some folks during the season, that's all. Thanks again, buddy." Ray said and held out his hand to the old man.

Back in the Big Daddy, Ray told the others what he had found out.

"He said a young man was with Leslie?" Carl asked. "Did he mention Liz?"

"No, he didn't see anyone but Leslie and the young guy. But he said they got gas and he gave us directions to the truck stop on Highway 309. We're real close. And don't worry, we're going to find them."

Ray took the wheel, and Brenda manned the passenger seat. Bob and Carl turned to go to the back. "I hope that young man isn't my replacement," muttered Bob.

Ray heard him, but didn't comment, even though he could have explained exactly who the young traveler was. He thought that would best be left for the girls to explain when they found them.

"Plane to Catch? This is Eagle One. Come in, please." Lulu had refused to climb down from the cab, so Les, Lyle and Eagle One were forced to crowd into the truck cab with her.

"Eagle One! We're heading your way. Less than thirty minutes, I think," said Ray. "But travel's slow on these back roads."

"Ten-four. Les, Lyle, and Lulu are here with me. We'll sit tight. What are your wheels?"

"A huge RV bus, not a truck. Long story. Looks like something Agent 007 would drive," replied Ray, laughingly.

"Ten-four. Over and Out." Eagle One clicked off the CB. The three men stayed in the cab talking and trading road stories. Some time later, a beat up old Cadillac pulled in just to the left of the rig. Three oddly dressed young men climbed out and made their way to another trucker standing nearby. Eagle One watched them as they ambled over to him and cracked his window enough to hear what they might be up to.

"Excuse us, sir. Can you give us some information about the homeless camp that's near here?"

"Hey, Les. You guys at camp taking on weirdoes like them?" asked Eagle One. "I guess it takes all kinds in this world, huh?"

Les nor Lyle answered. They had heard nearly the same comments about themselves before.

The three boys finished their conversation with the trucker and turned to go into the truck stop.

"Look, there's a big bus pulling in now," Lyle said.

"Looks like that might be our rescuers," smiled Eagle One. He blinked his headlights twice to signal to the driver.

"Eagle One, is that you?" blared the CB.

"Ten-four, buddy. Good to see you."

Ray pulled up on the right of the rig, and he and Brenda made their way out of the RV door to meet the three men and Lulu piling out of the other rig.

"Oh, there's my Lulu!" Beulah exclaimed, pounding her hand against the window that separated her from her beloved pet. "She looks wonderful!"

Ray held the door of the Big Daddy and the small group climbed aboard. Lulu rushed straight to Beulah, licking her all over. "You're such a brave, smart girl, Lulu," Beulah crooned. "I love you so much, and I've missed you, too." Lulu lapped up the kind words and attention.

After all the introductions were made, Les showed Bob and Carl the letter Lulu had delivered to him.

"But what do you have to do with Liz and Leslie?" Carl asked. "And why were they going to a homeless camp?"

"Oh, you two have a lot to catch up on when we find those two Queenies," smiled Beulah. "For now, just be thankful we are so close to reaching them."

"Okay, let's make some plans, then. Eagle One, can you stand a little adventure in your life?"

Eagle One nodded. "My curiosity is really up with this one, now. No way can I back out. I'll unhitch the trailer and Les and Lyle can ride with me to the camp. That seems to be ground zero."

When the cab was ready to go, Ray climbed behind the wheel of Big Daddy with Brenda Babe riding shotgun, and Les and Lyle left to join Eagle One. Lulu rushed after Les. Beulah was a bit surprised, but she let her go, sensing that Lulu's mission was not over quite yet.

The group pulled slowly to the highway and turned left, headed for the homeless camp. The old Cadillac cruised just behind them. "Whew, Mama!" said Winston. "Look at the RV rig. Now, that's traveling in style! Wonder where they're headed?"

# Chapter 50

## Hold On, I'm Coming

Eagle One and Ponderosa Man pulled their vehicles up close to the railroad tracks. Everyone piled out to stare at the empty rail cars and the huge bonfire that blazed in a snow cleared circle just in front of one of the cars. They all turned to stare as the old Cadillac pulled up to them and stopped.

"It's those weird guys, again," said Eagle One to the group. "I heard 'em asking for directions to this place back at the stop."

"Better go find out," replied Ray.

Winston stared as the two huge truckers strode toward the car. "Here come the two big guys. They're the ones we followed all the way here. I wonder what they're up to? It's just too strange that we ended up in the same place. Let's get out." The boys climbed out of the car to greet Eagle One and Ray. The rest of that group wandered over to the fire and then turned to stare.

"Man, those guys look like freaks!" said Carl. Bob shifted from foot to foot trying to stay warm and ward off his nervousness. Ray and Eagle One turned to walk toward them and the weird boys followed.

"Well, folks, it seems these guys are out to rescue our ladies, too. Meet Winston, Ronnie, and Kenny." Ray grinned, enjoying the look on both Bob and Carl's faces.

"Just how many guys have Leslie and Liz met on this trip of theirs?" Carl demanded. "We're liable to find a motor home full of men!"

"It's not like that, sir," explained Winston. It's a long story, but it's all innocent. Leslie and Liz will explain it all to you, I'm sure." He reached over to hug Beulah and pat Lulu's head.

"What is this? You all seem to know each other! Are Bob and I the only ones who are clueless here?" Carl's voice rose with agitation. "What the hell is going on with my wife?"

"It's like this, sir," said Winston and began to explain most of their story. Bob and Carl listened intently as the young men and Beulah filled in details of their meeting.

"So, you all had a regular pajama party together, huh?" Carl asked. "And they helped you out a bit, and now you show up here looking for them. Did they ask you to come rescue them?"

"Oh no, sir, they didn't do that. We contacted them by email, and they said they were stuck near a homeless camp, and we just got worried and thought we'd come find them. We decided on our own to do that. They never asked. Besides, we're going to be helping with the new website." Winston shook his head emphatically to make his point.

"What website?" Bob demanded.

Winston looked nervously at Kenny and Ronnie. "Oh, Leslie and Liz can tell you all about that, too, sir. Don't worry. We're just here to help out."

"Well, it looks like we've got more members for our search team. Les, since you know this area best, maybe you should lead the way. Didn't you say something about a church located near here?" Ray asked.

"Okay, let's travel," Eagle One said. "Les will guide me, then Big Daddy's crew, and these boys can bring up the rear. "Lulu's got a nose for searching, so we'll rely on her to guide us."

Everyone moved toward their rides. Only Les hung back. He looked up at Eagle One. "I don't know if I ought to come along," he said. I'm not sure Darlene really wants to see me, and I'm not sure I'm ready to face her."

"Well, he'll just have to get over it," shouted Beulah. "We've got to have him to help track those girls down." She stomped over to Bob. "You got anything of Leslie's or Liz's with you? Something that has their smells on it?"

"Well, I think I might," Bob answered. He made his way into the Big Daddy and returned holding an over-sized tee shirt. Red-faced he held it out to Beulah. "I've been sleeping with it since she's been gone. It smells like her." Beulah ripped the shirt from his hand. "Perfect," she said.

"Come 'ere, Lulu." She held the shirt in front of Lulu's nose and then lifted each front paw and slipped the garment onto the dog. "Now, get yourselves in the vehicles and let's get hunting," she commanded.

Lulu climbed up between Eagle One and Les. The others revved their engines, and slowly the rescue caravan pulled back out onto the road.

Sirens greeted them.

"Eagle One, this is Plane to Catch. I think the Smokies have finally caught up with us. But I don't know how they can pull us over in these conditions."

"Ten four," said Eagle One. "We'll just keep moving."

The blue lights pulled right up behind the Cadillac. Winston watched warily in his rear view mirror. "They must be after the truckers. If they stop them, we might not ever find Leslie and Liz. Hang on tight, guys."

Winston pulled out from behind the Big Daddy. The cops followed. He flew past Eagle One and raced down the slippery road. A quarter of mile beyond the caravan, he slammed on brakes. The Cadillac spun around, sending them speeding away in the opposite direction. The cops did a three-point turn and followed.

"Look at those crazy fools!" said Ray as he called Eagle One. "Got a regular little Rockford Files team with us."

"That was smart," acknowledged Eagle One. "He's keeping the heat off of us."

In the rear view mirror, Ray watched as the two vehicles disappeared, swerving from one side of the icy road to the other. The tactic would give them some good lead time, at least.

At the fork in the road, Les motioned for Eagle One to stop. "Well, here we are. Gotta make a choice. Right or left?" He looked at Eagle One.

"Hell, one's as good as the other for all we know. I guess we'll just flip a coin," Eagle One laughed.

Ray pulled behind the rig and walked up to Eagle One to find out what was up.

"Les has taken us as far as he can. He doesn't know which way to go," explained Eagle One.

"Well, then, let's see what Lulu has to say." He opened the cab door and called for Lulu to climb down. She trampled over Les and Lyle and stumbled clumsily from the cab. The men followed her.

Lulu stood for a minute, sniffing the air, first one way, and then the other. Les bent to rub her nose again with the tee shirt and Lulu turned immediately and trotted to the west.

"Looks like Lulu knows where she's headed," said Ray. "Let's follow her in the vehicles."

"I can't believe we're actually following a dog through a snow storm," grumbled Carl, as they crept along behind Lulu.

Beulah punched him in the shoulder. "Don't you question my Lulu. She's smarter than any of you put together, you hear? You just sit back and shut up. Let Lulu do her job."

"Yes M'am," replied Carl meekly. And no one in the RV dared laugh.

# The Homecoming…

# Chapter 51

## You're Simply the Best

Lulu trudged along ahead, climbed the mounds of snow the scrapers had edged to the side of the road, and stood sniffing the air around her. Her tail began a flirtatious dance and she trotted off behind a mound of snow.

"It must be near here. Look she's headed off the main road." Eagle One radioed Ponderosa Man that they would be stopping. Les jumped from the cab and called to Lulu. She loped back over the embankments of snow and returned to his side, only to run circles around him and bark. The rest of the group deboarded and gathered at the front of the convoy.

"Okay, Lulu. Let's find 'em," commanded Les. The big dog galloped off to the west with the rescue caravan following slowly on foot behind her.

"She's gonna leave us behind. Everyone follow us, come on," laughed Les, already feeling excited about the possibility of finding Darlene again, but anxious as well that he would not be a welcome visitor, in spite of the note she had sent.

"What the hell…?" Les shouted.

Everyone rushed up as fast as they could and trekked through the sludge carefully without slipping and falling. Les pointed to his left where Lulu crashed through the snow and fallen branches, and then disappeared from sight.

But they couldn't have followed even if she'd slowed down. Open-mouthed, they stood where she'd led them, staring at the line of colored underwear hanging like risqué flags from tree branches stuck deep in the snow drifts covering the road that led into the forest. Bob walked up to one particular branch and fingered a delicate yellow lace bra. The group stood silently watching, and then heard the bubbling sound of laughter, at first soft, and then uproarishly coming from Bob.

"It's Leslie's! By God, what a woman! Who else…?"

The group made a rush to join him, but was stopped dead in their tracks as sirens blared and a patrol car flashing lights barreled down on them. It screeched to a halt.

"Uh, oh," muttered Carl. "What next?"

Lulu raced toward her prize. Deeper in the forest, The Screamer stood bleakly tipped toward its rear in the ditch. She was out of fuel. The generator was down. Leslie and Reggie had tried the emergency switch that tied both batteries into one unit in an effort to keep each charged, but it was no use. There was no more heat. No more food. And night was coming fast. Inside, the group closed the blinds and bundled up under what blankets they could find.

Rachel and Reggie left the somber atmosphere inside to walk through the snow. They were deep into hopeful plans for their future when the sound of sirens and what they thought were far-off voices stopped them. Through the brush, they could see a big truck, a huge motor home, a police car, and another car. Rachel moved closer to Reggie's side and then screamed.

"It's Lulu! Look, it's Lulu! She's come back!"

Reggie grabbed her hand, and the two raced toward Lulu who promptly sat down and held up a paw to greet them. After much licking, the dog settled down, and the threesome made their way back to The Screamer.

Reggie busted through the door. "Hey everybody! Look here. Lulu's back!"

The excited dog was greeted with more hugs and kisses, and when he could speak and be heard above the laughter, Reggie announced, " There are sirens out by the highway. And trucks and other vehicles and police lining the road where I hung the underwear. Do you think they're looking for us? Are they going to arrest y'all for kidnapping?" He was clearly frightened.

The thought made Leslie squirm, and she scolded herself silently not to get worked up because there were no more dry underwear to be had.

Darlene shushed the young man. " Relax, son. Lulu's done exactly what we sent her to do. She got us help. Those people are here for us, I'm certain! I better go get ready." She waddled back to the bedroom and shut the door.

Lulu immediately whined and scratched at the door.

"I think she wants to go back out," Leslie said.

"Turn her loose," Liz said. And out the door she went, moving faster than any of them had ever thought possible. They lost sight of her and settled back onto the sofas behind the closed blinds to wait.

Lulu retraced her steps and bounded up onto the snow embankment just above the officers' heads. Brenda Babe had them cornered there. She had edged her way closer and closer to them, and they had retreated until they could no longer go backwards because of the plowed snow mounds lining the road.

"What's she telling him?" Carl asked Ray.

"Patience guys. Brenda's got a way with these guys. She'll have 'em eating out of her hand before you know it. Of course, she could also be threatening them with disclosing certain secret information to their wives. With Brenda, who knows? But it'll be okay, you'll see."

Sure enough, Brenda sashayed herself back to Ray's side, grinning. "All clear," she grinned. "We can go now."

"What did you say to him?" asked Carl.

"Oh, I just spun a little tale about a sick woman stuck back there in the woods, and how we are all trying to rescue her. No big thing. They're cool. They're going to stay right here until we get them out. Then they'll make sure we're all okay and lead us back to town."

From a distance, the boys in the Cadillac watched and wondered. When they saw the group cross the mounded snow and move down into the forest, they got out of the car. The underwear flags danced in the wind before them. "Those Queenies can handle just about anything, can't they? My, what pretty undies," Winston laughed.

The group trudged behind Lulu through the snow, stepping over fallen limbs and dodging snow dropping from the limbs above them.

"Hey, look there. That's The Screamer!" Beulah was ecstatic.

"Okay, so maybe we better not all go rushing up at once. They might shoot us or something," Carl said and stepped back from the crowd.

"Yeah, Leslie may have taken her pistol and won't be shy about using it if she feels threatened," agreed Bob. Everyone stared at him.

"Okay, tell you what. I'll go first. They know me. They'll see me and Lulu and then y'all can come up behind me." Beulah struggled forward through the drifts. The others watched her go, calling to her to be careful.

"It's Beulah!" screamed Liz! The others huddled around her staring out the window.

There was a mad scramble to the door, and they tumbled out and over each other to get outside and reach Beulah. Lulu bounced from one to the other. It was only then that Leslie noticed what the dog was wearing.

"This looks like the tee shirt I sleep in at home," she said and looked at Beulah questioningly.

"Well, now," Beulah said, gasping for breath after the flurry of hugs and delighted screams. "You're a little slow on the uptake, huh, Queenies?" She smiled and then said, "If this ain't some situation you two done gone and caused. Why half the state is on the lookout for you. And I brought the other half with me." She turned slightly and pointed to the group of people huddled in the distance.

Lulu barked twice, and Beulah waved them forward. Slowly one by one, the people began to walk toward The Screamer.

Darlene stepped up beside Leslie. She had applied fresh lipstick and sported her tiara. In her hand were two more, which she promptly tossed to Liz and Leslie.

"Here," she said. "Us Queen's need to look the part when we're rescued, don't you think?" She grinned, and then pulled nervously at her clothes.

Liz and Leslie slapped the tiaras on their head, too nervous about who might be approaching to really care how they looked. They strained their eyes trying to identify the bundled up bodies that came toward them.

Bob was the first to approach. Lulu rushed back and forth between him and the others, as Leslie made her way toward him.

"Oh, my!" sighed Leslie as she embraced her husband.

Carl was next. He shuffled along, suddenly shy with so many watching. Liz rushed out to him and jumped into his arms, which sent them both tumbling to the snow.

Ray and the others eased into the group, and they all gathered outside The Screamer in a tight circle. There was enough laughter to keep them all warm for some time. Even Winston, Ronnie, and Kenny joined in, and Eagle One forgot to worry about standing too close to Winston.

"This is just too good to be true," Leslie sighed. "We might have learned a lesson about being too proud to ask for help. Thank you all for coming to our rescue."

"Well, it was Lulu's doing. She's the hero, here," said Ray.

"Yeah, Lulu and Les," added Eagle One. With the mention of Les's name, the crowd grew instantly silent."

"Hey, where is Les, anyway?" he asked. In the commotion of reuniting, they had lost track of him.

Leslie looked around for Darlene, but she was nowhere to be seen either. So she made her way to the rear of The Screamer. In the distance, she could see a man's back. He was facing Darlene who stood with her hands on her hips, lips pursed and her rhinestone tiara sparkling in the sunlight. Leslie watched for just a moment, but when she saw Darlene smile, she realized the man must be Darlene's long lost love—Les, and she quietly backed away.

"Uh, Darlene and Les are just around the corner. Let's give them a few minutes." She snuggled up to Bob and dropped her head onto his shoulder.

"Okay, I know you all have lots of questions and stories, but those will have to wait. Right now, we need to get you people out of here. There's a cop waiting back at the road for us. And we've got some explaining to do to him. After that, we'll head back to the nearest motel and set up camp for the night. With any luck, we'll be able to get back here tomorrow and pull The Screamer out of that ditch."

There was a group yell, and the girls scrambled to collect the things they would need overnight. Liz grabbed Darlene's bag and the group tromped back out in the snow.

"Darlene, we've got to leave now. Come on," Leslie called to her.

Darlene nodded and motioned for the others to go ahead.

After some long explanations to the patrolman concerning the renegade rigs, the discovery of two missing young people in the group with the women, and haggling over who was to ride where, the group divided up and engines began to rev. Winston and the boys loaded the Cadillac with extra luggage from The Screamer, retrieved the undies from the side of the road, and invited Reggie and Rachel to ride with them. Brenda Babe grabbed hold of Ray and they climbed into the cab of Eagle One. That left Carl, Liz, Bob, Leslie, Beulah, and Lulu in Big Daddy. They were just about to pull away when Liz yelled for them to stop.

"Where's Darlene? She's not here. We can't leave Darlene! And where is Rosie?" Leslie and Liz rushed to the door and jumped into the snow determined to find them. They climbed up over the embankment at the side of the road and stood for a moment at the top, then lost their balance and tumbled to the bottom. As they struggled to their feet, laughter exploded from behind them. Darlene, with Rosie in her arms, stood hand in hand with Les staring down at the two silly white women wearing tiaras and wallowing in the snow.

"I done 'bout seen it all, now," Les said.

"You ain't seen nothin' yet, baby," Darlene quipped and stretched out her hand to help Leslie and Liz up from the snow. The girls stood before her, embarrassed, but she gently reached over and straightened their tiaras. Then touched her own. And the foursome joined the others for the ride home.

# Epilogue...

## We Are Family

There was much explanation all around for the next few days. Not everything turned out perfectly, but for the most part, my and Liz's little adventure turned out to be an adventure for all involved. Not one of us escaped some major life lessons.

In a matter of weeks, our show was on the air, and the ratings were all over the board. Liz and I did the inaugural Holiday shows and then turned the helm over to Darlene and Beulah who were after all, the real Queens in the group. We held satellite shows at Nursing Homes, Battered Women's Shelters and Troubled Young Women's Homes, in addition to the regular radio broadcast. If anyone needed to be a Queen for The Day, these were the women who were prime candidates.

Additionally, Darlene cut a new CD and donated the proceeds from its sales to help the homeless. My friend Brent, who owned the station, took a real liking to Les and made him the station manager. Winston and Company were hired for technical support to manage the website. Reggie and Rachel returned to Nashville and got married. Ray and Brenda consolidated their trucking careers and took to the road together. Eagle One met his destiny with a caller via the Queen Motor Home Radio Show. And Darlene's granddaughter found her through the show and came to live with her and Les.

We didn't forget Lulu and Rosie, either. They became the official mascots for the show. My mom even got involved as our marketing person soliciting sponsorships for prizes, and Sisters on Wheels became major sponsors of the show. Della and Lerline even convinced a major motor home manufacturer to donate a motor home as a grand prize for the first year show anniversary. Their sales, in turn, doubled, with eighty per cent of the new buyers being women.

Liz and Carl were working hard on reworking their marriage. Liz boasts that Carl is now getting in touch with his more sensitive side. Our boys, Billy and Rex are still in college and doing great. They're both thrilled at the changes in our lives.

As for Bob and me, we've simplified our lives. We have a motor home of our own now—The Silver Queen Screamer, herself. And we travel constantly, listening to Darlene's CD as we head off into the sunset together, singing along with her... "Side by Side."

*Follow the Continuing Adventures and life experiences of Leslie and Liz.*

**COMING SOON BY PATT FERO**

**The Reunion**

**Home Sweet Home**

**Sex on Wheels**

Visit us at: www.queenmotorhome.com

5726058R0

Made in the USA
Lexington, KY
09 June 2010